DOOMED
TO DIE

Also by Dorothy Simpson

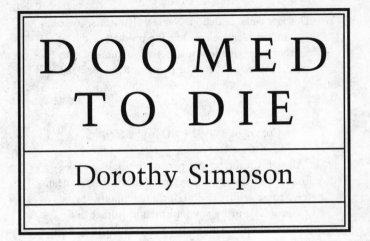

DOOMED TO DIE

Dorothy Simpson

CHARLES SCRIBNER'S SONS
New York

MAXWELL MACMILLAN INTERNATIONAL
New York   Oxford   Singapore   Sydney

Charles Scribner's Sons
Macmillan Publishing Company
866 Third Avenue
New York, NY 10022

Macmillan Publishing Company is part of
the Maxwell Communication Group of
Companies.

Printed in the United States of America

To Emma and Allan

1

On the evening of the day Bridget left home Thanet took Joan to the cinema. He hoped that the distraction would help him to forget that image of the train pulling away from the station platform, taking his beloved daughter out of his life. But it was no good, throughout the film the sense of loss remained, a dull persistent ache lurking at the back of his mind, ready to ambush him whenever he allowed his guard to slip.

One of the advantages of living in the small Kentish town of Sturrenden is that everywhere is within easy walking distance, and the Thanets had decided to leave their car at home. Outside it was a crisp, dry autumn evening with a hint of frost in the air. Joan shivered and turned up her collar, then glanced up at Thanet and took his arm.

'Come on, darling. Cheer up. She'll be home again at Christmas.'

Bridget had for many years been set on a career in cookery and now, at the age of eighteen, had left for a year's cordon bleu and housekeeping course at a well-known cookery school on the far side of London.

Thanet gave a shamefaced grin. 'I know. Stupid, isn't it? We spend all these years equipping them for independence and then when they finally achieve it we're sorry we succeeded! No, I don't mean that, you know I don't.'

Joan squeezed his arm. 'I know.'

'It's just that the break seems so final, somehow.'

'Not final in the true sense of the word. But I know what you mean. There is a sense of finality about it because it's the end of an era, isn't it? And however pleased we might be for her, because she's doing what she's always wanted to do, we can't help feeling sad for ourselves because our lives have lost a dimension.'

'That's it, exactly!' said Thanet. He sighed. 'Time seems to go so quickly. One minute they're toddlers, underfoot all the time, the next they've gone.'

Joan gave his arm a little shake. 'Come on, cheer up. It'll be another four years before Ben goes to university.'

'If he gets in.'

'My goodness, you are gloomy tonight! Of course he'll get in! He's unusually bright, he's working hard . . .'

The ache had eased a little and Thanet was able to leave the subject alone. They walked on in companionable silence, their footsteps echoing through the quiet streets as they passed the familiar squares of lighted windows behind which people were eating, sleeping, watching television, arguing or sharing jokes in the rich emotional chaos that is family life.

Ben heard the key in the front door and came to meet them.

'Sergeant Pater rang. Said it was urgent. I told him you'd ring back.'

The Station Officer. And at this time of night . . . In a flash the last vestiges of Thanet's depression had vanished as the familiar tingle of excitement pricked at his scalp. 'Right, thanks.' He went straight to the phone.

Joan pulled a face and headed for the kitchen. 'We all know what that means.'

Thanet dialled. 'Bill? Sorry, I've only just got in. What's up?'

'Report of a suspicious death, sir. Timed at 9.40 p.m.'

Thanet glanced at his watch. Ten-twenty. Someone should have reported in from the scene by now. 'Heard anything more?'

'Victim's a woman in her thirties. Looks like murder. Scalp wound and plastic bag over the head.'

'Right. What's the address?'

'Barnewell Oast, Melton.'

Pater's tone made Thanet pause. Melton is a couple of miles out of Sturrenden, on the Cranbrook road. And of course, Barnewell Oast was where Mrs Broxton lived!

Vanessa Broxton was a barrister, known to many of the police at Sturrenden because of her work for the Crown Prosecution Service. Hence that note in Pater's voice. Thanet had himself worked with her on a number of occasions. She was in her late thirties, able and ambitious; he had been surprised when, a couple of years ago, she started a family, and unsurprised when she had been back in Court a short time after the baby was born. This year she had taken another brief break to have a second child. Presumably Mrs Broxton herself was not the victim or Pater would have said so.

'I see. Mrs Broxton's place. Who rang in?'

'She did, sir.'

'She all right?'

'Sounded a bit shaken, naturally, who wouldn't be?'

'I'll get out there as soon as I can. Everyone else organised?'

'Yes, sir. Sergeant Lineham is already there and Doc Mallard is on his way. So are the SOCOs.'

'Good. Got any directions?'

Thanet scribbled them down as Pater talked. When he put the phone down Joan was holding out a Thermos flask. 'You'll be needing this.'

He kissed her. 'Thanks, love. Don't wait up.'

With so little traffic about it took only ten minutes to drive to Melton, a few minutes longer to find the Broxton house. Barnewell Farm and the converted Oast which had originally belonged to it stood in a quiet lane on the outskirts of the village. The two houses were about a hundred yards apart, the boundary between them delineated by a row of young silver birches. Thanet recognised Lineham's Ford Escort and the police surgeon's cherished old Rover among the cars already parked in the wide gravelled drive. Mrs Broxton's distinctive red Scimitar was presumably in the garage.

He got out of his car and stood for a few moments taking in the geography of the place. Over to his right, behind the delicate tracery of the birches, he could see the lights of the farmhouse and, at an upper window, the motionless silhouette of someone watching the police activity next door. A potentially useful witness?

Ahead of him the twin cones of the oast houses, linked by a barn, peaked against the sky. The lower roofs of a series of smaller farm buildings attached to them extended left and then forwards in an L shape. The one nearest to him, he noticed, had triple garage doors, but the rest had obviously been incorporated into the house.

As he crossed the drive, feet crunching on the gravel, the front door opened and Lineham came out with the uniformed constable who had been on duty there when Thanet drove in.

'Ah, there you are, sir. Packham came to tell me you'd arrived. The doorbell doesn't work.'

'Hullo, Mike. What's the story?'

'Don't suppose I know much more than you, yet. You know it's Mrs Broxton's house?'

'Yes. Pater told me.'

'She's pretty upset, of course, so I thought it best to leave questioning her until you arrived. A WPC is with her.'

'Has her doctor been sent for?'

'Yes. He was out on a call but he'll be along as soon as he can.' Lineham turned to lead the way inside.

Thanet nodded a greeting to Packham as they went by. 'I gather it was Mrs Broxton who found the body, Mike?'

'Yes. It's her nanny who's been killed.'

Thanet looked at him sharply. 'The children all right?'

Lineham nodded. 'Fast asleep, upstairs.'

'And it looks like murder.'

'Not much doubt about it, I'd say. Well, you'll see for yourself.'

Thanet paused, ostensibly in order to look around, but really to give himself a moment or two to brace himself for the ordeal ahead. Even after all these years he still could not face the prospect of that first sight of a corpse with equanimity. Somehow he always managed to conceal the complicated jumble of emotions which invariably assailed him—pity, anger, horror, sadness, but he had never managed to come to terms with the way this particular experience affected him, or to understand why he felt the way he did. And in this case, well, scalp wounds in particular could be messy, very messy . . . He forced himself to take in his surroundings.

This was presumably the barn which linked the twin oasts. He was standing in a spacious entrance hall which soared two storeys high right up into the exposed roof timbers. On the floor of polished stone flags oriental rugs created pools of glowing colour, and handsome pieces of antique oak stood here and there against the creamy walls. To the right a wide staircase of polished oak boards led up to a galleried landing.

'Impressive, isn't it?' said Lineham admiringly.

Thanet gave an inward smile. He could guess what was coming.

'But then, we knew they couldn't be short of a penny.'

Guy Broxton was a successful businessman and the Broxtons' combined income must indeed be substantial.

Thanet concealed his amusement with difficulty. Confront Lineham with any house bigger than a semi and his reaction was always the same.

'We're not here to study the Broxtons' life-style, Mike. Which way?'

Lineham gestured. 'In the kitchen.'

The diversion had helped and Thanet followed the sergeant along a short corridor leading off the hall on the right, as ready as he was ever likely to be for what was coming.

Lineham pushed open a door. 'In here.'

This was the ground floor of one of the oast houses and unusual in that it was an oval not a circular oast. In the days when home-brewed beer had been the norm and every sizeable farm had its own oast house, this was where the hops would have been dried. The kitchen, which had been built into it following the curves of the walls, was every woman's dream, of a type familiar to Thanet from the illustrations in Joan's favourite magazine: custom-made wooden units, a green Aga cooker set into a deep chimneybreast of mellow brick, glass-fronted wall cupboards containing an attractive array of china and glass, a floor of polished terracotta tiles, a central pine table and chairs and an old pine dresser displaying a carefully designed clutter of plates and jugs. Cream linen curtains patterned with sprays of wild flowers hung at both windows. The activity in the room was a shocking contrast to what Thanet imagined to be its normal atmosphere of warmth, light and decorative richness. The Scenes-of-Crime team was busy taking samples and photographs and Doc Mallard, bald head gleaming, was kneeling beside the body, which was huddled on the floor beyond the far corner of the table on the same side of the room as the Aga.

Thanet approached. 'Hullo, Doc.'

Mallard glanced up over the top of his gold-rimmed half-moon spectacles. 'Careful, floor's slippery. Spilt milk. Better come round the other way.'

Glad of the momentary delay Thanet paused to inspect the pool of milky liquid and the small saucepan lying on the floor against the base of the wooden units before walking around the table and approaching the body from the far side. He steeled himself, looked.

For a flicker of time he couldn't make sense of what he saw. In his dread of this moment he had temporarily forgotten the plastic bag which Pater had mentioned, and the unnatural sheen of blood-smeared plastic encasing the woman's head caught him unawares. Then his brain reassimilated the information and he saw that she was lying on her side, her face partly obscured by the mass of curly fair hair which had fallen across her cheek. She was small and slender, neat buttocks encased in tight green corduroy trousers stained now by the voiding of the rectum common in cases of suffocation, her tiny feet encased in fashionable brown suede laced ankle boots. Her knitted jacket was a glorious kaleidoscope of greens, browns, creams and near-black neutrals. If he hadn't already been told that she was in her thirties, from what he could see of her he would have guessed that she was much younger, even in her teens, perhaps. The richest years of her life should have lain ahead.

Thanet welcomed the familiar surge of anger, the anger which invariably spurred him on and gave an edge to his determination to succeed in each new murder investigation. No one, under any circumstances, had the right to deprive another human being of the most precious gift of all, life.

Mallard put a hand on the floor to heave himself up. 'We could turn her over now, if you like. I didn't want to move her until you'd seen her.'

Thanet glanced at Trace, the SOCO sergeant. 'Got all the photographs you need?'

'Yes, sir. Sir . . .'

'What?'

'The back door. I thought you'd like to know. It's unlocked.'

'Is it, now? Interesting. Thanks.' Thanet studied the position of the body for a moment longer, then glanced at Lineham. 'Give me a hand, Mike.'

Together they bent down and gently rolled the woman over. Her bulging eyes stared sightlessly up at them, her congested features further distorted by the plastic. Her trousers were spattered with the spilt milk, Thanet noticed, the heel and side of one boot still wet with it. He stood back while Mallard continued his examination and tried to work out what had happened. Careful not to touch he bent to inspect the corner of the kitchen table nearest to her. It was smeared with blood. He pointed it out to Lineham.

'There must've been a quarrel,' said the sergeant, 'in the course of which the saucepan of milk was knocked over. She stepped back, slipped in the greasy liquid and fell, banging her head on the corner of the table. Then someone decided to put the bag over her head and finish her off.'

'Looks like it,' agreed Thanet. 'What d'you think, Doc?'

'That's your department,' said Mallard, levering himself to his feet again. 'We'll know more after the PM, of course, but on the face of it, yes, the fact that the head wound bled so much indicates that she was alive when she hit her head, and it would seem pretty obvious that she was then suffocated.'

'When did it happen, d'you think?'

'I was waiting for that one.' Mallard glanced at the Aga. 'It's warm in

ere, so it's tricky.' He considered. 'You know how I hate committing
myself at this stage but, well, say within the last four hours, to be on the
safe side.'

Thanet glanced at his watch. Ten-fifty-five. Some time between 7 and
9.40, then, when Mrs Broxton had rung in.

Mallard snapped his bag shut. 'Right, well, I think that's about it for
the moment. I'll let you know when we fix the PM.' He held up a hand
as Thanet opened his mouth. 'Don't bother to say it. Yes, it will be as
soon as possible.'

Thanet grinned. 'Thanks, Doc.'

'Bridget gone yet?' asked Mallard, as Thanet escorted him to his car.

Helen Mallard, his wife, was a professional writer of cookery books
and had for a number of years encouraged Bridget in her choice of
career. She and Bridget regularly met to dream up new dishes and it
was through Helen that Bridget had first landed a commission to write a
children's cookery column in the *Kent Messenger*.

Thanet grimaced. 'Saw her off this morning.'

'Helen will miss her.'

'So will we! Oh, give Helen our congratulations, by the way. I saw her
latest book in Hatchards in Maidstone this week. *Eat Yourself To Life*.
Good title.'

'We thought so. I'll tell her. Thanks.'

After several attempts the Rover's engine coughed into life.

'You never know,' said Thanet through the car window, 'if it makes
enough money you might even be able to afford a new car.'

Mallard was always having to put up with good-natured teasing on
the subject of his car.

Mallard switched his lights on and engaged first gear with a flourish.
He raised his chin in pretended affront. 'I will ignore that remark, or
this could be the end of a beautiful friendship.'

Thanet gave the Rover an affectionate pat as it went by and stood for
a moment smiling indulgently at its vanishing tail-lights. He had known
Mallard since childhood and he and Joan had always been fond of him,
had remained loyal friends during the bad years after the lingering
death of Mallard's first wife from cancer. The tetchy, irritable, scruffy
Mallard of those days was virtually unrecognisable in the spruce, buoyant man he had become since he met and married Helen, and Thanet
never ceased to marvel at the transformation.

Back in the house there was a lot to do. Briskly he issued instruc-
tions, sending the solid, reassuring Bentley, accompanied by a WPC, to

interview the owner of the silhouetted figure glimpsed at that upstairs window in the farmhouse next door, in case it turned out to be a woman living alone. He hoped it would. Solitary women often took a lively interest in the affairs of their neighbours.

Finally he turned to Lineham. 'Right then, Mike. Let's go and see what Mrs Broxton has to tell us.'

2

Vanessa Broxton was huddled miserably in a corner of one of the deep, soft sofas in the drawing room, feet tucked up beneath her, discarded shoes on the floor. WPC Barnes, who had been keeping her company, stood up as Thanet and Lineham entered the room.

'D'you want me to stay, sir?' she asked quietly.

'Yes, please.'

Mrs Broxton glanced up. 'Hullo, Inspector Thanet, Sergeant Lineham.' She grimaced. 'I never thought we'd be meeting under these circumstances.'

'No. May we . . . ?'

'Yes, of course.'

She swung her legs to the floor, tugging the hem of her skirt down, and slipped her shoes on.

Thanet chose a chair opposite her and Lineham retreated to one slightly behind him and off to one side. This room, the ground floor of the other oast, was also oval. Floor-length curtains in shades of apricot and turquoise hung at the windows, the colours echoed in the apricot fitted carpet and sofas and chairs upholstered in shades ranging from deep cinnamon to peacock blue. Between two of the windows a floor-to-ceiling bookcase revealed that this was a literate household where the printed word was considered just as important as the ubiquitous small screen—more so, perhaps; the television was conspicuous by its absence. Silk-shaded lamps cast warm pools of light on furniture that glowed with the unmistakeable patina of age.

Vanessa Broxton was wearing a straight charcoal grey skirt and white tailored blouse, part of her workaday uniform, no doubt. Slung loosely around her shoulders was a thick blue knitted jacket and as Thanet watched she crossed her arms and tugged it more closely around her, hugging herself as if to contain the shock she must have sustained. He had never seen her look so vulnerable before. Of medium height, she seemed to have shrunk since he last saw her, and her usually immaculate short straight dark hair was dishevelled as though she had been running her fingers through it. Her long narrow face was striking rather than beautiful, with heavy dark brows and prominent nose, and her best feature by far was her eyes which were a very dark brown, almost black. In Court Thanet had seen them glitter like anthracite but tonight, as they watched him, waiting for him to begin, they were soft, bewildered and, not surprisingly, afraid.

'Do you feel up to answering some questions?'

'Yes, of course.' She sat up a little straighter, bracing herself.

'The dead woman was your children's nanny, I gather.'

'Yes. No. Well, not exactly.' She ran her fingers through her hair and gave an embarrassed little laugh. 'Sorry, I'm sounding positively incoherent, aren't I? Let me explain.' She took a deep, ragged breath. 'My usual nanny, Angela—Angela Proven—has been with me ever since I had Henry—that's our first baby, he's twenty months now—but yesterday she was rushed into hospital for an emergency appendectomy. This left me in a terrible fix. My husband is away in Brussels on business and I had a case starting in Norwich this morning. I have a housekeeper who comes in daily, but she has two children herself and can't be here at night. As it was a Sunday none of the staffing agencies was open, of course, and neither my mother nor my mother-in-law lives close enough to take the children. I just didn't know what to do. You'll appreciate the problem with my particular line of work, Inspector. It's not like an office where if you take a day off you can catch up later. If a barrister fails to turn up in Court on a day when there is only one case in the list, not only the judge but the Court officials, the jury, all the witnesses, everyone has to go home . . . And apart from the fact that it doesn't help your career to acquire a reputation for unreliability, this particular case was important to me. Work is always slow to pick up after such a long break and this was my first decent case since I started back after Alice was born. It was expected to last about three weeks and involved my staying away from Monday to Friday in Norwich . . . I'm just trying to explain how it came about that I asked Perdita to look after the children for me.'

'That would be Perdita . . . ?'

'Perdita Master. I've known her for years, we were at school together. Not that we've ever been close friends, but living in the same area we've run into each other from time to time and kept up with each other's news. So when I met her at the hospital, it seemed like an answer to a prayer when I found she'd just left her husband and was looking for somewhere to stay for a few days while she sorted herself out. Sorry, I forgot to say, she was a trained nanny, before she got married—'

'I'm sorry to interrupt, but you said, at the hospital . . .'

She raked her fingers through her hair again. 'Yes. Oh God, I'm not doing very well, am I, I feel such a fool . . .'

'You've had a severe shock . . . I assume you accompanied Miss Proven, when she was admitted to hospital.'

'Yes. Well, she went by ambulance and I followed by car, with the children—as I say, I had no one to leave them with . . . Anyway, I waited for a bit and then Angela was taken into the theatre and it seemed pointless hanging around for hours, especially with the children, so I decided to go home and on the way out I ran into Perdita. She'd been visiting her mother, who was in for some tests. Naturally we each explained what we were doing there, and when she heard about the fix I was in she suggested we could do each other a good turn. If she came and looked after the children until the weekend, when I could interview for a temporary nanny until Angela gets back, she could have a few days respite in which to sort out what she was going to do . . .'

'She'd just left her husband, you say?'

'Yes, on Saturday, the previous night. There'd been a frightful row, I gather, and she'd walked out on him. She'd gone to her mother's, but Giles had followed her there and—'

'Sorry, would that be Giles Master the estate agent?'

She nodded. 'Yes.'

The firm of Master and Prize was one of the larger estate agents in the town and had been founded by Giles Master's father, who had died a few years previously. Thanet knew most of the businessmen in Sturrenden by sight and some of them quite well; like Master, who was a few years younger than Thanet, many of them had attended the same school as he. He hadn't liked Giles much as a boy and had had no reason to change his opinion since.

'Anyway, as I was saying, when she walked out he guessed she'd go to her mother's house and followed her there, made an awful scene banging on the door and shouting because her stepfather wouldn't let him in. So when I saw her on Sunday afternoon she was trying to think of somewhere to go—not too far away, because of her mother being in hospital—where he wouldn't be able to find her . . . He's terribly jealous and possessive, she's had a hell of a time with him, poor girl . . .' For a moment the flow of her narrative halted as the memory of Perdita's fate caught up with her again. Then she shook her head, took another deep breath and went on. 'Anyway, we both thought it would never occur to him to look for her here . . .'

'You think that's what happened?'

Mrs Broxton hesitated, frowned down at her lap. 'How can I say?'

She paused and Thanet waited. She had remembered something, he was sure of it, and was debating whether or not to tell him.

'I don't actually know anything other than what happened to me.'

So she had decided against it. Could he have been wrong? He decided to go along with her, for the moment. 'And what was that?' Thanet had been wondering: if Mrs Broxton was supposed to be on a three-week case in Norwich, what was she doing here, at home? Unless the case had gone short, of course.

'My case went short,' she said. 'After the mid-day adjournment the defendant entered a plea. So naturally I decided to come straight home —well, I had to go back to the hotel to collect my stuff and pay the bill, of course. Anyway, I got away about three. I didn't bother to ring Perdita, I thought I'd easily be home between five and six.' She grimaced. 'Unfortunately my car broke down on the M11.' She ran her hand through her hair again. 'Oh God, what a day! There wasn't much traffic about and no phones in sight. I didn't dare get out of the car and set off to walk to the next one.'

Thanet nodded sympathetically. Ever since the motorway murder of Marie Wilkes, a young woman who had been seven months pregnant at the time and who had had to walk only a few hundred yards in broad daylight to telephone for assistance, women travelling alone whose cars broke down on motorways had been advised to lock the doors, stay inside and wait until help arrived, however frustrating the delay.

'It really does make me so angry, that women have lost the freedom to behave normally.' Briefly Mrs Broxton's eyes flashed with remembered fury and frustration. 'I was kicking myself for not having had a phone put in the car, or at least getting one of those emergency kits I read about, with a sign one can put up in the back window. I thought no one was ever going to stop, but eventually a police car pulled up and sent for the RAC. But it was another three-quarters of an hour before they arrived . . . I assure you I really heaved a sigh of relief when I at last arrived home. And then, of course—'

'Sorry, what time was that?'

'About half past nine, I think.' She waited a moment, in case Thanet had a further question, then went on, 'When I got to the front door I could hear Henry screaming. He always insists on having his bedroom door left open at night and with the galleried landing sound tends to carry, you can hear him if he so much as whimpers. Inside, I called Perdita, but there was no reply so I went straight up to the nursery. He was in a terrible state, practically hysterical . . .'

'Presumably he still sleeps in a cot.'

'Yes, thank God, or . . .' She shuddered and put her hands over her eyes, as if to blot out the images conjured up by her imagination.

'What about the baby? Alice?'

The first hint of a smile, there. 'Sound asleep, thank God. She sleeps like a log, always has. Fortunately she's in a separate room, so that there's no chance of Henry disturbing her. He does tend to wake in the night and make a fuss until someone comes.'

'Right. So you comforted Henry . . .'

'Yes. I thought he'd take ages to go to sleep, he was in such a state, but in fact he went out like a light, within minutes. I think he had cried himself to the point of exhaustion.'

'So then what did you do?'

'Well, naturally, the first thing I did was go and look for Perdita—that is, I glanced into her room, it's across the corridor from Henry's . . .'

'Is that normally Miss Proven's room?'

'No, that's next door to Henry's—well, between Henry's room and Alice's, actually. This is just a spare room, Angela sometimes has a friend to stay and she'll sleep in there . . . Anyway, Perdita wasn't in there, I didn't for a moment think that she could have been, and not heard Henry screaming . . . So then I went downstairs . . .'

Suddenly, as if impelled from her seat by an invisible force, Vanessa Broxton stood up and walked around to pick up a cigarette box from a sofa table behind the settee upon which she had been sitting. She opened it, peered inside then slammed it down in frustration. 'Oh God, I'm sorry, has anyone got a cigarette?'

Thanet looked at Lineham and WPC Barnes, both of whom shook their heads. 'Go and see if you can find one,' he said to the woman police constable.

Vanessa Broxton had returned to her seat. 'I haven't had a cigarette for over two years, I gave up when I was pregnant with Henry.'

'I think, under the circumstances, you can allow yourself a little laxity,' said Thanet.

WPC Barnes returned with a packet of Silk Cut and offered it to her.

'Thank you. There's a lighter on the table there . . .' Mrs Broxton put the cigarette to her lips with a hand that shook and inhaled deeply, closing her eyes. 'That's better.' She opened her eyes and gave a shamefaced grin. 'It's disgusting, but it helps.'

Thanet smiled, content to wait. He knew she was bracing herself for the worst part of her story.

3

After a few more puffs Vanessa Broxton pulled a face, reached for an ashtray and stubbed the cigarette out. 'I think I can manage without this after all. Sorry, where was I?'

'You went downstairs . . .'

'Ah, yes. I glanced in here, first. I thought perhaps she'd fallen asleep on the settee, or had been listening to music with headphones on, but the room was empty. So then I went to the kitchen . . . and . . . and found her. Well, you saw for yourself . . .'

'Did you move the body at all?'

'No.' She shuddered, compressed her lips. 'I did touch her, though. I felt her pulse, just to be sure . . . But I could see she was dead . . .' She shook her head. 'I couldn't believe it. It seemed like a nightmare, there in my own kitchen . . .'

'Did you touch anything else?'

'I don't think so, I may have done.' She pressed her fingers to her temples again. 'I don't really know. I'm sorry.'

'So then what did you do?'

'Went straight to the phone, of course, to ring the police.'

'That would be the phone in the kitchen?'

'No. I couldn't . . . Not with Perdita . . . I used the one in the hall.'

'Mrs Broxton, when I asked you just now if you thought Mrs Master's husband had found out she was here, I had the impression you remembered something . . .'

She gave a wry smile. 'One thing I should have remembered is that nothing much escapes you, Inspector. Yes, there was something . . . I suppose I was just giving myself time to make up my mind whether to mention it or not . . . I didn't want to be unfair to Giles. But of course, it's not a matter of being unfair, is it? Apart from the fact that if I don't tell you someone else is bound to, with the work I do I really ought to know that I *have* to tell you everything, down to the last detail . . .'

'So what was it, that you remembered?'

'Well, yesterday, when Perdita and I came out of the hospital, we could see that Giles was waiting for her, by her car. I suppose he'd guessed she'd probably visit her mother some time during the day and had decided to hang around so that he could catch her on the way out. At this point Perdita and I separated. Perdita was going to drive to her mother's house to collect her things, and then come on to mine. She and Giles had a brief argument, then she got into her car and drove off.'

'Did he follow her?'

'No. Not to my knowledge, anyway. He stood looking after her for a moment or two, then went to his car. He was still sitting in it when I left.'

'So what are you suggesting?'

'I'm not suggesting anything, Inspector, merely telling you what happened.'

But it was clear why Mrs Broxton had thought the incident could be significant. Master didn't sound the type to give up easily: if he had decided to try again, later in the day, to see his wife, had gone to her mother's house only to find that she was not staying there any longer . . . He could well have remembered seeing her with Vanessa at the hospital and put two and two together.

'Mr Master knows where you live?'

'Yes, he does.' She ran a hand wearily through her hair again. 'Oh God, what a mess . . .'

The brown eyes were dulled now, almost glazed. Shock was beginning to catch up with her.

'We've nearly finished, Mrs Broxton, then you can rest. I wonder, do you happen to know the address of Mrs Master's parents? We'll have to let them know what's happened.'

'Oh God, yes. As if they didn't have enough to cope with as it is, with her mother so ill in hospital . . .'

'We'll tell her stepfather, first, I think, and leave him to break the news to his wife when he feels she can cope with it. If you could just give us his name?'

'It's Harrow. They live in Wayside Crescent, Sturrenden. On the Pilkington estate. I don't know the number, I'm afraid.'

'Not to worry, we can easily find out. The next thing I wanted to ask you was this. These keys were in Mrs Master's pocket. Do you recognise them?' Thanet held them out.

She leant forward to inspect them. 'Yes. They're the keys to this house. I gave them to her. Front door, back door.'

'Why d'you think she would have been carrying them?'

Vanessa Broxton shrugged. 'She probably took the children out for a walk this afternoon and didn't want to carry a handbag. I've done the same myself.'

Thanet nodded. A reasonable enough explanation. 'Yes, of course. The next point is, do you happen to have noticed if there is anything obviously missing from the house? There seem to be no obvious signs of forced entry or disorder, I don't suppose you've even thought to check, in the circumstances . . .'

She again ran a hand through her hair, glanced about the room. 'Oh God, no, I haven't. It just didn't occur to me, everything seemed to be in order, as you say . . .'

'Tomorrow, perhaps, when you have time.'

'Yes, of course.'

'I only ask because I don't know if you realised . . . Your back door was unlocked when we arrived this evening.'

This brought her head up with a jerk, eyes now alert and wide open with shock. 'Was it? Oh God, I never thought to check . . . What a *fool* . . . He could still have been out there, after I got home. All I could think of was getting away from . . . getting out of the kitchen, ringing the police, getting somebody here, anybody . . .' Her hands were clasping, unclasping, kneading each other in her agitation.

There was a knock at the door. WPC Barnes opened it and went out, came back a moment later. 'Mrs Broxton's doctor is here, sir.'

Just at the psychological moment, by the look of it. Thanet stood up. 'Good. Bring him in.'

The doctor was short, middle-aged, brisk. He nodded at Thanet then went straight to Mrs Broxton, took both her hands in his. 'Vanessa, my dear, what a terrible business. How are you?'

'Better for seeing you, Peter.' She gave him a wan smile. 'But I think the appropriate expression in the circumstances is, "As well as might be expected."'

'I'd better take a look at you.' He glanced at Thanet, raised his eyebrows.

'Yes, we've finished here for the moment,' said Thanet. Then, to Mrs

Broxton, 'WPC Barnes will stay here tonight, so if you need anything . . .'

'Thank you, Inspector. You've been very kind.'

At the door Thanet turned. 'Oh, just one small matter . . . We'd like to take a look at the room Mrs Master was using . . .'

Vanessa Broxton waved a hand. 'Please, whatever you need to do, just do it. Anything, anything at all . . .'

'Thank you. If you could just tell us where it is?'

'Up the stairs, turn left, then straight along the corridor. It's the second door on the right. The children's rooms are opposite and Henry's door is open, so if you could be as quiet as possible . . .'

'Of course.'

Outside in the hall Perdita Master's body was just being removed by two ambulancemen. Thanet watched them leave before going in search of the dead woman's bedroom.

'If the back door was unlocked it could have been an intruder, couldn't it?' said Lineham as they mounted the stairs.

Thanet shrugged. 'Or whoever killed her unlocked it to get out.'

'You think it might have been the husband, and she let him in herself?'

'Early days, Mike. Early days. Let's not start speculating too soon.'

'In any case, it's odd that Mrs Broxton didn't think to check that the back door was locked before ringing us, don't you think?'

'Oh, I don't know. I think it's quite feasible that she was too shaken to be thinking clearly.'

On the galleried landing Thanet paused to look around. Above him massive honey-coloured oak beams lit to dramatic effect by strategically-placed spotlights rose in graceful curves, horizontals and diagonals. Below, the generously proportioned hall added a further dimension of light and space.

Lineham was concentrating on more mundane matters. 'But she's not stupid. In the circumstances you'd think her first thought would be to make sure the house was secure. After all, as she says, for all she knew the murderer could still have been around.'

Thanet shrugged. 'You know as well as I do, Mike, that people don't always think or act logically in situations of stress.'

They turned left as instructed along a broad corridor. More ancient beams straddled the ceiling and at one point they had to duck to pass beneath. Ahead of them, on the left, a door ajar indicated that they were approaching Henry's room and Thanet glanced at Lineham and put a finger to his lips. Henry had had enough traumas for one evening.

The room which Perdita Master had so briefly occupied was pleasant and comfortable, with a green fitted carpet, cream-washed walls and sprigged floral curtains. Double doors on a fitted cupboard opened to reveal a neat washbasin built in to one half, hanging and shelf space for clothes in the other.

She had brought very little with her: toilet things, several changes of underwear, another pair of cord trousers, cream this time, a couple of blouses, a pair of flat shoes. The most interesting item was a sketchbook on the bedside table. It was relatively new, the first pages taken up by sketches of flowers, grasses and trees. The last ten or twelve were a different matter. One was full of quick studies of two children, a small boy and a baby—Henry and Alice?—the last two of more detailed portraits of a man, drawn from several different angles.

He showed them to Lineham.

'Her husband?' said Lineham.

Thanet shook his head. 'I know Master. That's not him.'

'Perhaps Mrs Broxton will know who he is.'

They both stared at the sketches. The subject was in his late thirties or early forties, Thanet guessed, with straight hair worn rather too long for Thanet's taste and a narrow, sensitive face. The eyes were deepset, depicted with a distant, somewhat contemplative expression, the mouth rather weak.

'A lover?' said Lineham.

'Could be.' Thanet was still looking at the drawings, admiring now the skill of the artist. 'She was good, wasn't she? I wonder if she was a professional.'

'Mrs Broxton said Mrs Master was a trained nanny, before she got married.'

'Before she got married. Exactly. I can't quite see Giles Master allowing his wife to play nursemaid as a career.'

Lineham raised his eyebrows. ' "Allowing"? Like that, was it?'

'Perhaps I'm judging him too harshly. Anyway, you'll see for yourself soon, no doubt.' Thanet tapped the sketchbook. 'If she wasn't a professional she was a very gifted amateur. If the other drawings are of Henry and Alice, then as these come afterwards we can only assume she must have done them since she got here yesterday.'

He could imagine Perdita sitting propped up against those pillows, lamplight turning that mass of fair hair to spun gold, totally absorbed in her task and finding solace in it. He tried to put himself in her situation. The breakup of a marriage is always traumatic to both partners, regardless of which one is choosing to initiate it. Perdita would still have been shaken, emotionally bruised by the row with Giles and having so precipitately left her home. She was at a major turning point in her life, living in a kind of limbo. What more natural than in that state her thoughts would have turned to her lover, if she had one? He would have been her life-line to the future.

'Mrs Broxton said that Mr Master was very jealous and possessive, sir. That Mrs Master had a "hell of a time" with him. If it was only on Saturday night that he discovered she had a lover . . .'

'Quite.'

'Looks as though this could turn out to be pretty straightforward, doesn't it?'

'Perhaps.'

'Mr Master next, then?'

'Yes. Someone will have to break the news to him anyway. Looks as though in this case it had better be us.' This was one task which, like every policeman, Thanet hated above all others. 'Better take a look at her handbag before we go.'

On a demure little easy chair covered with the same sprigged material as the curtains lay a bulky brown leather shoulder bag. Lineham emptied its contents on to the bed and sat down beside them.

Thanet continued to study the drawings. He would know this face again when they met it. And if this were Perdita's lover, here was a second person about to receive a crushing blow. Thanet wondered if the man were married, had a wife and family . . .

'Doesn't look as though there's anything of any significance here, sir. Just the usual stuff.' Lineham was putting things back into Perdita's bag.

'Right. Let's go, then.' Thanet tucked the sketchbook under his arm. If Vanessa Broxton was still around he wanted to show her the portraits. But in case she wasn't, first of all . . .

Outside in the corridor he paused outside Henry's room. Silence. With a gesture to Lineham to remain where he was Thanet pushed the door open a little wider and tiptoed in. A nightlight in the shape of a red-spotted mushroom with a rabbit perched on top illuminated the cot. Henry was sound asleep, flat on his back with arms outflung in the careless abandon of childhood. One glance was enough to tell Thanet that this was indeed the small boy in the sketches. Perdita had been very talented, there was no doubt about that.

He returned to the corridor. 'The drawings are of Henry,' he whispered to Lineham.

On the galleried landing they met Mrs Broxton's doctor and WPC Barnes coming from the opposite direction. Presumably the Broxtons' bedroom was on the first floor of the far oast.

'Would it be possible to have a quick word with Mrs Broxton?' said Thanet.

The doctor shook his head. 'Sorry, she shouldn't be disturbed again tonight. I've given her a sedative. Constable Barnes has kindly agreed to listen out for the children.'

Thanet gave a resigned nod. Too bad. Identification of the man in the sketches would have to wait until morning.

Downstairs Bentley had just returned from interviewing the neighbour.

'Any luck?' asked Thanet.

'She's a Mrs Barnes, sir. A widow. Says she was putting the cat out at about 8.30 this evening and heard some kind of commotion over here—someone hammering on the front door and a man shouting, she says. She couldn't hear what he was saying, but after a few minutes the shouting stopped. She went back indoors then and just happened to go upstairs.' Bentley grinned. 'The landing window overlooks the drive of this house, so I'd guess she went up deliberately, to see what was going on. Unfortunately, she's got arthritis in both hips, so it took her some time to get there and by the time she did all she saw was a car driving away.'

'Any description of the car?'

Bentley shook his head. 'Nothing of any use. Big and dark in colour, that's all. And it was too dark for her to see who was driving, or how many people were in it. One interesting point, though. She did say she was aware of an unusual number of cars around this evening. She noticed because it's usually pretty quiet at night here.'

'What did she mean by "around"? Did she mean driving past her house, or coming into the drive of this one?'

'She couldn't be sure. Her sitting room is on the front corner nearest to the drive of the Oast, so it would have been difficult to tell.'

'And what did she mean by an unusual number?'

Bentley shrugged. 'She couldn't be very specific. When I pressed her she said between four and six.'

'Close together, or spaced out?'

'Between the incident we spoke of and the time the police cars started arriving.'

'Between 8.30 and, say, 10, then . . . Could mean anything or nothing.'

'She said she'd wondered if there was one of those supper safaris—you know, when a group of people have the first course at one house, the main course at another and the dessert at a third. They tend to go in for that sort of thing around here, apparently.'

'Remember to ask the men to check that, when you're doing house-to-house enquiries in the morning.' Thanet glanced at his watch. Ten past twelve. 'It's too late to start tonight. Lineham and I are going now to break the news to Mrs Master's husband, and I'd like you to do the same with her stepfather.'

A shadow flitted across Bentley's round, normally placid face. 'Right, sir.'

Thanet left Lineham to check the number of the Harrows' house and also the Masters' address in the telephone directory, while he went to see how the forensic team was getting on in the kitchen.

Five minutes later they were on their way.

4

Outside Thanet shrugged deeper into his overcoat and shoved his hands into his pockets. The temperature had dropped still further and the roofs of the cars were frosted over. The sky was thick with stars.

'Shall we go in separate cars, sir?' said Lineham.

'Where does Master live?'

'Nettleton.'

'Ah.'

They knew Nettleton well, from a case they had worked on together some years ago. Carrie Birch had been an apparently innocuous middle-aged cleaning woman, whose body had been found crammed into an outside privy behind a cottage near where she lived. Nettleton was only a couple of miles from Melton and it shouldn't take more than ten minutes to get there at this time of night.

'We'll go together in yours and pick mine up on the way back.'

'Right.'

Lineham sprayed de-icer on to his windscreen. 'The Super isn't going to like this, is he?' he said as he got into the car.

'You mean, because Mrs Broxton is involved? No. It could be tricky.'

Superintendent Draco, a fiery little Welshman, had arrived to take charge of Sturrenden sub-divisional headquarters a couple of years previously, full of zeal and enthusiasm to make his patch the best-policed area in the South of England. The ensuing period of change and adjustment had been painful for all concerned, but the results had been impressive: the record of arrests had gone up, morale had improved dramatically and although everyone grumbled about the demands Draco made upon time and energy he was universally accorded unqualified respect and even a grudging affection.

'Come to think of it, though, it's odd he hasn't turned up tonight, don't you think, sir?'

Draco liked to have his finger on the pulse of his division and the previous year had even gone through a period of turning up unexpectedly during the course of an investigation and sitting in on interviews with witnesses. Thanet had not enjoyed having the Superintendent breathing down his neck and had heaved a sigh of relief when Draco had turned the spotlight of his attention elsewhere. It was certainly unusual for him not to have been present for something as important as the start of a murder investigation, especially as the crime had been perpetrated at the Broxtons' house. Draco prided himself on good relationships with other professions concerned with the maintenance of law and order.

There had been so much to take in this evening that Thanet had not noticed Draco's absence until now. 'Yes, you're right, Mike. It is. Actually, I was thinking the other day . . . Don't you think he's been rather subdued, lately?'

'Now you mention it, yes, I have. I wonder . . .'

'What?'

'Well, Louise said she saw Mrs Draco in town the other day and she didn't look at all well. Louise wondered if we'd heard anything. I meant to ask you.'

'No, I haven't heard a word. But if she is ill, it would explain a lot.'

Thanet would never forget the first time he had met Angharad Draco. Shortly after Draco's arrival in Sturrenden the Thanets had been invited to a Rotary dinner and during the preceding reception Joan had nudged him.

'Who is *that?*' she'd whispered.

Following the direction of her nod Thanet had beheld one of the most beautiful women he had ever seen in his life. Tall and willowy, with a cloud of gleaming copper-gold hair and flawless complexion, the woman Joan had indicated was surrounded by a crowd of admiring males. She was in her early thirties, he guessed, and her lovely body in its simple floor-length sheath dress of sea-green silk would have had any sculptor reaching for his tools.

'No idea. Good grief—look!'

The group of men around the woman had shifted slightly, revealing the shorter man who stood beside her, smiling up at her. As the Thanets watched she put a proprietorial hand through his arm and returned his smile.

'Draco,' breathed Thanet. 'Surely that's not his wife.'

But it was. Later in the evening the Thanets had been introduced to her by a Draco whose uxorious smile held a distinct tinge of amusement; he was clearly used to the effect Angharad had upon others, and to the politely concealed disbelief that he should have won such a prize. It had been obvious then that he adored her and that his feelings were reciprocated.

Thanet had eventually come to understand that in fact the Dracos complemented each other: she needed his ebullience and volatility as much as he needed her cool, calm reserve. They had no children and apparently did not feel the lack of them; in such a mutually exclusive relationship any third person would perhaps have been superfluous.

Now, if Angharad were ill, if there were something seriously wrong with her . . . How would Draco bear it? Thanet remembered Doc Mallard's long years of near-disintegration, and shivered inwardly.

'I'll ask Louise to keep her ear to the ground,' said Lineham.

His wife was a trained nurse and had many friends in the medical profession, having worked for some years as a Sister at Sturrenden General Hospital.

'How is Louise, by the way? I haven't seen her for ages.'

Lineham did not reply immediately. Thanet thought that this was because they were approaching a T-junction, but after slowing down, waiting for a car to pass and turning left, Lineham still said nothing. Perhaps he hadn't heard?

Thanet glanced at him. It was dark, of course, but even so the dim illumination from the dashboard was sufficient to reveal the grim expression on Lineham's face. Thanet revised his opinion. The sergeant had heard, and either he didn't want to reply or he didn't know what to say. In either case Thanet had no intention of repeating the question.

But Lineham, it seemed, had merely been considering his answer. 'To be honest, sir, I think she's a bit confused.'

This was unexpected. Louise was a very decisive sort of person, with positive views on pretty well everything and a black and white outlook on life which Thanet would personally have found very difficult to live with. 'Oh?' he said, warily. Dare he ask what about? Was Lineham expecting him to?

Thanet decided to follow one of his own rules: when in doubt say nothing. If Lineham wanted to pursue the matter, he would. But if so, he would have to make up his mind quickly. Another half a mile or so and they would be in Nettleton. Having been brought up in this area

Thanet knew most of the roads around Sturrenden. He knew, for instance, that the camber was wrong on the next bend ahead, that if Lineham didn't slow down a little the car might well drift across the centre line . . .

Lineham slowed down.

'About going back to work, that is.'

'I'm not sure what you mean,' said Thanet, cautiously. He knew from his own experience what a minefield the question of working wives could be.

'Well, you know how keen she's always been to get back to work when both the children are at school, how difficult she's found it to adjust to staying at home, while they were small?'

'Yes.' Only last year Louise's restlessness had almost resulted in Lineham leaving the force; unable to find a satisfying outlet for her own energies she had for a while tried instead to persuade her husband to strike out in a new direction. Fortunately Lineham had found the strength to resist and on Thanet's advice had, instead, persuaded Louise to find a part-time job for the few hours a week when Mandy, their youngest, had been at playgroup.

'Well, as you know, Mandy will be starting school at Easter and I thought Louise would be over the moon at getting back into nursing, but no, now she's saying she's been out of the profession too long, that she's lost touch with all the latest developments in medicine, that she wouldn't be able to cope . . .'

'But surely there are refresher courses, for people in her position?'

'That's what I say to her. But I don't know . . . I think the truth is, she's lost confidence in herself.'

'That's not unusual. In fact, I understand it's quite common for women who've been at home for a few years to feel like that. Joan did, herself.'

'Did she?' said Lineham eagerly. 'I didn't know that.'

'Oh yes, she certainly did. Look, if it would be any help, I'm sure Joan would have a chat with her.'

'Would she?' Lineham's tone was still eager, but it changed as he said doubtfully, 'I'm not sure that Louise would be too pleased if she thought I'd been talking to you about it. Unless Joan could bring the subject up casually, without her knowing . . .'

'I'm sure she could. She's pretty good at that sort of thing.'

'Yes, I know.' Lineham was silent for a few moments, then said,

'D'you think you could ask her, then? If the situation arises, that is, when she could do it tactfully?'

'Of course.'

'Thanks. I really would appreciate it. Nothing I say seems to make any difference. Perhaps Louise will listen to someone from outside the family who's been through the same thing herself.'

Lineham pulled up at the main Sturrenden to Maidstone road, then crossed it to enter Nettleton. It was now just after midnight and apart from a single light in the bedroom of one of the cottages the village was dark and silent.

'D'you know where the house is?' said Thanet.

'In Wheelwright's Lane. It's a turning to the right, just past the post office.'

The black and white timbered building, formerly a private house, which housed the general shop and post office loomed up on their left.

Lineham signalled and turned right. Wheelwright's Lane was narrow and winding, with a scatter of cottages which soon gave way to open fields and clumps of trees, their branches etched black against the night sky.

'Now,' said Lineham, leaning forward to peer through the windscreen, 'if it's where I think it is . . . Yes, it'll be one of these.'

Ahead lay a cluster of buildings: a pair of cottages on the right and several larger, detached houses strung out along the road on their left.

'What's it called?' said Thanet.

'Applewood House.' Lineham slowed down as they came to the first drive entrance.

'This is it,' said Thanet, peering out. The name was stamped in black letters on a white board attached to the right-hand gatepost.

Lineham reversed, then drove in, wheels crunching on the gravel.

Despite the hour there were lights on in the house, a sizeable red-brick house of relatively recent design, with white-painted window-frames which gleamed in the darkness.

There was no knocker and after a moment or two of groping and peering Lineham found an iron loop which he thought must be the bell. He pulled it.

No response.

'Try again,' said Thanet.

A minute or two later a man's voice called out, 'Who is it?'

'Police.'

The scrape of a key, the rattle of a latch and the door swung open. A man peered out.

'Mr Master? It's Inspector Thanet, Sturrenden CID.'

Master swayed. 'Ah, Thanet, yes . . . What is it? What's the matter?' The words were slurred and it was clear that he had been drinking.

'If we could come in for a moment . . .'

Master stepped back unsteadily to let them in and led them through a small, square hall into a room on the left. Inside he turned slowly to face them. 'What is it?' he repeated.

A thrill of interest and curiosity coursed through Thanet's veins at his first clear view of Master's face. He was familiar with Master's conventional good looks, well-cut tweed suits and generally well-groomed appearance; he and the estate agent were both out and about a lot in the area in the course of their work. Tonight, however, Master sported a black eye and severe bruising of the left cheek. His tie was loosened and his usually sleek brown hair was dishevelled. He was clearly in no condition to receive such news as this—if news it was. On the other hand, if he were innocent, perhaps the fact that his perceptions were blunted would help to cushion the blow.

In any case, Thanet had no choice. 'Won't you sit down, Mr Master?'

Master simply stared at him with alcohol-dulled eyes.

'Shall we all sit down?' Thanet moved decisively to the nearest armchair and sat.

Following Thanet's nodded instruction Lineham stepped forward and, putting one hand gently under Master's elbow, guided him to a chair and lowered him into it.

Master continued to stare blankly at Thanet.

Come on, get it over with, thought Thanet. 'I'm afraid we have some bad news for you.'

No change in Master's expression.

'It's . . . it's about your wife. She . . . I'm sorry, there's no way I can make this easier for you . . . She was found dead earlier this evening.'

Master continued to stare and it was a full minute before a glimmer of comprehension and disbelief crept into his eyes. 'Dead?' he whispered. His voice grew louder, thickened. 'Perdita? She's not. Can't be.'

'I'm sorry. It's true.'

'No!' Master rubbed his hands over his face, his eyes, shook his head violently as if to clear it. 'Must be mistake. All right s' evening.'

'You saw her this evening, then?'

'Just said so, didn't I?' Master raked his hair with his hands, made an
obvious effort to pull himself together and speak clearly. 'There must
be some mistake,' he repeated stubbornly.

Thanet shook his head. 'I'm afraid not.'

There was a brief silence, then Master muttered, ' 'Scuse me,' and
blundered out of the room.

At Thanet's nod Lineham followed him. The sergeant left the door
open and it was soon clear that Master had merely crossed the hall to a
cloakroom; from the sound of it he was dousing his head in water.

Thanet glanced around. A dying log fire smouldered in the hearth
and a near-empty bottle of whisky and half-full glass showed where
Master had been sitting. A television set still murmured in a corner and
Thanet crossed to switch it off before studying the room more closely. It
was large, and spacious, with windows on three sides, French doors
which presumably opened on to the garden and a high ceiling decorated
with plaster mouldings. Interestingly, however, despite the big, soft sofas and chairs and tastefully disposed antique furniture, the impression
was curiously chilly and impersonal. Thanet frowned, trying to work out
why. Perhaps it was absence of clutter—books, newspapers, magazines?
Or perhaps the predominance of blue? Blue and cream carpet, deep
blue or cream upholstered chairs, cream brocade curtains . . . Only
one bright pink chair and a brilliant explosion of colour in a picture on
the wall opposite the fireplace redeemed the room from coldness.
Thanet crossed to take a closer look at the painting, which had caught
his eye earlier. Indeed, it could hardly fail to catch the eye. A thought
occurred to him: perhaps, if Perdita Master had painted it, the room
had been designed around it, to accord it just this degree of promi-
nence?

It was, he realised as he drew closer, a watercolour, not an oil painting as he had at first thought. He was no connoisseur of art, and had
always supposed that such vibrancy of colour could only be associated
with oils. This was, he supposed, a painting of a garden, or of a
flowerbed, depicting a waving forest of brilliant fuchsia-pink exotica—
lilies, perhaps?—in a dense, lush undergrowth of writhing greens and
purples. And yes, it had been painted by Perdita Master; her signature
was in the lower righthand corner.

He was still studying it when Lineham returned, followed a moment
or two later by Master, whose hair was wet and roughly combed. The
estate agent certainly looked more alert, and Thanet wasn't sure

whether the glazed look residual in his eyes was due to shock or alcohol. It shouldn't take too long to find out.

Master plumped down in his armchair, automatically picked up his glass, looked at it, then slammed it down again so forcibly that the liquid slopped over on to the table-top. 'Oh, sit down, for God's sake. No point in standing there like a couple of tailor's dummies.' He buried his face in his hands, shaking his head and massaging his forehead with hooked fingers.

They sat.

'I really am sorry,' said Thanet gently.

Master looked up. 'Are you?' he said fiercely. Then he leaned back, closed his eyes. 'Oh God, I'm sorry. It's not your fault . . .' His eyes snapped open, suddenly dark with apprehension. 'You haven't told me yet what happened, how she . . .'

There was no way Thanet could soften the blow. 'Your wife was found dead in the kitchen of Mrs Broxton's house. And I'm afraid it was no accident.'

Master stared at him, trying to take in the implication. 'No accident? What d'you mean? Are you saying . . . ?'

'I'm sorry. Yes. She was killed, deliberately.'

Master's eyes were wide with shock. 'Murdered?' he said, his voice rising. 'You're saying Perdita's been *murdered?*'

If the man was acting he was carrying this off superbly. But then, he would have a lot to lose . . . Thanet nodded. 'Yes.'

'But how . . . ?'

'It looks as though there was an argument, a quarrel . . . So far as we can tell at the moment, Mrs Master fell, knocking herself out—'

'And the bastard just left her there to die!'

Master's voice was hoarse with outrage and Thanet did not contradict him. If Master were innocent there was no point in turning the knife in the wound by giving further details.

Master moaned and again buried his face in his hands. From time to time he shook his head in disbelief or despair.

Thanet sent Lineham to make some coffee. 'Hot and strong.'

When Lineham returned Master accepted the mug of steaming liquid and sipped at it as obediently as a small child. Eventually he said wearily, 'I suppose you'll be wanting to ask me some questions.'

'When you're ready.'

'I'm as ready as I ever will be.'

'Very well . . . You say you saw your wife earlier on this evening?'

A nod.

'Would you tell us about it?'

The man hesitated, clearly marshalling his thoughts. 'You obviously know that she was staying with Mrs Broxton . . .' He waited for Thanet's nod. 'Well I got there about half past eight, twenty to nine . . .'

'I'm sorry to interrupt, but was this meeting prearranged?'

Master looked uncomfortable. 'No. I just called in on the off-chance . . .' He waited, but Thanet remained silent. 'Anyway, she agreed to come out for a drink with me . . .'

'What about the children?' said Thanet.

Master waved a dismissive hand. 'Oh, that was all right. They were sound asleep.'

Thanet's face must have shown his disbelief, because Master burst out angrily, 'If you don't believe me you can ask the landlord of the Green Man in Melton. There weren't many people there, he should remember us.'

Master must be telling the truth, the story could so easily be checked.

'I think it only fair to tell you that Mrs Broxton said your wife had left you.' Thanet paused, but Master said nothing. 'She also says that you have since attempted to talk to Mrs Master on at least two occasions, once on Saturday night, when you followed her to her parents' house, and once on Sunday afternoon, at the hospital. She says that Mrs Master had gone to stay with her in the hope of a few days' peace when she could sort out what she wanted to do . . . You must see that in the circumstances I find it very difficult to believe that she willingly went for a drink with you this evening, especially as it would have meant leaving the children alone in the house at night.'

'No, well . . .' Master was realising that some explanation would have to be given. His hand moved to pick up his glass of whisky, stopped. 'Oh hell, what's the point of pretending. The truth is, I made her come with me . . . Don't look at me like that! Don't you see, I *had* to talk to her. And she wouldn't let me in.'

Thanet could understand why. Once Master had got his foot over the threshold there would have been no way that Perdita could have got rid of him.

Abruptly, Master stood up and began to walk about. 'She was my *wife,* for God's sake! Surely a man's entitled to talk to his own wife!'

'Mrs Broxton's neighbour has told us that around 8.30 there was some sort of commotion outside Mrs Broxton's house. A man shouting, she said. I assume, from what you're saying, that that was you.'

Master swung around and faced Thanet. 'I told you, Perdita wouldn't listen! And don't think I can't see where all this is leading, Thanet.' He advanced until he was standing only a few paces in front of Thanet, looming over him threateningly.

Bracing himself in case of attack, out of the corner of his eye Thanet was aware of Lineham also tensing in readiness for action.

Master was pointing an admonishing finger, punctuating practically every word by stabbing the air. 'Just get this into your head, will you? I did *not* kill my wife. I wouldn't have harmed a single hair of her head . . .' His tone suddenly changed. 'Can't I make you understand? I loved her!' His belligerence had evaporated and he now sounded more bewildered than anything else. 'I loved her more than anything on earth, and now . . .' Abruptly he plumped back down into his chair and his eyes filled with tears, which began to spill over and trickle down his cheeks. Tugging a handkerchief from his pocket he dashed them away impatiently.

Only the most consummate actors can cry at will. The man's distress was genuine, Thanet was sure of it—but based on what? Grief at the news of the death of his wife, or remorse at having brought it about? Thanet was as aware as the next man that the most likely culprit in a case of domestic murder is the husband or wife, and this fact had caused him some of the most uncomfortable moments in his career. Always, in this first interview with a bereaved partner, he was torn between compassion in case the suspect were innocent and determination that if he were guilty he couldn't be allowed to get away with it.

'Look, Mr Master, you shouldn't jump to conclusions. I assure you that at the moment we have a completely open mind on the subject. I'm just trying to get you to see that you have to be frank with us—'

'All right, all right, you've made your point!' The man's natural aggression was already beginning to reassert itself. He blew his nose loudly and put the handkerchief away.

'So let's start again from the beginning, shall we? You got there at about 8.30 . . .'

5

At a signal from Thanet, Lineham took over the questioning. It was some time before the full story emerged.

Master had arrived at the Broxtons' house between 8.30 and 8.40. In response to his knock Perdita had come to one of the front windows, being understandably wary of opening the front door at night in such a quiet country area when, apart from the children, she was alone in the house. At first, seeing that it was Giles, she had simply gone away, but he had persisted, banging more loudly on the door until she had come to the window again and this time opened it.

'Giles! Stop making all that noise, you'll wake the children. Go away!'
'Let me in! I have to talk to you.'
'I've got nothing to say to you. We said it all on Saturday night.'
'Perdita, please . . . I won't stay long, honestly.'
'I'm sorry, Giles, I just don't feel I can trust you to keep that promise.'

Thanet guessed that she had also felt she couldn't trust her husband to keep his temper.

'But I will! I will, honestly . . . OK, look, in that case, let's go down to the pub in the village, for a quick drink. We won't stay long, I promise. You can leave whenever you like . . .'
'And leave the children alone in the house? Don't be ridiculous. It's out of the question!'

And she had closed the window and gone away again.

'So then what did you do?' said Lineham.

'Well I wasn't going to give up, was I? No way!' Master shook his head. 'After all, as I say, all I wanted to do was talk to her, for God's sake! So I thought, Right, if that's the way she wants it . . . If she doesn't mind the children being woken up, that's fine by me. And if Mrs high-and-mighty Vanessa Broxton doesn't like having the police called around to her house, then that's just too bad.'

'So what did you do?'

'Hammered on the door and shouted fit to wake the dead,' said Master with retrospective satisfaction.

It was perhaps the fact that the word was at the end of the sentence that made it seem to hang on the air, reverberate. The brief animation which Master had displayed while he recounted this incident fell away and his expression changed as he returned to the present with a thud. 'Oh God . . .'

Thanet waited for a minute or two before saying, 'This needn't take much longer, sir. If you could just finish telling us . . .'

Master nodded, took a deep breath, then expelled it slowly. 'She didn't hold out long, of course. I knew she wouldn't.'

After a few minutes Perdita had returned to the window and reluctantly agreed to talk to him outside. A moment or two later she had come out, shutting the front door behind her.

Presumably so that her husband wouldn't force his way in, thought Thanet.

Master had stopped.

'Then what?' said Lineham.

'I was hopping mad,' said Master sullenly, 'at the way she was treating me. After all, she was the one who was in the wrong. She was the one who'd walked out on me, not the other way around . . .'

Lineham said nothing, waited.

'I didn't see why it all had to be on her terms.'

'So?'

'I told you, I was furious with her . . .'

Thanet guessed that Master was ashamed of what he had done next, and this was why he was prevaricating. He could also guess what was coming.

Lineham was still waiting.

'I made her get into the car,' muttered Master shamefacedly.

Lineham opened his mouth, shut it again.

Thanet imagined the sergeant had been going to say, 'Made her? How?' and had thought better of it. Sensible perhaps to gloss over the use of force at this point. But it wouldn't have been difficult. Perdita had been small and slight, Master must be a good fifteen stone.

'Then what?' said Lineham.

Master shrugged. 'I'd left the keys in the ignition, so it was easy. I just took off. We went to the pub, as I said.'

Lineham was shaking his head. 'Sorry, sir. After all that I can't see Mrs Master meekly going along and having a drink with you. How did you manage to . . . persuade her?'

Master shot him a venomous look. 'All right, so I'm not very proud of myself now . . .'

Lineham raised his eyebrows.

Master jumped up and went to stand in front of the fire, his back to them. 'Oh hell . . .' He swung around to face them. 'I simply told her that if she didn't I'd just keep on driving, and the kids would be left alone all night. But if she agreed, I'd guarantee to get her back to the house in half an hour.'

It had been Hobson's choice for Perdita.

All this had taken no longer than ten or fifteen minutes and they had arrived at the Green Man in Melton at about ten to nine. In the event, it had been a pointless exercise. Perdita had remained adamant. She refused even to consider going back to him and had repeated that nothing would change her mind about seeking a divorce. In the end he had given up. He took her back to the Broxtons' house, arriving there at about twenty past nine and had left at once.

'You didn't go into the house?' said Lineham.

'No. I didn't bother to ask. She'd only have refused. Anyway, there would have been no point. Her mind was made up. I just dropped her off then drove away.'

Lineham glanced at Thanet, eyebrows raised. *Anything else you want to ask?*

Thanet nodded and picked up the plastic carrier bag in which he had put Perdita's sketchbook. He took it out. 'We found this amongst your wife's belongings.' He flicked through it, held up the full-face sketch. 'Can you identify this man?'

The muscles of Master's face froze but he couldn't control the expression in his eyes. Shock, pain, anger, all were there. 'Yes. That's our next-door neighbour, Howard Swain.'

'Drawn by your wife, I assume?' Thanet glanced at the painting on the wall. 'She was an artist, I gather.'

'Yes. She's . . . she was, very talented.' Master nodded at the drawing and said, with an attempt at lightness, 'She was always persuading friends to sit for her. She preferred to draw people she knew than to hire a model. I imagine those are preliminary sketches for a portrait.'

Thanet didn't believe him. The fact that these had been drawn in such detail and probably from memory strongly suggested an emotional involvement on Perdita's part. But if so, Master was doing his best to play it down. Why? Because he couldn't bear to think of her having a lover? Or because knowing that she had a lover would give him a stronger motive for killing her, in the eyes of the police? It was interesting that Swain was their next-door neighbour. Perhaps he, too, was sporting a black eye.

Master looked exhausted. His eyes seemed to have receded deeper into their sockets, the pouches beneath them to have become more pronounced.

Thanet took pity on him. If the man were innocent he needed a respite; he had suffered enough for one evening. And if he were not . . . well, it was obvious that at the moment nothing would shake his story. Further questioning would have to wait until they had something specific to go on. He stood up. 'About the formal identification . . . I'll send someone to pick you up, in the morning.'

Master's lips tightened. 'What time?'

'Nine o'clock?'

A nod. 'Right.'

At the front door Thanet paused. 'That's a nasty black eye you've got there, sir. What happened?'

Master's mouth tugged down at the corners. 'Believe it or not, I walked into a door. I feel such a fool . . . Got up to go to the bathroom during the night, didn't switch the light on . . .'

That old chestnut! In Thanet's opinion Master would have had to run into a door at top speed for the impact to have had that effect. But he merely nodded, murmured his thanks and left.

'Walked into a door!' said Lineham as they got into the car. 'I bet this chap Swain was the reason she was leaving him and after the row on Saturday he went steaming around there and they had a fight.' He peered through the windscreen at the house next door, which was all in darkness. 'Are we going to see Mr Swain now?'

Thanet glanced at the dashboard clock. Nearly one a.m. 'I don't think we've got enough evidence to justify hauling him out of bed at this hour. No, he'll keep till tomorrow. I think we'll call it a day.'

* * *

Next morning, he and Ben were having breakfast when the phone rang.

'I'll get it,' called Joan, who was on her way downstairs.

'Yuk!' said Ben, surveying the array of cereal packets on the table. 'Bran, bran and more bran. Oh, sorry, bran, bran, muesli and more bran. Why can't we have rice crispies, or sugar puffs, or even corn-flakes . . . ?'

'Stop grumbling,' said Thanet, with only half his attention on the conversation. The phone call was probably for him. 'High fibre is good for you.'

The door to the hall was ajar and he heard Joan say, 'Oh, no! When was this?'

Her tone told him that this was bad news. His stomach lurched. Bridget. Something had happened to Bridget. He got up and went to the door.

Joan was facing him, clutching the phone in both hands. Her expression confirmed that this was serious. In a series of lightning vignettes his ever-fertile imagination presented him with a succession of images, each more horrendous than the last: Bridget lying in the road, injured and bleeding; Bridget flying through the windscreen of a car, her face cut to shreds; Bridget lying, as he had seen so many people lie in premature death, sheeted in the morgue, a label on her toe the only vestige of her identity . . . Joan covered the receiver, whispered, 'My mother. Heart attack.'

The relief was only momentary. Thanet was very fond of his mother-in-law, had got to know her particularly well when she had come to live with him and the children while Joan was completing her training for the Probation service. He put his arm around Joan's shoulders. 'She's not . . . ?'

Joan shook her head.

This time the relief was heartfelt.

Joan said, 'I'll get there as soon as I can.' She put the phone down. 'That was Mrs Parker, Mum's next-door neighbour. They were sup-posed to go shopping together in Maidstone this morning and wanted to leave early, to get in before the rush. She went out to get the milk at half past seven, noticed Mum's curtains were all still drawn, no lights on. There was no answer to her knock so she let herself in; she's got a key . . .'

'What's the matter?' Ben was standing at the kitchen door, listening. 'Is it Gran?'

Joan nodded, biting her lip.

'She's not . . . ?' said Ben, echoing his father.

'No, of course not! She's . . .' Joan hesitated, clearly wondering how much to tell him.

'What?'

Joan glanced at Thanet. *Shall I?*

'Oh *Mum!*' said Ben. 'Come on! I'm not a baby, you know. What's the matter with her?'

'She's had a heart attack.'

Ben's fingers tightened on the doorpost. 'Oh . . .' He put the question that Thanet had been waiting to ask. 'How serious is it?'

'Mrs Parker didn't know. But fortunately it seems to have happened not long before she got there—Mum had just got out of bed, they think . . . Mrs Parker called an ambulance and they got there very quickly. They've taken her to Sturrenden General.'

The muscles of Joan's shoulders were rigid with tension beneath Thanet's arm.

'I must go,' she said. She put her hand to her head. 'Let me think. What have I got to do, first? I'll have to let them know, at work . . .' She glanced at her watch. 'But that'll be all right, I can do that later.'

'I'll do it for you, if you like.'

'No, it's all right, I'll have to speak to Janice myself, get her to reorganise my day. Fortunately there's nothing especially . . . Oh no . . . There was one particularly important appointment this morning. With Sharon . . .'

Sharon Strive was a young single parent with two small children who after a long history of shoplifting was making a serious attempt to go straight. Joan had been working with her for some time.

'She's not on the phone, either, there's no way of getting in touch with her.'

'Someone from the office will go around and explain, I'm sure. She'll understand, in the circumstances. First things first.' He pushed Joan gently towards the stairs. 'Go on, get ready.'

'I just hate letting people down, especially someone like her, who hasn't got anyone else.'

'Get your coat,' said Thanet. 'I'll see to everything here. And I'll ring the hospital and get along as soon as I can.'

'No, don't worry, I'll ring you as soon as I find out the position.

You'll be so busy today, with this new case. How long will you be at the office?'

Thanet thought rapidly. 'Till about 9.30, I should think.'

'Right.' Joan hurried upstairs and Thanet went to move his car out of he drive, so that she could get hers out of the garage.

For once Thanet arrived in good time at Draco's morning meeting. Very little of interest had come in overnight and he had left Lineham to organise various tasks for the team: a preliminary, low-key call at the Swains' house, an interview with Mrs Broxton's housekeeper, house-to-house enquiries in the vicinity of the Broxtons' home. The PM had been fixed for that afternoon.

Draco was standing at the window when Thanet entered, looking out at the forecourt, hands clasped behind his back.

'Ah, good morning, Thanet. Take a seat. Sorry I couldn't get along last night.'

He offered no explanation, Thanet noted.

Draco sat down heavily at his desk.

There was definitely something wrong with him, thought Thanet. All the Superintendent's usual bounce and verve had drained away. The jet-bright blackness of his eyes was dulled and even his crisp, dark, springing hair seemed more limp and lifeless than usual. Perhaps it was Draco himself who was ill, or at least well below par.

Chief Inspector Tody, Draco's deputy, sidled in in his usual irritatingly deferential manner, followed soon afterwards by Inspector Boon of the uniformed branch, a long-time friend and colleague of Thanet.

The meeting began as it always did with a brief summary of the previous day's proceedings by each of them. The murder of Perdita Master at Melton was by far the most serious crime to report, and of necessity Thanet's report was the longest. Draco would normally have peppered Thanet with questions, but today his interest was little more than cursory. Apart from a brief flare of interest at the fact that the murder had taken place at Vanessa Broxton's house ('You'll have to be careful not to tread on too many toes there, Thanet'), he said little until Thanet had finished. Then, with a visible effort, he said, 'Not much to go on at the moment, then?'

'No, sir. Only the polythene bag.'

'Well, you never know what we might learn from that. Every contact leaves a trace, remember, Thanet. Every contact leaves a trace.'

'Yes, sir,' said Thanet, suppressing his irritation. He did wish Draco wouldn't treat him like a raw recruit half the time! Boon's ironic wink made him feel a little better.

'Right,' said Draco, laying both palms flat on his desk.

This was the usual signal for the meeting to end and all three men began to rise.

'Er . . . There's just one other thing,' said Draco.

They subsided into their chairs again.

Draco picked up a pencil and began fiddling with it, tapping on the desk and turning it in his fingers. 'Er . . .' Thanet and Boon glanced at each other. What was coming? Draco was usually positive, decisive, the words tumbling over each other in his haste to get them out, or rolling forth in the sonorous, measured cadences of a Welsh preacher.

'I had hoped it wouldn't come to this, but . . .' Draco compressed his lips. 'I'm afraid, however, that it looks as though I am going to have to make somewhat heavier demands than usual upon you, so . . .'

He glanced at each of them in turn, his gaze sombre, assessing.

'It seems likely,' he said carefully, 'that in the near future I shall have to take time off occasionally.' He lifted his chin, almost pugnaciously, as if preparing himself to meet whatever blows fate had in store for him. 'My wife is ill, and she is going to have to go to London from time to time for treatment. Naturally I shall go with her . . .' He was looking at his desk, unable to meet their gaze, afraid perhaps that the sympathy in their eyes would unman him.

There was a moment's silence while his three subordinates glanced at each other, united in shock and sympathy. Then Tody cleared his throat and said, 'We're very sorry to hear that, sir. We hope the treatment will be effective very quickly and meanwhile, please, don't worry about what will happen at work. I know I speak for all of us when I say we'll be only too willing to stand in or work overtime whenever it's necessary.'

Draco risked a glance at them. 'Thank you.'

It was obvious that his self-control was precarious and in unspoken agreement his three subordinates rose and left the room. Outside they conferred in low tones. 'Sounds serious,' said Tody gloomily.

'If it is, it'll hit him hard,' said Boon.

'Don't talk as though she's dead already!' said Thanet. 'We don't know what's wrong yet. Could be something that'll respond to treatment.'

Boon shrugged. 'Let's hope so.'

When Thanet told Lineham the sergeant snapped his fingers. 'I forgot to tell you . . . Louise told me this morning that she'd run into one of her friends from Sturrenden General yesterday and she'd told her that Mrs Draco has leukaemia.'

'Oh, no . . . How serious is it? Aren't some types of leukaemia curable nowadays?'

The phone rang: Joan, with news of her mother. Mrs Bolton was in intensive care and the nursing staff would say no more than that it was too early to tell. Joan was going to stay at the hospital all day, if necessary.

'I'll probably have to see someone in the hospital later on this morning,' said Thanet. 'I'll try and get along to see you at the same time.' He wouldn't tell Joan about Angharad Draco at the moment.

'Oh good. See you then.'

Thanet put the phone down. 'Bit of an avalanche of doom and despair this morning, eh, Mike?'

'I expect we'll survive, sir. We usually seem to. Meanwhile . . .'

Meanwhile, thank God, there was work to be done.

'Who first, then, sir?'

'Better go and see Mrs Master's parents, I suppose.'

'Not Mr Master? Or Mr Swain?'

Thanet shook his head. 'Mr Master is doing the identification at the moment. And anyway, as I said last night, I want to see if we can get something a bit more concrete before we go back to him. With any luck Perdita Master confided in either her mother or her stepfather. And Mr Swain can wait. He won't run away.'

'We hope,' murmured Lineham *sotto voce,* as they picked up their coats and headed for the door.

6

In comparison with today's sprawling conurbations the Pilkington estate in Sturrenden is positively cosy, consisting of no more than a few pleasant tree-lined streets of 1930s houses. Wayside Crescent backs on to school playing fields and Perdita Master's mother and stepfather lived in one of the few detached houses. It was typical of the era, with generous bay windows upstairs and down and an arched entrance porch floored with quarry tiles. The place was spick and span, with neat front garden, weed-free drive, fresh paintwork and shining windows.

The man who opened the front door was, Thanet guessed, usually equally neat, the type who feels most comfortable in suit and tie and whose only concession to leisure wear would be to discard his jacket in favour of a knitted cardigan. This morning the suit was appropriately sombre, dark grey worsted, with white shirt and black tie. The tie, however, was ill-knotted, a shoelace on one of his highly polished black shoes was trailing, and there was a small whitish patch on his jawline where he had cut himself while shaving and dabbed the spot with a styptic stick.

'Mr Harrow?' Thanet introduced himself and Lineham.

Harrow's jowls quivered as he clenched his teeth. 'I still can't believe it . . .' He stepped back. 'Come in.'

He was in his mid-fifties, shortish and plump, verging on fat, with a round face, double chin, pale watery blue eyes and a few strands of hair trying to conceal the fact that he was virtually bald.

He led them into a stiflingly hot sitting room which was neat if somewhat insipid, with pale green walls, deeper green curtains and a fitted carpet in shades of green and beige. It was comfortably furnished with settee, matching armchairs, and bookshelves in the alcoves on either side of the gas fire with its imitation logs. The most striking feature was the painting on the opposite wall, one of Perdita's, Thanet guessed. Here was a night-time garden, the pale disc of the moon floating through swollen, swirling masses of sombre cloud. In the foreground was a forest of white lilies, ghostly in the moonlight, their pale, delicate trumpets upturned as if in worship of the silver goddess of the night.

Harrow acknowledged Thanet's evident interest. 'Perdita painted that. A birthday present for my wife. Do sit down.'

Excess flesh strained against fabric at shoulder, thigh, stomach and crotch as Harrow lowered himself into an armchair.

Thanet sat on the settee, deliberately choosing to turn his back on the painting. It had a kind of magnetic power, drawing the eye and nailing the attention, altogether too distracting while conducting an interview. Even so, he could visualise it, almost *feel* it on the wall behind him, exerting its strange fascination.

Lineham took the other armchair. He and Thanet preferred not to sit next to each other at interviews. It was important for them to be able to see each other's face. Unspoken communication was an essential part of their routine.

'Such a waste,' said Harrow, shaking his head.

Thanet was already beginning to feel uncomfortably hot. How could people live in such a temperature?

Lineham was also feeling the heat. Like Thanet, the sergeant had already removed his overcoat and was unbuttoning his jacket.

'I'm very sorry about your stepdaughter. It must have been a terrible shock to you.'

Harrow inclined his head. 'Yes. And the worst part of it is, I've still got to tell my wife. She's in hospital.'

'Yes, I know.'

Harrow leaned forward anxiously. 'You haven't told her yourself, I hope?'

Thanet shook his head. 'We thought it best to leave it to you.'

'Good.' Harrow pulled a face. 'I say "good" but I'm dreading it. She's got enough on her plate to cope with as it is. Anyway, I guessed you'd come around this morning so I thought I'd wait to visit her in case you had any news. Have you?'

'It's too early yet, I'm afraid. We came to see you to fill in a little of the background.'

'In what way?'

'It's important that we should understand what has been going on lately in your stepdaughter's life.'

'You're not saying she was . . . that this has happened . . . that someone she *knows* was responsible for her death? I assumed it was some maniac who had broken in . . . One hears so much of that sort of thing these days.'

'At this stage we simply don't know. So if we could . . .'

Harrow heaved himself up out of his armchair and began to walk about. 'But that's impossible! Ludicrous! Unless . . .'

Abruptly, he stopped walking and turned to stare at Thanet.

'Unless what?'

Harrow shook his head. 'Nothing.'

'Oh come, Mr Harrow. Obviously a thought struck you, just then.'

But Harrow again shook his head, stubbornly. 'It was nothing, really.'

Thanet guessed that Harrow was thinking of Perdita's husband, of the quarrel. He decided not to press the point at the moment. 'Anyway, it's essential that at this point we take as broad a view as possible, and gather some background information. So if you could answer a few questions . . . ?'

Harrow returned to his chair, sat down again. He lifted his sausage-like fingers in a gesture of surrender. 'Of course. Anything to help.'

Thanet was beginning to sweat. 'I wonder if, before we begin, we could perhaps have the door open?'

'Of course.'

Lineham jumped up with alacrity, opened it as wide as it would go.

'Sorry,' said Harrow. 'I always forget how hot people find it. I've got used to it by now, of course. It's my wife. She can't stand the cold, always has to have the place like a hothouse. Only yesterday, in the hospital, she was complaining about the temperature in there. All the other women were sitting up in frilly nighties and she was practically shivering. When I went back in the evening I had to take a woollen bedjacket in for her. Sorry, I'm rambling . . . I can't seem to think straight this morning . . . What did you want to know?'

As arranged, Lineham began the questioning and they soon learnt that Perdita's father had died when she was ten and that her mother had remarried two years later. The young girl had been very fond of her father and despite every effort on Harrow's part had found it difficult to adjust to having a stepfather.

Harrow shook his head sorrowfully. 'I'm afraid she never really forgave me for taking her father's place. I've often thought it was just as well Stephanie didn't come along until we'd given up hoping she might —that's our other daughter. She's thirteen now.'

Perdita would have been in her twenties by then, Thanet worked out.

'I think Perdita would have found it even more difficult, if she'd had to share her mother with a baby. As it was, by the time Steph arrived Perdita had been away to college and when she did come home to visit she was more like a mother than a sister to her.'

'How is Stephanie taking the news of her death?'

Harrow compressed his lips. 'She doesn't know yet. I haven't been able to pluck up sufficient courage to tell her.'

'What did you tell her last night, after my men had called? Or didn't she wake up?'

'She wasn't here. She's staying with a friend while her mother's in hospital. You know what girls of that age are like. Any excuse to stay at one another's houses . . .'

Thanet grinned. 'My daughter was just the same.'

'It's very convenient, really. My hours are rather irregular. I'm Deputy Head at St Michael's Primary and I often have to get to school early, or leave late. Steph goes to Sturrenden High and it's always Ros —my wife—who does the school run. So when Stephanie suggested staying with Diana . . .'

Thanet nodded. Harrow didn't exactly fit Thanet's image of a deputy head, but then the man couldn't be expected to be at his best this morning.

'Steph was here over the weekend, of course. Actually, that was another reason why I was glad she suggested staying with Diana. If Giles —that's my son-in-law, Perdita's husband—was going to keep coming around here causing trouble . . . I didn't like the idea that he might come when I was out and Steph was here alone. I'm not sure she'd have been able to cope . . . You did know that Perdita and her husband had separated?'

'Yes,' said Thanet. 'And we knew Mr Master had come here once, on Saturday night, but you said, *keep* coming around and causing trouble . . . He came more than once, then?'

'He came back on Sunday and then again on Monday.'

Thanet glanced at Lineham. 'Let's take it in sequence, go back to Saturday night.'

'What, exactly, did happen on Saturday night?' said Lineham.

Briefly, so briefly that Thanet wondered if he had imagined it, some memory or thought flickered in Harrow's eyes, was quickly suppressed. Then he ran his hand over his head, gingerly patting the carefully layered strands. 'Perdita arrived at about—let me see—ten o'clock or thereabouts. She didn't say much, just that she and Giles had had a row and could she have a bed for the night? Naturally I said yes. She had just gone upstairs when Giles rang to see if she was here. Perdita refused to speak to him and asked me to tell him she didn't want to see him. The next thing we knew he was banging at the door, demanding to be let in.'

'And did you let him in?'

'No, of course not.' Harrow contrived to be both brusque and self-righteous. 'If Perdita didn't want to see him, that was that, as far as I was concerned. He kicked up a dreadful row, half the street was on the doorstep wondering what was happening . . . In the end I said if he didn't leave I'd call the police. So he went away. But he was back by ten the next morning. Fortunately Perdita had already gone out, so he went off fairly quietly.'

'Where had she gone?'

Harrow shook his head. 'No idea. I got up late and she had already left.'

'Had she taken her stuff with her?'

'No, not then. Not that she had much, just a small grip. She came back and collected that in the afternoon.'

'Did she say where she'd been?'

'To visit her mother in hospital, she said. I knew she was going, we'd arranged it the night before—that she'd go in the afternoon and I'd go in the evening.'

'What about Stephanie?'

'She was going on a school trip to London on Sunday afternoon, some exhibition at the Barbican . . . When her mother was unexpectedly called into hospital Steph said she wouldn't go, but my wife insisted that nothing would be happening, medically speaking, on a Sunday and it was pointless Steph missing her trip for no good reason.'

'Did Mrs Master tell you where she was going, when she collected her bag?'

'Yes. She said she'd run into an old school friend of hers at the hospital, and she was going to stay with her for a few days. She gave me the address and telephone number, in case I needed to get in touch with her about her mother, and asked me not to tell Giles where she was.'

'And did he come back?'

'Yes. He was knocking on the door at eight o'clock next morning. He was furious that I wouldn't tell him where she was.'

'So Mrs Master left here on Sunday morning some time before ten o'clock and didn't get back until . . . ?'

'About four.'

'And apart from the time she spent visiting her mother, you've no idea where she was or who she went to see?'

'No idea at all.'

Lineham glanced at Thanet. *Anything else?*

Once again Thanet produced the sketch.

Harrow frowned at it, holding it at arm's length. 'I'm pretty certain—yes, that's Perdita and Giles's neighbour. Swain, that's his name. Howard, I think. Arty-crafty type. Knits.'

Lineham's eyebrows shot up. 'Knits?'

Harrow waved a hand. 'Calls himself a knitwear designer. His wife's something high-powered in TVS.'

'Were he and Mrs Master anything more than friends?' asked Thanet.

Harrow looked taken aback. 'Were they having an affair, you mean? I've no idea. It's possible, I suppose. They both worked at home, so there was plenty of opportunity. But if so, it's the first I've heard of it . . . Perhaps that's what the row was about, on Saturday night.'

'Did you know that Mrs Master was asking for a divorce?'

Harrow's plump lips pursed into a silent whistle. 'No wonder Giles was in such a state! He's always been somewhat, shall we say . . .' He broke off, aware perhaps of the potential significance of what he was saying.

'Possessive?' said Thanet. 'Jealous, even?'

Harrow looked uncomfortable. 'He's always been very fond of Perdita . . . Look, Inspector, if there's nothing else . . . I feel I really must get along to the hospital as soon as possible, in case my wife hears about it from someone else.'

'Don't worry. Your stepdaughter's name is not being released until this afternoon.'

Harrow looked relieved. 'Oh good. But still . . .'

Thanet hesitated. He very much wanted to go to the hospital himself, to find out how his mother-in-law was. He had intended to go later, after seeing Swain. But perhaps it would be useful to talk to Mrs Harrow, first, if she were well enough to be interviewed. Thanet's guess was that if Perdita and Swain had been having an affair, it might well have been Swain she went to see on Sunday morning. If she had confided in her mother when she saw her on Sunday afternoon Mrs Harrow might be able to confirm this. He made up his mind, stood up. 'We'll come along to the hospital with you.'

Harrow looked alarmed. 'You're not going to talk to my wife? She won't be up to it. She was very fond of Perdita, this is really going to hit her hard.'

'Don't worry,' said Thanet. 'If your wife doesn't want to talk to us, she needn't. It'll be entirely up to her. I have to go to the hospital anyway, for another reason.'

Harrow was still looking doubtful. 'I wouldn't want to put any pressure on her. She's got enough on her plate at the moment, without this.'

'Don't worry,' said Thanet gently. 'We're not inhuman, Mr Harrow. We won't do anything to distress your wife, I assure you.'

Harrow stood up reluctantly. 'I'll get my coat.'

7

'How is she?' said Thanet.

He had gone straight to intensive care, leaving Lineham with Harrow. On the way to the hospital it had been agreed that Harrow should see his wife alone to break the news to her as best he could, and that they would then enlist medical opinion to try to assess whether or not she was up to talking to Thanet and Lineham.

Joan's smile of greeting faded as she shook her head. 'Conscious. I've seen her . . . She's holding her own at the moment but we won't know for some time, apparently, whether she's going to be all right. She could have another attack at any time, we just have to wait and see . . . The risk is greatest, apparently, in the first twenty-four hours.'

Thanet comforted Joan as best he could. She and her mother—her father had died some time ago—had always been close and this was very hard for her, he knew. Then, after a brief glimpse of his mother-in-law alarmingly surrounded by wires and machines, he made his way through the labyrinthine corridors of the hospital to the women's medical ward, where he found Lineham leafing through a tattered copy of *Homes & Gardens* in the waiting room.

'He's still with her,' said Lineham, tossing the magazine on to a low table. 'He said he'll tell her we'd like a word with her and see how she reacts. The Sister is being very helpful, she understands the situation. She says there's no reason why we shouldn't talk to Mrs Harrow as long as she is willing.'

'Good.' Thanet was relieved. He had meant what he said to Harrow: if Mrs Harrow didn't want to talk to them, then that would be that. All the same, he hoped that she would agree to do so. He very much wanted to learn more about Perdita Master.

'What, exactly, is she in for?'

'A whole battery of tests. Harrow says she's never had very good health but this time she's apparently been ill for months with one of these mystery viruses that no one can identify. Now they're making one final attempt to get to the bottom of it.'

A few minutes later a pretty young coloured nurse came into the room. 'Sister says you can talk to Mrs Harrow now. We've transferred her to one of the side wards.'

The Ward Sister met them at the door. 'I've told Mrs Harrow that it's up to her to say when the interview is to stop.'

Thanet nodded. 'That's fine by us.'

His first sight of Rosamund Harrow shook him and he at once understood the general aura of protectiveness which seemed to surround her. She was sitting in a chair beside the bed, wearing a thick woollen dressing gown. On top of that, around her shoulders was draped a blue woollen bedjacket, presumably the one Harrow had brought in the previous evening, and over her knees was a tartan rug. Even so, despite all this camouflage, nothing could disguise her emaciation. The ankles which protruded from beneath the rug were mere sticks, the hands bundles of bones, the head little more than a skull encased in skin stretched tight. To him it looked as though this was a hopeless case, that disease had already almost won the battle against medical science. If he had known she was in this condition he wouldn't have dreamt of interviewing her unless it were absolutely essential. However, it was too late to back out now without causing her embarrassment. Harrow was sitting beside her, one arm around her shoulders.

'Mrs Harrow, I really am sorry to trouble you.'

Her lips quivered and she pressed them hard against each other for a moment before speaking. 'I . . .' She cleared her throat, tried again, 'I do understand that it's necessary. In the . . .' She shook her head as tears began to spill over and trickle down her cheeks.

'Look, let's just forget this, shall we? It's not essential that I speak to you at the moment. I'll come back later, when you've had a little time . . .' Privately, Thanet was resolved not to come back at all unless it were absolutely unavoidable. It had been stupid anyway, even to consider interviewing a sick woman five minutes after she'd heard her daughter had been murdered. What could he have been thinking of?

She shook her head, wiping her eyes with a balled-up handkerchief. 'No. It's all right, really. I'd like to help, if I can.'

Thanet was already at the door. He hesitated, glancing at Harrow.

Harrow said, 'I think my wife really would prefer you to stay.'

'Yes, I would. Please, Inspector, do sit down—if you can find something to sit on, that is.'

'You're sure?'

She nodded.

Thanet felt he had no choice. 'Fetch us a couple of chairs, would you, Sergeant?'

Lineham disappeared, returning a few moments later with two plastic-topped stools.

'If you feel you've had enough at any point, just say the word.'

She nodded, attempted a smile. 'Thank you. You're very kind.'

Thanet didn't feel in the least kind, he felt a monster. 'It's just that we thought you may be able to fill us in a little on your daughter's background.'

She waited, her brown eyes huge in their sunken sockets.

'We understand Mrs Master came to see you on Sunday afternoon?'

She nodded. 'Yes. She . . . She wanted me to know that she and Giles—her husband—were splitting up, that she'd asked for a divorce.' Mrs Harrow gave Harrow an apologetic glance. 'She also told me that she'd fallen in love with someone else. I'm sorry, love, I couldn't tell you that before, she asked me not to say anything to anybody at the moment.'

'Did she say who the man was?' said Harrow.

His wife shook her head. 'No. But I certainly can't blame her, after what she went through with Giles, can you?'

'So,' said Thanet, 'her news didn't exactly surprise you?'

'Only in that I couldn't believe she'd actually plucked up the courage to tell him. No, I knew she hadn't been happy with Giles for a long time.'

'Why was that, do you know?'

'Several things, really. Giles had always been, well, difficult.' She glanced at Harrow.

'I told you,' said Harrow. 'Jealous. Very possessive.'

Mrs Harrow sighed. 'Oh, incredibly. You wouldn't believe . . . He had to know every single thing she did. Perdita even had to account to him for every penny she spent. She loved pretty things, nice clothes, but Giles . . . He always seemed to think she was dressing to attract other men. I remember once he even tore up a new shirt she'd bought, said it was too revealing, too transparent. I don't know how she stuck it as long as she did.'

Talking seemed to have calmed her down and Thanet was beginning to feel more comfortable about the interview. 'So when she told him she wanted a divorce . . . ?'

'He went berserk. Locked her in the bedroom. Would you believe, she had to get away by climbing out of the window? Luckily there's a little extension at the back and she was able to drop down on to the roof, or she'd have been stuck there.'

'It sounds as though you were really quite relieved to hear they were splitting up.'

'Well, when your daughter's unhappy like that, over a period of years, it's very hard to bear. No, she knew I'd be pleased, that's why she wanted to tell me, and especially about the fact that she'd found some-one else.'

'And she really gave no hint as to who he was?'

'No . . . though I think I can guess. But perhaps I shouldn't have said that. He's married and now that she's . . . I wouldn't want to make trouble for him. Perdita wouldn't want me to, I'm sure.' Mrs Harrow shook her head, the tears welling up and spilling over once more. She dabbed them away. 'It seems so unfair. She's had such a rotten time of it and now, just when it seemed . . . It wasn't just her husband, you see, it was her mother-in-law too. She made everything ten times worse.'

'In what way?'

'She couldn't stand Perdita. To tell you the truth, I don't think she could have accepted anyone Giles married. He's an only child, you see.' Mrs Harrow frowned, skin creasing against bone in slack folds. 'The trouble was, it was all done so . . . subtly, I don't know that Giles was even aware of what was going on half the time. But Perdita knew. Oh yes, Perdita knew, all right. And Mrs Master knew she knew.' Mrs Harrow shivered and hugged the dressing gown more tightly around her. 'Horrible woman.'

'I'm not sure I quite understand what you mean.'

'Well, that's the trouble, it's so difficult to explain . . . It's just that whatever Perdita did—or didn't do, whatever she said—or didn't say, Mrs Master would somehow twist things to show that Perdita was wrong, or her method was unsuitable or inferior or naïve or *some*thing. And Perdita herself was too sweet-natured to retaliate. She just put up with it. It used to make me so angry . . . And as I say, I'm not sure whether Giles genuinely had no idea of what was going on, whether he knew but chose to ignore it, or whether he did nothing because he simply didn't know how to deal with it. Though I think he did get fed up with his mother always being on their doorstep. She was always round there in the evenings and at weekends.'

'She's a widow, I believe?'

'Yes. A pity, I've always thought, as far as the young people were concerned. If she'd had a husband of her own to look after . . . Though I understand she's always been very possessive about Giles. She doesn't seem to have much of a life of her own, does she, Ralph?— no close friends, so far as I know, or other interests.'

Harrow was nodding. 'Could never stand the woman, myself.'

Thanet was aware of Lineham shifting uncomfortably beside him. Perhaps all this was a little too close to home for the sergeant's comfort. He too was an only child and had had to suffer the claustrophobic attentions of a widowed mother.

'She and Giles didn't have much of a social life, either—virtually none, in fact. Giles almost invariably said no to invitations and in the end people stopped asking them. I don't think he could stand the way other men looked at her. Perdita was always very attractive to men, you see. I don't know what it was about her, but right from the time when she was in her teens she used to have a string of boys after her. Actually, when she started work it was a nuisance—she never stayed long in any one job because sooner or later her employer would start hanging around her and either she'd get fed up with it and move on or the wife would get suspicious and give her the sack.'

'Did she enjoy all this admiration?'

'Well it was flattering, of course, when she was younger, but no, I think she found it more of a nuisance than anything else, especially after she was married, with Giles being so jealous. No, I think the only reason she was able to stick with the marriage so long was because she found her satisfactions elsewhere—in her painting, chiefly, and in her garden. She loved her garden.'

'I've seen some of her work,' said Thanet. 'She was very talented.'

'She was always mad on painting and drawing, right from the time she was a little girl. She should have gone to Art School. She could easily have gone to Maidstone College of Art, or Medway, but no, she had to go and train as a nanny. I know she always loved kids, but it seemed such a waste . . . I blame myself really. She was at the age when if I said "Black", she'd say "White". I was always on at her to go to Art School but the more I pressed the more determined she became not to go. I should have seen what was happening and just shut up, let her go her own way. If I had, I think she would have gone.'

'She never had any children of her own?'

'No. That was a great disappointment to her. Though now, perhaps it's just as well—' Mrs Harrow suddenly clutched at her husband's hand. 'Ralph! I've just thought! Stephanie! Does she know yet?'

'No. I wanted to tell you first.'

'You must go. At once. I couldn't bear it if she heard from someone else. She'll be so upset, she was so fond of Perdita . . .'

Harrow patted her hand. 'It's all right, don't worry. She won't hear from anyone else. The police are not releasing details until this afternoon, are you, Inspector?'

Thanet shook his head. 'No.'

'Oh. But you will make sure . . . ?'

'Of course I will. I promise.'

'Sorry,' she said to Thanet.

'If you'd like to stop, now?'

Mrs Harrow shook her head, slowly, as if her thin neck could not sustain too vigorous a movement. 'No, it's all right. It's just . . . No, if there's anything else you want to ask . . . I'd rather get it over with.'

'Very well. Her husband, Mr Master did he mind not having children?'

Her answer was what he expected.

'No. I think he was glad, really. He preferred to have her all to himself.' Her lips quivered again, but she took a deep breath and continued. 'It's so sad, really. I think she was very relieved to have come to a decision, to have actually managed to tell Giles she was leaving him. She looked happier and more optimistic than I'd seen her in years . . . Looking back, you know, I don't think she ever really got over her father's death.' She glanced at her husband, squeezed his hand. 'Not that it's any reflection on you, Ralph, but she never did accept you, did she? She'd always been a Daddy's girl, you see, and she changed a lot. Became, well, withdrawn and gloomy. I thought she'd get over it, but she never did. I remember once . . .' She stopped and her eyes darkened with pain at some memory.

'What?' said Harrow.

She shook her head, sorrowfully. 'I was just thinking . . . At one time, in her teens, she used to be obsessed with death. She was forever asking questions about it, questions I couldn't answer. And then, a few years ago, when she was going through an especially difficult patch with Giles, she said to me, "Still, I don't suppose it matters much, does it, Mum? I don't expect I'll have to put up with it much longer." And when I asked her what she meant, she told me that she'd always thought she would die young.' Mrs Harrow's face was becoming even more skull-like, as if the thin layer of flesh upon it were melting away before their eyes. She was staring at her husband without seeing him, looking back into the past and relating it to the present in a way which was evidently almost too painful to bear. 'It's almost,' she whispered, 'as if she knew . . . that she was doomed to die before her time.'

Abruptly she turned her head into Harrow's shoulder and began to weep, harsh, racking sobs which were painful to witness.

Thanet glanced at Lineham. *Time to go.*

Unobtrusively, they withdrew.

8

Outside in the corridor, Thanet said, 'If I'd known she was in that condition . . . Why didn't anyone warn us?'

Lineham shrugged. 'Doesn't sound as though Mrs Master had much of a life, does it? If you ask me we won't have to look much further than her husband. If he could tear up her new blouse simply because he couldn't bear to think of other men seeing her wear it, imagine how he'd react if she told him she'd fallen for someone else! He'd go berserk! I bet you anything he got that black eye in a fight with Swain on Saturday night. I bet that's why he locked her in the bedroom, so that she wouldn't be able to get away while he was beating Swain up. He didn't reckon on her climbing out of the window though, did he?' The thought evidently gave Lineham satisfaction.

'I agree, he does seem the best bet so far. I wonder if forensic will come up with anything useful on that polythene bag. That's what bothers me as far as—'

He stopped as they turned a corner and ran into Vanessa Broxton, casually dressed in jeans and knitted jacket. Her eye shadow was unevenly applied, her mascara smudged, her eyes anxious in their shadowed sockets. The strain of the last twenty-four hours was taking its toll.

She had left the children with the housekeeper. 'I don't think Angela's really up to having Henry bounce all over her yet,' she said, with an attempt at lightness. 'How are things going, Inspector?'

'Too early to tell at the moment, I'm afraid.'

'If you need me, I'll be at home. I'm not going back to work until I find a reliable temporary nanny. Fortunately, the fact that my case went short means that I'm free at the moment.'

'Have you managed to get in touch with Mr Broxton yet?'

She grimaced. 'No. He's moving about, it's difficult. I expect I'll hear from him this evening, though. He rings every other day, when he's away.'

Back at the car there was a message on the radio. The men who had been to interview Howard Swain reported that Swain appeared to have been in a fight; he too was sporting a black eye.

'Told you!' said Lineham triumphantly. 'Do we go and see him next?'

Thanet nodded. He was curious to meet the third person in the triangle which had seemingly brought Perdita Master to her death. He was inclined to agree with Lineham. It was looking more and more likely that Master was their man. Though, as he had been about to say when they ran into Vanessa Broxton, the polythene bag puzzled him. It seemed out of character. He could see Master losing his temper with his wife, lashing out at her in a jealous rage, but he would have thought that having knocked her down, Master would then have been more likely to be overcome with remorse rather than resort to such a cold-blooded and calculated way of finishing her off. Still, time would tell, no doubt.

Meanwhile, Thanet was content to enjoy the brief drive out to Nettleton. It was a glorious autumn day. The frost which had lain thick upon the grass when he got up this morning was long gone and the sun, now high in a sky of pure unblemished blue, illuminated the glowing colours of the foliage in trees and hedgerows: the gold of oak, the lemon, butter-yellow and apricot of field-maple, the scarlet of hawthorn berry, the frothy cream of old man's beard, all set against the tender green of winter wheat and the rich chocolate furrows of newly-ploughed fields. Thanet loved the gentle, rolling curves of the Kentish landscape, the undulating skyline of the North Downs, the sense that the countryside was gradually preparing to settle down into its winter sleep.

Apart from the occasional tractor the roads were quiet, Nettleton asleep in the noonday hush. As they approached the Masters' home Lineham slowed down so that they could take a better look at it by daylight. It was a substantial house, built probably in the sixties, Thanet guessed. Its proportions were good, the windows generous and the grounds extensive and well maintained. They glimpsed a man with a wheelbarrow raking up leaves on the lawn.

'Full-time gardener by the look of it,' said Lineham.

'I doubt it. Her mother said that Mrs Master loved her garden and implied that she spent a lot of time in it. He probably comes in once or twice a week to do routine maintenance.'

'What would two people want with a house that size anyway? And I wonder how he got planning permission?'

Thanet didn't respond. He was used to Lineham's twinges of envy over other people's life-styles.

'This'll be the Swains'.'

A five-barred gate stood open at the entrance to another gravelled drive, but the house was very different, a long low black and white timbered Elizabethan dwelling with a tilting roof-line and leaded windows.

'Ve-ry nice,' said Lineham as they got out of the car.

The Masters' house, Thanet guessed, had been built in part of the original grounds of this one, perhaps replacing a range of stables or outbuildings. No one would get away with that these days. In the country old was now considered sacred. Thanet often thought that it was a pity the same principles had not been applied to the towns. The county town of Maidstone, for instance, had been ruined by the wholesale destruction of old buildings replaced by characterless blocks of offices and ugly warehouse-style temples to consumerism.

But the charm of a house like the Swains' would never fade. It sat in the landscape as if it had grown there, the very materials of which it was constructed hewn from local timber, culled from local tilefields, local earth. Thanet's own preference was for brick and tile-hanging, but he couldn't help admiring such a picturesque tribute to the skill of Elizabethan craftsmen.

Lineham was already wielding the heavy iron ring-knocker on the front door, the hammer-like blows reverberating in the still, sun-drugged air. Thanet walked across to join him, admiring the late-blooming yellow roses trained across the front of the house, the well-tended borders crammed with cottage-garden plants. Here was another keen gardener, it seemed. Perhaps that was how Perdita Master and Swain had first got to know each other well—over the garden fence, so to speak.

'Yes?'

A shock of recognition. Despite the purple and yellow bruising around Swain's left eye, the strip of plaster along his jawbone, he was immediately recognisable as the man in Perdita Master's sketches. She had captured exactly his air of sensitivity, the impression of a mind engaged elsewhere in some aesthetic activity.

'Oh, not again,' said Swain, when they introduced themselves. 'I've had you lot around once this morning already.'

'Yes, I know, I'm sorry. But I wouldn't trouble you if I didn't think it necessary.'

Swain stood back with ill grace. 'You'd better come in.'

The room into which he led them was low and square, with massive overhead beams and a huge inglenook fireplace. It was comfortably if conventionally furnished with chintz curtains and matching loose covers on chairs and sofa. Through an open door at the rear Thanet caught a tantalising glimpse of a kaleidoscope of colour: floor-to-ceiling shelves on one wall held a rainbow of coloured cones of wool, and the other visible wall was a huge pinboard covered with vivid sketches, designs and samples of knitted swatches trailing multi-coloured strands.

Here was more common ground between the two. Perdita and Swain were both artists, united in their love of beauty, colour and form.

Swain himself was presumably wearing one of his own creations, a rugged masculine heavy-knit sweater in an abstract design of muted earth colours—browns, greens and a deep, rich aubergine.

'I don't know what more I can tell you,' he said as they all sat down.

'Perhaps I ought to show you this,' said Thanet. He took out Perdita's sketchbook and opened it, held it up.

The shock showed in the clenching of Swain's fists, the tightening of his lips, the determined effort he made not to betray emotion. It was clear that he had recognised not only himself but the hand of the artist.

'We found it amongst Mrs Master's possessions, at the house where she was staying. And it's clear, from the preceding sketches, that these were done from memory. An excellent likeness, I'm sure you'll agree.'

'She . . .' Swain paused to clear his throat, take a deep breath to steady his voice. 'She had brilliant recall.'

'Interesting that during her very brief stay at Mrs Broxton's house, Mrs Master should have spent most of her spare time drawing you.'

Swain said nothing, just shook his head slightly, perhaps to deny involvement with Perdita, perhaps to hold emotion at bay.

'It's only fair to tell you that we know Mrs Master wanted a divorce because she had fallen in love with someone else.'

Still Swain did not speak. Perhaps he couldn't trust himself to do so.

'We know too that she told her husband of her intentions on Saturday night, and that they had a row about it . . . And of course, we find it very interesting that both you and Mr Master have obviously been involved in a recent fight.'

This time Swain opened his mouth, but Thanet held up a hand, fore-stalling him. 'Please, don't insult us by telling us that you, too, walked into a door. We're not idiots, Mr Swain. The inference from all this is quite clear, and sooner or later the truth is bound to come out. It would be easier all round, I think, if you were frank with us now.'

Swain was looking down at his hands, rubbing the side of one thumb with the other, his jaw muscles clenched.

Thanet waited, to give the man time to think it over, and then said softly, 'Don't think that we don't understand your position, Mr Swain. It must be an unbearable strain on you, to have lost the woman you loved and not be able to mourn her openly.' He meant it. Although in his heart he could not condone adultery, he could recognise and sympathise with suffering when he saw it.

Compassion prevailed where reason had not. Swain made a small, choking sound and jumped up, went to stand with his back to them at one of the windows, his shoulders jerking with stifled sobs. After a few moments he took out a handkerchief and furtively wiped his eyes, blew his nose.

Why were so many men ashamed of showing emotion? Thanet wondered. What could be more natural than to show grief at the death of a loved one? The tradition of the stiff British upper lip had a lot to answer for. Far better to mourn openly, acknowledge and come to terms with a sense of loss, than to drive it underground to fester perhaps for years to come.

At last Swain turned to face them again. 'I must apologise, Inspector.'

'Please don't. It would be presumptuous to say I know how you feel, because I've never been in your position. Shall I just say that I find your reaction entirely natural.'

Swain managed a faint smile of gratitude now, and returned to his chair. He blew his nose once more then put his handkerchief away, in control of himself again. 'You're right, of course. What's the point of denying it? Perdita and I were in love . . .' Briefly his voice wavered and he took another deep breath. 'We had planned to marry, eventually, when we were free . . .'

Thanet waited, willing for Swain to set the pace. Now that the man had begun to talk he would go on.

'She had a terrible time with him, you know. He was impossibly, insanely jealous. He wanted her all to himself, all the time. He didn't want her to go out or do anything, ever, except with him. She was becoming virtually a prisoner in her own home. It hadn't got to the tage where he actually locked her in, but she could see that coming, in he not-too-distant future. He'd ring her up at all times of the day, to make sure she was there, and if she wasn't, when he came home he'd question her. Where had she been? Who had she seen? What had they done? What had she bought? Which shops had she been into? It was as f he wanted to be with her physically or vicariously twenty-four hours a day, and as you can imagine she was suffocated by it.' Swain shook his head. 'I'd have gone mad, if someone had invaded my privacy to that extent . . . I often wondered why she chose me, you know, and I suppose the answer is quite simple. I was *there*.'

Thanet risked a question. Swain was well launched now. 'Wasn't Mr Master suspicious of you, living next door and working at home?'

'Oh God, yes. In fact, Perdita and I had to pretend we couldn't bear the sight of each other. In public we treated each other with icy politeness, no more. We knew that if either of us showed even the slightest sign of interest in the other Giles would up sticks and go, and then Perdita would have been totally isolated . . . And that wasn't all she had to put up with. There was his mother, too. She couldn't stand Perdita. Well, I don't know if that's strictly true. What she couldn't stand was the thought of her son having a wife, with first claim upon him. Especially if he was as obsessed with her as Giles was with Perdita. Not that she showed it overtly, mind. On the surface she was all sweetness and light, but she never missed a chance, by innuendo, to underline Perdita's failings and make her miserable. But it was all done so subtly that I don't think Giles was even aware of it . . . Anyway, it got to the stage where we were both sick and tired of the situation, and decided to pluck up the courage to tell our respective partners simultaneously, on Saturday night. We were both dreading it, but Perdita especially, as you can imagine. She was afraid of what he might do. I begged her to let me be with her when she told him, but she was adamant that she wanted to do it alone. She said she owed him that much, not to humiliate him in front of me . . . So we arranged that I would be here and that if there was any trouble she would ring me . . .'

He paused, gave Thanet a rueful glance. 'You've guessed what happened, or some of it, anyway. There was an almighty row and Giles dragged Perdita up to their bedroom and locked her in. Fortunately there's an extension below their window, and she managed to climb out and get away while he was here. He came around straight away, of course, as soon as he'd locked her up. The second I opened the door he came bursting in, knocked me flying. I tried to retaliate, but he's much

bigger and stronger than me and it only took a few blows to floor me
Swain's hand went up and gingerly touched the strip of plaster along hi
jawline. 'I hit the back of my head on something and passed out. Ap
parently he just stood there shouting at me to get up and fight like
man, but when he saw I was out cold he gave me one final kick in th
ribs and stormed off.' This time Swain's hand massaged the left side o
his rib cage. 'I've got the most psychedelic bruise you ever saw, dow
here.'

'You said, "apparently". Your wife was a witness to all this?'

'Yes. It was she who told me what happened after I passed out. Th
whole thing was a nightmare.' Swain rubbed a hand wearily across hi
eyes. 'Thank God the children are away at boarding school.'

'And it was presumably Mrs Master who told you how her husband
reacted when she broke the news to him.'

'Yes, when she rang me on Saturday night, from her mother's house
We arranged to meet on Sunday morning, to discuss what she was goin
to do next. Obviously she couldn't go home again . . .'

So that was where Perdita had gone. Her stepfather had told them
that she had already left when he got up on Sunday morning. Thanet
was pleased that they were gradually building up a picture of her move
ments over the last couple of days before she died. 'How long did yo
stay together?'

'Until after lunch. She was going to visit her mother in hospital in th
afternoon. Mrs Harrow has been ill for some time, and they've neve
succeeded in finding out exactly what is wrong with her. She's been
waiting for a bed at Sturrenden General so that they could take her ir
and really try to get at the root of it. Apparently they rang up on
Saturday morning to say that a bed had unexpectedly become available
and could she come in straight away. She didn't tell Perdita because she
didn't want to worry her. She knew Perdita was having a bad time at
home, and she was only going to be in for a few days. It wasn't as
though they were going to operate . . .'

'So when Mrs Master went to her mother's house on Saturday night
she didn't know Mrs Harrow wouldn't be there?'

'No. She didn't find out until she got there.'

'Was she upset, that she hadn't been told?'

'Yes. And angry with her stepfather, that he hadn't let her know in
spite of her mother's wishes.'

Remembering how ill Mrs Harrow had looked, Thanet wasn't sur
prised. If Perdita had been fond of her mother, as apparently she was,

she would have wanted to know exactly what was happening, however worrying it might be.

'So when you parted, after lunch on Sunday, Mrs Master had no specific plan in mind?'

'No. She said she'd probably go and stay in a hotel for a few days, give Giles a chance to calm down and get used to the idea that she'd meant what she said, about a divorce. She said she'd be in touch, when she found somewhere. But then later, oh, it must have been about six, she rang to tell me she'd run into an old friend at the hospital, Mrs Broxton. She said Mrs Broxton was in a fix because her nanny had been rushed into hospital with appendicitis and she herself had a case starting the next day which involved her staying away from Monday to Friday—she's a barrister, well, you must know that by now, of course. So they'd agreed to help each other out. Perdita would look after the children until Saturday, while Mrs Broxton tried to find a temporary nanny. Perdita thought that Giles would never find her there . . .'

The implication was strong. *But she was wrong, wasn't she?* Here was someone else who was convinced of Master's guilt.

Thanet would have loved to know how Swain's wife had taken all this, but felt that it would be better to find out for himself. It could be highly relevant. Mrs Swain could be considered to have as good a motive as anyone for getting rid of her rival. Harrow had said she was 'something highpowered in TVS', so presumably she wouldn't be the type to take this sort of situation lying down. Yes, a visit to Mrs Swain should come fairly high on the agenda, depending on how the next interview with Master went.

Meanwhile, there was one more question he wanted to ask and there was no way of putting it tactfully. 'Did you see Mrs Master last night?'

'Last night?' Briefly, something flickered at the back of Swain's eyes, then he shook his head. 'No, I didn't.'

The statement was so unequivocal that Thanet felt there was no point in pursuing the matter at the moment. He was in no mood for a patient breaking down of Swain's resistance at this stage of the interview. But he was left wondering: what was the question he should have asked?

9

'Why didn't you ask him where he was last night?' said Lineham, as they walked to the car.

Thanet shrugged. 'Didn't seem much point. He was so positive about not seeing her it would have taken a lot of pressure to get him to change his tune. And frankly, I wasn't prepared to exert it at that stage. I felt he'd had enough for today. Anyway, I really don't think he's involved. What possible motive could he have?'

'With respect, sir . . . What are you grinning at?'

'You. Every time you say, "With respect, sir", I know you're going to disagree. And before you go on, just put through a call to headquarters, will you? Get them to fix up an appointment with Mrs Swain at TVS at 2.30 or thereabouts.'

This took a little longer than expected, owing to the fact that at work Mrs Swain was apparently known under her maiden name of Edge. When the appointment was at last arranged Thanet suggested having lunch at the village pub before seeing Master again. 'We could do with a break.'

'Good idea. I must admit I'm feeling a bit peckish.'

When they had collected their beer and sandwiches and were seated in a quiet corner Thanet picked up their interrupted discussion, quoting Lineham with a grin. ' "With respect, sir . . ." '

Lineham grinned sheepishly. 'It's just that I don't necessarily agree with you about Swain. Just say, for example, that he and Mrs Master arranged to meet at the Broxtons' house last night. When he gets there she tells him she's decided not to go ahead with the divorce after all, that she can't face all the hassle it would involve with her husband. They're in the kitchen, she's about to make a hot drink. They have an argument, he grabs her, she pulls away, knocking the saucepan of milk off the cooker. She's off balance and, as we said before, she slips, knocking her head on the corner of the table—'

'And when he sees she's passed out, instead of trying to revive her he whips a handy polythene bag out of his pocket, slips it over her head and waits until she's stopped breathing before leaving. Oh yes, highly credible, I must say!'

Lineham said nothing, just looked slightly crestfallen and took a large mouthful of ham and tomato sandwich. He chewed for a few moments and then shook his head. 'It's that polythene bag that's the trouble, isn't it?'

'Yes. Mind, even if there were no polythene bag I find it difficult to imagine Swain resorting to violence. He's just not the type.'

'I'm not talking about violence, sir. Not really. Just a heated argument which got out of control.'

'Yes, I appreciate that. It was the wrong word to use, for the scenario you were describing. Nevertheless . . .'

'I still think it's possible. We all know that even the mildest of men can get pretty worked up, given the right circumstances. And in this case'—Lineham leaned forward in his eagerness to convince—'in this case, if she was telling him the affair was over . . . I mean, he'd naturally have been upset wouldn't he, if he was in love with her? And pretty angry too, going through all that for nothing!'

'All that?'

'Telling his wife he wanted a divorce, for one thing. She might have known nothing about the affair until he told her, on Saturday night. And getting beaten up by Master, for another . . . All, as I say, for nothing!'

'I suppose so.' But Thanet was still doubtful. 'This is all wild guesswork, of course. But even if you're right, it's still, as you say, that polythene bag that's the problem. Not so much in terms of availability, it could well have been lying around to hand somewhere in the kitchen, but in terms of the murderer's behaviour. There's a world of difference between causing someone to slip and fall during the course of an argument and cold-bloodedly putting a plastic bag over her head to finish her off. I'm not sure that I could see Master doing that either.'

'I disagree with you there! He's a nasty bit of work, if ever there was one. I can just see him standing there looking down at her and saying to himself, "If I can't have her, no one will." He might regret it afterwards, when he had time to think about it, but at the time . . . For that matter, I found it difficult to swallow that after taking her back to the Broxtons' last night he just went meekly home.'

'I'm not so sure. He could have decided to give her a few days to cool off, before trying again.' Thanet opened up his beef sandwich, and peered inside. 'They've been a bit lighthanded with the mustard.' He took another bite, chewed. 'The impression I've got is that he wasn't going to give up easily. If he didn't succeed in persuading her one day, he'd just come back the next. And the next. No, I think that whoever killed her truly wanted her dead. And I don't think you could say that about either Master or Swain.'

'Truly wanted her dead,' repeated Lineham thoughtfully. 'The only person I can think of who might possibly fit that description is Mrs Swain.'

' "Might" is the operative word. For all we know she's been longing to get rid of her husband for years and Mrs Master is the last person in the world she'd want dead. No doubt we'll find out when we see her this afternoon.' Thanet drained his glass. 'Finished, Mike?'

'We're still going to see Mr Master next?'

'Of course. Despite what I said about the polythene bag he's still top of our list. Statistically, he has to be.'

There was a silver-grey Peugeot 205 parked in Master's drive alongside his Mercedes.

'Visitors,' said Lineham, as they got out of the car. 'I wonder who.'

'From what we've heard about her, could be his mother.' Thanet hoped it was. He was curious about Mrs Master senior.

While they waited for the door to open he looked around at the garden. Here again was evidence of devotion, skill and artistry. Carefully trained climbers clothed the walls of the house, tubs of winter-flowering pansies stood on either side of the front door, and mixed borders of shrubs and perennials curved away around the beautifully tended lawn, each group of plants a harmonious composition of colour, form and habit.

The door opened.

Not Mrs Master senior, then. This woman was in her mid-forties, a good ten years too young. She was slim, elegant in black and grey silk dress, expensively-styled dark hair curling around her narrow, sharp-featured face. Her reception was cool. 'Yes?'

'Could I have a word with Mr Master, please?'

'He's not seeing anyone at the moment. Can I help? I'm his mother.'

Astonished, Thanet looked again more carefully, but she still didn't look any older to him. No one's idea of a mother-in-law, this.

She was evidently used to this reaction. She was watching him with a spark of amusement in her eyes.

He introduced himself.

'How can I help?'

'We really do need to see Mr Master, I'm afraid.'

'Really! Must you bother him at a time like this?'

'I wouldn't be asking if it weren't essential, Mrs Master.'

'Well I think it's disgraceful! He's shattered, poor lamb, absolutely shattered. He's only just got back from identifying the . . . from the mortuary. I believe it was you who arranged it, Inspector.' The implication was clear. *I'm blaming you for the state he's in and the least you can do is leave him alone.*

'I know. And I'm sorry. But we really must talk to him again.'

She frowned, deep creases appearing between the neatly plucked eyebrows. 'Couldn't you at least leave it till later?'

'I'm afraid not. We have a great deal to do, as I'm sure you can imagine. And now we're here . . .'

She hesitated for a moment longer, clearly debating whether to hold out, calculating her chances of success. She was obviously used to getting her own way. Then she sighed, capitulated. 'Oh, very well, if you must. But do try not to upset him any further.'

Reluctantly she stood back and let them in. She indicated a door at the back of the hall. 'In the kitchen. I was just trying to persuade him to eat. He's got to keep his strength up.'

She followed them into the room and Thanet did not demur. He was eager to observe the relationship between mother and son. Perdita had apparently found it very difficult to cope with. Thanet wasn't surprised.

Master was sitting head in hands at the kitchen table, which was laid for two: silver cutlery, crisply folded napkins and shining crystal wine glasses. Again, the message was clear. *She's gone, but I'm still here to look after you.* The arrangement of yellow chrysanthemums in the centre of the table was a small explosion of colour in the room, which was all white—white ceramic tiled floor, white units, white furniture. It was, Thanet thought, as clinical and impersonal as an operating theatre. Perdita's choice? he wondered. If so, what did it say about her? Apart from the painting in the sitting room he had as yet seen nothing of her personality imprinted anywhere in the house. Yet she had lived here for years . . . It was as if she had deliberately chosen to hide herself from public view. Perhaps she'd had some private corner to which she could withdraw and truly be herself. Of course, her studio! No doubt she had one. If so, Thanet determined to see it.

'It's the police, Giles. They insisted on seeing you.' Frosty disapproval in Mrs Master's voice.

As Master raised his head she edged around the two policemen to stand behind his chair and rest her hands on his shoulders.

Thanet saw the barely perceptible flinch. Mrs Master must have felt it too for her forehead creased and she withdrew her hands, sat down beside Master instead.

So his mother's attentions were unwelcome. A brief glance at Lineham's face told Thanet that the sergeant had missed none of this.

'They're only doing their job, Ma.'

Mrs Master's lips tightened, but she said nothing, merely flicked her hair back from her face with an impatient gesture and folded her hands in her lap. The knuckles were white, Thanet noticed.

'May we sit down?'

Master waved a hand. 'Help yourself.'

'How cosy!' The muscles along her jawline tightened. 'Am I supposed to offer you a drink, Inspector? Or lunch, even?'

'Ma, please! What did you want to ask me, Thanet?'

Master looked haggard. His eyelids drooped as if he had not slept at all last night, and the extensive bruising to his left cheek didn't help. He had cut himself shaving and there was a smear of blood on the collar of his shirt—the same shirt that he had been wearing last night, Thanet realised. The jacket of fine tweed draped over the back of Master's chair was also the same, Thanet now noticed. It looked as though the man hadn't even bothered to go to bed.

There was no doubt about his grief and once again Thanet suppressed the twinge of compassion. A woman had been murdered and it was his duty to get to the bottom of it.

'I think that you were perhaps less than frank with us last night, Mr Master.'

'What do you mean?' Wary.

'We've just interviewed your next-door neighbour, Mr Swain.'

Master's eyes darkened, his teeth clenched. 'So?' Slowly he straightened up. Despite his distress his instinct for self-preservation was asserting itself.

'So he too is sporting a black eye.'

Master shrugged. 'Coincidence.' It was a poor attempt at nonchalance. He must realise that Swain would have had no reason to conceal the truth.

'That's not what Mr Swain says.'

'Really, Inspector!' Mrs Master cut in, eyes flashing. 'What are you implying? That my son and this . . . person, have been in some sort of vulgar brawl?'

'Ma, please! If you're going to keep interrupting—'

'I am not "keeping interrupting"! It's the first time I've spoken! And I was merely pointing out the unlikelihood—'

'Ma,' said Master wearily. 'Shut up. And if you can't shut up, perhaps you'd better go. You don't know what you're talking about.' He waited for a moment to see if she would follow his suggestion, but she didn't move, just compressed her lips as if to prevent errant words escaping and sat back in her chair folding her arms. *Nothing will make me leave if I don't want to.*

Thanet was interested. He wondered just how much Master had told his mother. He had obviously not confided in her.

Master turned back to Thanet. 'I take your point, Inspector. I can see there's no point in denying it. Yes, Swain and I did have a fight. On Saturday night.' He cast a warning glance at his mother, who had just opened her mouth.

She shut it again.

He picked up one of the table napkins and begun rolling the corner between his fingers.

His mother could restrain herself no longer. Her hand shot out to grasp his arm, red talons digging into flesh. 'Why?' she demanded fiercely. She gave his arm a little shake. 'Why did you have a fight?'

She looked eager, Thanet thought, as if she were about to receive some news for which she had been waiting a long, long time.

'Oh, for God's sake!' He erupted out of his chair, tossing her hand off his arm so violently that she rocked back in her chair. 'Can't you guess what all this is about? They were having an affair! Perdita and Swain were having an affair! Perhaps now you'll be satisfied!'

She too jumped up and stood facing him. In profile, thus, the family resemblance was unmistakeable. Her expression was of apparent disbelief. But she was a bad actress, Thanet thought. He could almost feel the satisfaction which was vibrating through her, lending her words of denial a spurious passion. 'Satisfied? What do you mean, satisfied?'

'You never did like her, did you? Ha! That's putting it mildly. You couldn't stand her, could you? You may have thought I didn't realise what you were up to, but don't think I didn't know you were always looking for ways to put her down! No wonder she got fed up with it, fed up with me! I should have had more sense, should have realised just how much it upset her, and told you I wouldn't put up with it! Well, now you've got what you always wanted. She's gone, dead, finished!'

Master appeared to have forgotten that Thanet and Lineham were there. Either that, or he was past caring.

'Giles! You don't know what you're saying! That simply isn't true! Perdita was a sweet girl . . .'

'Mother, for God's sake, stop playing the hypocrite. I *know* how you felt about her, I tell you. What's the point in pretending any more?'

Mrs Master clearly didn't know what to say, how to react. It looked as though this was the first time her aversion for Perdita had ever been brought out into the open. She shot the two policemen an embarrassed glance. 'I'm so sorry, Inspector. My son is overwrought.'

'Overwrought?' shouted Master. 'OVERWROUGHT? Of course I'm overwrought! What do you expect? My wife has been murdered, she's lying there now stretched out on a marble slab . . . Oh God, I can't bear it . . .' He plumped down into his chair, put his elbows on the table and lowering his head clasped his hands over the top of it as if to cling on to his sanity.

Thanet glanced at Lineham. The question in the sergeant's eyes was clear. *Don't you think we ought to go?*

Thanet shook his head. *No.*

To witness this degree of distress in another human being was always painful, but he could not allow embarrassment to deflect him from his task. He had to remember that the cause of Master's distress could be not simple pain at the death of a beloved wife but remorse at having brought that death about. Jealousy is a fearsome emotion, violent and uncontrollable, and despite Thanet's doubts about the polythene bag he had to remember that Lineham was right. A dog-in-the-manger attitude was not uncommon. *If I can't have her, no one else will.*

Mrs Master was still standing and now she put out her hand as if to rest it on her son's bent head in a gesture of sympathy. But she thought better of it. The hand hovered for a moment and was then slowly withdrawn. She shot Thanet a venomous glance. *Now, look what you've done.* It was clear that she was not in the habit of accepting responsibility for the consequences of her behaviour.

'Mr Master,' he said gently. 'Look, I know how painful this is for you, and I'm sorry. I have no wish to cause you more distress. But if I am to

ind out what happened to your wife, I must know everything, abso-
utely everything, about the circumstances leading to her death. Now I
:an, if you wish, leave this for the moment and come back another time.
But I think it would be better, don't you, if we could get it over with.
Then we can go away and leave you in peace.'

Silence. Master shook his head and then unclasped his hands, slowly
sat back, eyes shut as if he could not bear to reveal the naked emotion
in them, see the effect his ravaged face was having upon them. 'I suppose so.' His voice was dull, exhausted. He opened his eyes and glanced
up at his mother. 'I think it would be best if you went.'

There was a note of finality in his voice. She opened her mouth to
object, glanced at Thanet and then, without a word, marched to the
door, high heels clacking on the polished tiles. Outside the sound
ceased abruptly as she moved into the carpeted hall.

Thanet wouldn't have put it past her to listen at the door and he
glanced at Lineham, nodded at it. *Go and check that she's not there.*

The sergeant rose and, moving quietly in his rubber-soled shoes,
crossed the room, opened the door and glanced outside. Satisfied, he
returned. *All clear.*

Now that Master was in a cooperative state of mind it didn't take
long to find out the facts. This time he held nothing back, confirming
what until now had been hearsay, information gleaned from others.

After Perdita had broken the news to him on Saturday night he had
grabbed her by the wrists and dragged her upstairs, locked her in their
bedroom. In a furious temper he had then left the house immediately to
confront Swain. After the fight he had returned home to find Perdita
gone. Realising that she had probably taken refuge at her mother's
house he had followed her there, but Harrow, her stepfather, had refused to let him in. Frustrated he had gone home and drunk himself
into a stupor.

On Sunday he had woken late with a fierce hangover and because of
this had missed Perdita, who had already left by the time he got to
Wayside Crescent. Harrow had answered the door and when Giles had
asked to see Perdita's mother in the hope of enlisting her aid in persuading Perdita to come back to him, he learnt for the first time that
Mrs Harrow had gone into hospital the previous day.

Realising that Perdita would no doubt visit her mother some time
that day he had driven straight to the hospital and waited there for
hours. He had seen her arrive, but had bided his time until she came

out, telling himself that she might be more willing to talk to him if sh
were not anxious to get away and see her mother.

When she did come out he had been annoyed to see that she was wit
Vanessa Broxton and the children, but they had separated and he ha
the chance of a few words with her. She had refused to talk with him a
any length, however, and he had decided that it would be best to let he
simmer down for a while and speak to her the next day, Monday.

On Monday morning he had again gone around to Wayside Crescen
and had been bitterly disappointed to hear that she had returned there
to pack her bags on Sunday afternoon and had then left, saying that sh
was going away for a few days. Harrow wouldn't tell him where she hac
gone, but Master remembered seeing Perdita with Vanessa the previous
day and on the off-chance that Vanessa might know had rung the
Broxtons' house. A woman had answered the phone.

> *'Hullo?'*
> *'Mrs Broxton?'*
> *'No, she's not here.'*
> *'Could you tell me when she'll be back?'*
> *'Who's speaking, please?'*
> *'My name is Master, I'm the husband of a friend of . . .'*
> *'Oh, it's Mrs Master you want to speak to?'*
> *'Ah . . . Yes. Is she there?'*
> *'I'll fetch her.'*

But Perdita had told him once again that she had no intention of
coming back. And no, she would not meet him in the meantime to
discuss the matter. Vanessa was away for the week and she had promised to look after the children until Friday evening. So he had decided
to go to the Broxtons' that night after the children were in bed.

The rest they already knew.

Thanet was nodding. The picture was gradually becoming clearer.

Master leaned back in his chair and closed his eyes. He looked exhausted. Perhaps the retelling of the events of Perdita's last days had
had a cathartic effect upon him, and now he would be able to sleep.

'I don't understand it.' Master was shaking his head in bewilderment.
'I really don't understand.' Suddenly his eyes snapped open and with
one last spurt of energy he leaned forward, clasping his hands together
so fiercely that his fingers made indentations in the flesh. 'What did I do
wrong, Thanet? I gave her everything, everything she wanted.' He

waved his hand, encompassing kitchen, house, garden. 'And I never so much as looked at another woman.' Suddenly he unclasped his hands and thumped the kitchen table so hard that Thanet and Lineham jumped, the glasses rocked, the cutlery clattered. The series of tiny noises drew his attention to the two places so carefully laid by his mother and with a small, inarticulate sound he laid his forearm on the table and swept everything off. Silverware crashed on to the floor, glasses smashed and one napkin ring flew across the room to hit the wall before rolling into a corner.

He was surveying the mess, face expressionless, as his mother burst into the room. 'Giles! What happened?' An accusatory glance at Thanet and Lineham. Perhaps she thought they had been resorting to strong-arm tactics. In any case, it was bound to be their fault.

'Don't fuss, Mother. A slight accident, that's all.' He looked at Thanet. 'Have we finished?'

'Almost. One question for you, Mrs Master.'

She had begun to pick up the debris and she straightened up, table napkins in hand. 'For me?' She was looking at Thanet as if he were a bad smell.

'Yes. Did you see Mr Master at any time, over the weekend?'

'Naturally.' She was picking up knives, forks, spoons, now. 'We see each other most days, don't we, dear?'

Master gave a resigned nod.

'When, exactly, would that have been?'

She dumped the handful of cutlery on the table with a clatter. 'Would you mind telling me what is the point of all this?'

'I'm just trying to build up as complete a picture as possible of the movements of everyone connected with your daughter-in-law, over the last few days before her death.'

'I can't see what possible relevance this could have . . .'

'You must allow me to be the judge of that,' said Thanet sharply.

'Very well. Giles came around for Sunday afternoon tea, as usual. He and . . . They always do . . . did.'

'That was when he told you Mrs Master had left?'

'Yes.' Her lips tightened.

Thanet could see her thinking. *Good riddance to bad rubbish.* And yes, buried deep but nevertheless discernible was a glint of elation in her eyes.

'And on Monday?'

'I popped around here late in the afternoon. Naturally I was anxious about my son.'

'Did he on that occasion tell you where your daughter-in-law was?'

'Yes, of course. With that Broxton girl.'

So Mrs Master senior had also known where Perdita had 'hidden' herself. Who hadn't? Thanet wondered.

He stood up. 'I'm afraid there's just one other matter I must trouble you with, Mr Master. I shall need to examine your wife's things. And I imagine she had a studio . . . ?'

Master was looking sick. Thanet wasn't surprised. The thought of a complete stranger pawing through his wife's belongings would be enough to upset any man, but for a jealous one the idea would be purgatory.

'I suppose it's essential . . .'

'It is. If you would just show us where to go, we needn't trouble you any further. We'll try to be as unobtrusive as possible.'

'Very well.' Wearily Master stood up. 'Where first?'

'Perhaps we could begin upstairs?'

10

On the landing Master turned left towards the front of the house and stopped outside a door. 'This one.'

He blundered back down the stairs.

Thanet and Lineham watched him go.

'Poor devil,' said Lineham. 'Doesn't know whether he's coming or going.'

'Not like you to be sorry for a murder suspect, Mike.' Thanet opened the door and light streamed into the corridor.

'Must be going soft in my old age,' said Lineham with a grin. 'Anyway, you must admit he's got a lot to put up with, with that mother of his.'

Ah, so that was the reason for Lineham's sympathy, thought Thanet as they walked into the Masters' bedroom. It was understandable that the sergeant should identify with Master in this respect.

'I must say, I'm glad she's not my mother-in-law.' Thanet thought of Joan's mother, lying in intensive care. *Please, God, let her be all right.* As soon as he was finished here, he'd ring the hospital to see if there was any news.

The room was spacious, light and airy, with luxuriously soft fitted carpet and floor-length curtains. The effect was comfortable but curiously impersonal, as if it were a hotel room temporarily occupied by tenants who had failed as yet to stamp their personalities upon it. The colours were muted, safe—predominantly pale green and cream. Thanet would have expected something a little more inspired from an artist, a woman to whom colour would surely have been one of the most important factors in her life. He was becoming more and more convinced that Perdita had not cared enough either for her husband or her home to employ her talents wholeheartedly in beautifying it.

He noticed that the duvet on the bed was tossed into an untidy heap on one side of the bed, as if someone had pushed it aside when getting up. It looked as though Master might have lain down fully dressed and tried to sleep. There was a damp patch on one of the pillows, Thanet noticed, and the other one lay part of the way down the bed, askew. He had a sudden, painfully vivid vision of Master giving vent to his grief in the early hours of the morning, clutching the pillow upon which his dead wife's head had rested . . .

Thanet shook his head and the image shattered, dissolved. 'What did you say, Mike?'

'Stacks of jewellery here. Look.'

Thanet joined Lineham at the dressing table. Standing amongst a clutter of expensive-looking perfume bottles, Perdita Master's jewel box was a sumptuous affair of soft white leather lined with red velvet, and it was crammed with necklaces, brooches, earrings, rings in every conceivable stone.

'Must be worth a fortune,' said Lineham. 'Let's hope he's got it insured.'

Thanet picked up a gift tag which had slipped down flat against one side of the box. *'To my darling wife. Jewels to a jewel.'*

He showed it to Lineham. 'Makes you wonder what it must be like, to be loved so . . . overwhelmingly.'

'As Mr Swain said, suffocated,' said Lineham with feeling. 'Desperate to escape.'

Well, Perdita Master had escaped, and enjoyed two brief days of freedom. And look at the price she had paid for it.

'I wonder *why* he was so jealous.' Thanet knew that violent jealousy is supposed to arise from a poor self-image. The theory is that you place so little value on yourself that you can't possibly believe that the object of your affections can love you. But Master's mother obviously thought the sun shone out of him. His father's influence, then? Jealous perhaps of his wife's attitude towards the baby, and taking it out on the child by constant denigration?

While they talked they had been looking around. There was a stack of glossy art books on one of the bedside tables and Thanet glanced through them. These, too, were presents from Master to his wife. *To darling Perdita, Christmas 1989. Happy birthday, darling! To my darling wife on our 15th anniversary.* How terrible unrequited love must be, thought Thanet. Popular opinion agrees that it is better to have loved and lost than never to have loved at all, but he wasn't sure that this was necessarily true. To love a woman with all your heart and to have to live with her indifference, year after year . . . To do everything in your power to please her, to win her, and to live always with the knowledge that you have failed . . . It must be soul-destroying.

And he, he told himself briskly, must be careful. He was becoming maudlin, and in danger of feeling too sorry for Master. All the same, this brief inspection of their bedroom had, he felt, given him a valuable glimpse into their relationship.

'There's nothing here, Mike. We'll go back down.'

Master had pointed out the door to Perdita's studio as they passed through the hall earlier. Downstairs all was silent and Thanet wondered what Master and his mother were doing. Eating a silent lunch in the kitchen? Or had Master retreated to his study, if he had one, to mourn in solitude?

Lineham led the way. He flung open the studio door and Thanet stopped dead, momentarily overwhelmed by the impression of light, space and visual richness. He had been seeking an imprint of Perdita's personality and here, at last, he had found it.

This room had been built along the back of the house, facing north, and was flooded with the clear, flat light so necessary to the serious artist. The wall facing the garden was glass from floor to ceiling and huge skylights had been set into the sloping roof. Along the back wall of white-painted brick hung panels of material, some plain, some richly textured and patterned in brilliant colours. Beneath them ran a long wooden bench cluttered in places with a diversity of objects doubtless used by Perdita in her paintings: curiously shaped pieces of wood, shells, pots and vases of all sizes and descriptions, fans, feathers, pebbles and stones, even pieces of bleached bones, including a skull. At intervals, in cleared spaces, a still life had been set up. Along one of the side walls were racks holding finished paintings and sheets of watercolour paper, and along the other, shelves stacked with reference books, sketchbooks, notepads, jars of pencils and brushes, paints, all the paraphernalia of the working artist. Draped over a chaise-longue was a dazzling variety of shawls, scarves and pieces of fabric. There were two easels, one freestanding and the other a large adjustable table model set up on a worktable at right angles to the tall windows. Thanet crossed to look at the painting taped to it.

Perdita had been working on another night-time landscape, a powerful disturbing work of rich, sombre hues. Distorted shadows were cast by the moon which floated behind the stark, silhouetted branches of trees and in the foreground was a tangle of undergrowth which only partly concealed the bleached bones of some long-dead animal.

'Wow!' Lineham brought Thanet out of his absorption with a jolt. The sergeant was standing in the middle of the studio, revolving slowly. 'Some place, eh?' He crossed to peer over Thanet's shoulder. 'Wouldn't like to hang that on my wall.'

'She was good, though, wasn't she?'

'I'm no judge of that, I'm afraid. But she certainly didn't lack for equipment.'

Thanet thumbed through some of the numbered sketchbooks ranged along the shelves. Book after book was filled with pencil drawings and watercolour sketches, some bold and rapidly executed, some fragmentary, some meticulously detailed, and covering every conceivable subject. It was obvious that to Perdita a pencil or a paintbrush in the hand had been almost an extension of her body. Thanet shook his head, sighed. What a waste of talent. And how desperate she must have been to get away, to have left all this behind her.

'Don't seem to be any personal papers here,' said Lineham.

'Depends what you mean by personal.'

'Letters, documents, that sort of stuff.'

'Wait a minute.'

Thanet had spotted something. Covered by one of the vivid shawls which Perdita had loved, a futuristic design of whorls, squiggles and geometric shapes, was what Thanet had taken to be a table and now realised was a filing cabinet. But if they had hoped for personal revelations they were disappointed. It merely contained a drawer of indexed photographs and immaculately kept business records: receipts, details of sales, exhibitions, letters from galleries and from Perdita's accountant. Having seen the power of her work Thanet was not surprised to see how successful she had become. She would certainly have been able to support herself, and Thanet wondered if Master in fact realised that by providing her with this elaborate cage and encouraging her to develop her gift he had unwittingly handed her the means to escape from him.

'Look at this! Two thousand quid!' Lineham was holding a receipt in his hand, looking dazed. 'She was getting two thousand quid for one painting!'

'Frankly, having seen her work, I'm not surprised. Don't look so astounded, Mike. People will pay, you know, for a fine work of art.'

Lineham was still shaking his head. 'But two thousand pounds . . .

How can anyone afford that sort of money—and for a modern artist. I mean, it's such a risk, isn't it?'

'Depends on whether you're acquiring the painting as an investment or simply because you like it. Anyway, I don't think there's anything more to see here. It's gone two. We'd better get a move on, if we're going to be in time for our appointment with Mrs Swain.'

There was still no sign of either Master or his mother and they let themselves quietly out of the house.

They stopped at the telephone box in the village for Thanet to ring the hospital. No change in his mother-in-law's condition.

As he got back into the car Lineham said, 'I've been thinking . . . What you said, about someone truly wanting her dead, what about Mr Master's mother? She certainly seems glad to see the back of her.'

'Mrs Master senior doesn't seem to be shedding any tears, I agree. But what motive could she have had? After all, Perdita was gone. She'd left her husband and no doubt her mother-in-law was delighted. But why bother to kill her?'

'To make sure she didn't change her mind, come back?'

'A bit thin, Mike.'

'Maybe, for a normal person. But Mrs Master is obsessive as far as her son is concerned and as you're always pointing out, people with obsessions don't behave normally.'

'I can't see that she'd have had any reason to go and see her.'

'She did know where young Mrs Master was. She admitted it.'

Thanet was shaking his head. 'I still think she'd have left well alone. I think she'd have been well satisfied just to know that Perdita was out of the picture. If there'd been any positive indication that Perdita was considering coming back, now, well, that would be different. But Master says that when he talked to his wife on Monday evening she was still determined not to do so. And I really can't see that he'd have any reason to lie about that, quite the reverse. I'd be much more inclined to think he was lying if he was trying to pretend that everything was all right between them.'

'True . . . Unless, of course, he was trying to protect his mother.'

'If she'd killed his wife! I should think he'd have been much more likely to turn on her with his bare hands! No, you're pushing this too far, Mike.'

'I was only going by what you said, about whoever killed her truly wanting her dead!'

'I know. I just don't think there's any point in pursuing this line of thought for the moment. If something turns up to make me change my mind, fair enough, we'll reconsider.'

The traffic was thickening and slowing down as they approached the section of the A20 where the new M20 motorway was being constructed. Alongside the old road excavations and earthworks disfigured the landscape, with their attendant turmoil of trucks, diggers, cranes and workers' caravans.

'What a mess!' murmured Thanet.

'The A20'll be much quieter when it's finished.' Lineham was a great fan of motorways.

Thanet merely grunted. He hated what was happening to Kent. Along with most of the other inhabitants of the county he bitterly resented the fact that the so-called garden of England was being turned into a through road to Europe. The Channel Tunnel was a blight on the county. For miles inland the coastal areas had been devastated to provide approach roads and loading depots, the M20 motorway link had laid waste a great swathe of countryside, and the dreaded High-Speed Rail Link was the worst threat of all. In order to match the High-Speed Link through France, where relatively uninhabited countryside made construction far easier, British Rail was intending to slice through ancient Kentish villages with a total disregard for history, tradition or the lives of the people who lived in them. Property values close to the proposed route had slumped and many had found their houses unsaleable. Driven to desperation, the placid inhabitants of Kent had taken drastic measures. There had been protests, marches, petitions to Parliament, they had even burnt an effigy of the Chairman of British Rail, all apparently to little avail. But lately there had been whispers: the cost of the Link had soared and it could prove too expensive an undertaking. Thanet fervently hoped that this would prove to be the case.

He glanced at his watch. Twenty past two. They were going to be late. At a snail's pace they crawled through Harrietsham then on past Lenham. Then came a glimpse of the battlements of Leeds Castle before they arrived at Hollingbourne corner. Here the traffic became virtually stationary as at the double roundabouts two lanes reduced to one. By now it was twenty to three.

Lineham thrummed his fingers on the steering wheel. 'Come on, come *on.*'

Thanet could sympathise. He too hated being late. 'No point in getting worked up about it, Mike. There's nothing we can do.'

At last they reached the Maidstone turn-off and were clear of the congestion. A couple of miles further on they turned right to the TVS Studios.

'Ever been here before, Mike?' said Thanet as the barrier was raised and they drove in.

Lineham shook his head. 'Nope. I must admit, I'm quite looking forward to it.'

TVS, which serves the densely populated South East, is an immensely successful Independent Television company. The modern building which houses its Maidstone studios has been built in the former grounds of a small country house, Vinters Park.

'Don't suppose we'll see much of it, Mike. We're hardly likely to get a guided tour.'

Thanet was right. Perhaps in retaliation for their lateness Ms Edge/Swain made them wait fifteen minutes in the foyer before she arrived. She then led them a short distance along a corridor before turning into a small room furnished with a low round coffee table and a few chairs.

When they were seated she glanced at her watch. 'Right, Inspector. How can I help you?'

A clear message. *I'm a busy woman. Don't waste my time.* Thanet had already apologised for being late, though she had not. He had no intention of being pressured or rushed through this interview.

'As I've no doubt you've gathered, we are investigating the murder of Mrs Perdita Master.'

Her lips compressed and the muscles along her jawbone tightened as she clenched her teeth. She was a complete contrast to Perdita, tall and heavily-built with straight blond hair cut very short and a broad, high-cheekboned, almost Slavic face which seemed incomprehensibly familiar to Thanet. He was sure he had never actually met her before or seen her on the box. She was wearing brown corduroy trousers, chestnut-brown leather boots and a beautiful mohair sweater in an abstract design of browns, neutrals and black—one of her husband's creations, Thanet assumed.

He wondered how she had felt about her husband's bombshell on Saturday night. Or perhaps it hadn't been a bombshell at all, maybe she had already known about the affair, or at least suspected it. Did she love her husband? he wondered. Perhaps she hadn't cared. She would at least have been able to support herself, jobs in television were notoriously well paid. But if she had cared, yes, she would be a formidable opponent. Capable of murder, to hold on to what she wanted?

He looked again at the firm, square jaw, the pugnacious blue eyes.

Thanet could see what Harrow had meant by 'high-powered'. He could well imagine that many people would find her intimidating.

However, she wasn't going to intimidate him.

'I'll come straight to the point, Mrs Swain. We have been to see your husband and he has been very frank with us. He has told us that he and Mrs Master were having an affair, and that on Saturday night he informed you that he was going to leave you, for her.'

She picked up the huge soft brown leather shoulder bag that she had deposited on the floor beside her chair, opened it and took out a packet of cheroots. Taking her time, she lit one and exhaled slowly, leaning back in her chair and blowing the smoke towards the ceiling. She smiled. 'My, we don't pack our punches, do we, Inspector. Are you saying that I am suspected of killing my rival?'

'That might be putting it a little too strongly. But clearly, you have a motive and therefore we have to consider the possibility.'

She took another puff, exhaled again. Then, suddenly, she leaned forward. 'Let me make my position quite clear, Inspector. Frankly, I'm glad that Perdita is dead. I never did care for her, I can't stand that boneless, helpless little woman type and she was always the same, even at school. Men like it, of course.' She rolled her eyes, cast them up to heaven in mock despair. 'They really go for it, and my husband was no exception. He thought I didn't know what was going on, but he was mistaken. I'm not blind and I'd seen it coming, for months.'

Briefly, her composure slipped and Thanet glimpsed the pain behind the façade. So she had cared. Deeply. His interest quickened.

'But, Inspector, and believe me, it's a very big "but", I did not kill her. I knew that in the end, you see, my husband wouldn't have had the . . .'

Guts? supplied Thanet.

'He wouldn't have been able to bring himself to leave. He enjoys his little comforts and I earn far more than he does. When he'd got around to the nitty-gritty, he'd have worked out that he couldn't afford to leave me and continue living in the style to which he has become accustomed.'

Thanet sensed rather than saw Lineham shift on the seat beside him. What had discomforted the sergeant? The note of contempt in Mrs Swain's voice, when she spoke of her husband? Thanet knew that Louise, Lineham's wife, could be pretty scathing at times. Was Lineham going to find himself in the position of identifying with yet another suspect?

'I'm not so sure of that, Mrs Swain. Mrs Master had become pretty successful, you know.'

She waved her hand and a worm of ash fell on the carpet. She put out her foot and rubbed it in. 'She may have sold a painting or two. But it's a pretty precarious living.'

Thanet was amused to find himself indignant on Perdita Master's behalf, had to restrain himself from arguing with Mrs Swain. Was she genuinely ignorant of Perdita's success? he wondered, or was she deliberately misrepresenting the facts? Perhaps it was simply wishful thinking on her part.

'Just now you said, "Even at school", Mrs Swain. You were at school with Mrs Master?'

'We both went to Sturrenden High.'

Of course, that was why Mrs Swain looked familiar!

Thanet's brain had produced a fleeting, vivid image: a group of girls walking along the pavement outside Sturrenden High, chattering, laughing and casting sidelong glances at the boys hanging around on the opposite side of the road hoping for just such a glimpse as this. In those days approaches to members of the opposite sex had been much more hesitant, tentative. She had always been in the same group, had stood out because she was a good head taller than the rest. Her hair had been glamorously long then, had swung to and fro like a golden bell as she walked, a magnet to the boys' attention. He suddenly realised that there was a rich vein of information he had not yet tapped—Joan. She, too, had been at Sturrenden High, and although she was a year or two older than Perdita and this woman, she might well know something about them. And about Vanessa Broxton too. Joan had been in bed when he got home last night and this morning there had been no opportunity to talk before the phone call about her mother took precedence over everything else. He hadn't even told Joan the name of the murder victim.

'So you know Mrs Broxton, too.'

She blew smoke again. 'Naturally. Cosy, isn't it? We were all in the same form.'

'Friends?'

She grimaced, shook her head. 'No. Vanessa was too much of a swot, and Perdita . . . Well, Perdita was always a bit of an outsider.'

'Why was that, d'you think?'

There was a knock at the door and a girl put her head around it. 'Oh, sorry.' She withdrew.

'If she was an outsider, she must have been different. In what way?'

Another shrug. 'She always seemed to live in a world of her own. You felt that half the time she didn't really see you even if you were standing bang in front of her. As if you were invisible or something. And who likes to feel invisible? No, she just didn't seem very interested in having friends, doing things with other people. She was always stuck in a corner by herself, drawing.' Briefly, a reminiscent smile touched her lips. 'She used to do some pretty good caricatures of the staff, I remember.'

'But this didn't make her any more popular?'

Mrs Swain shook her head emphatically. 'I told you, she just wasn't interested.'

'Unusual, in a teenager.'

'And of course,' said Mrs Swain, blowing a smoke ring and watching Thanet with a glint in her eye, 'she was pretty, well, for want of a better word, retarded.'

'Retarded?' Thanet's eyebrows rose. Then he realised that her choice of word had been deliberate. She had wanted to jolt, to shock.

'Don't look so astonished, Inspector. I don't mean mentally. Sexually.'

'She just wasn't interested in boys?'

'Exactly. Pretty rare, in an adolescent, wouldn't you say? Of course, to begin with she was a late developer. Small, skinny. She was in the fifth form before her periods started. We all knew, because she was never excused gym. We used to joke about it.'

And pretty cruel such teasing could be, Thanet thought.

'We'd all had boobs for years before Perdita began to sprout them. And then, suddenly, we realised that the boys were sniffing around her. We could never understand the attraction.' She smiled, a slow, lazy, almost seductive smile. 'A mystery, isn't it? S.A.?'

'Sex appeal?'

Again the smile, with a hint of appraisal as well as amusement in it as she glanced at Lineham, who always seemed to emanate a prudish disapproval when sex was openly discussed, even after all his years in the force. 'Don't you like talking about sex, Sergeant? That must make life difficult for you.' She raised her arms above her head and stretched, her heavy breasts lifting beneath the soft, caressing surface of her sweater. 'Me, I find it highly stimulating.'

Lineham, apparently impassive, made a note and Thanet read it, out of the corner of his eye.

Likes sex!

Thanet suppressed a grin. It might be misinterpreted. 'And Perdita had it, you say? She was sexually attractive?'

'She must have been, mustn't she? Why else would the boys suddenly have been around her like bees around a honeypot? As I say, we could never understand it.'

'And she encouraged them?'

'That was the interesting thing. No, she didn't. But it sure didn't put them off, no sirree. Back they came for more. And yet, the odd thing was . . .'

'What?'

She leaned forward, stubbed out the cheroot. 'Well, you know what it's like when you're at school. You're always being asked what you want to do when you leave, having to make subject choices, filling in questionnaires . . . We all envied Perdita in that respect because we thought she'd be saved all the agonising. It seemed so obvious that she'd go to Art College, be a painter, or a designer, or an illustrator. We just couldn't believe it when it came out that she intended to train as a nanny.'

'She never once said she wanted to go to Art School?'

'Not to my knowledge. So off she went to some college and got herself trained. Not that she was a great success, by all accounts.'

'Why not? Wasn't she good at it?'

'I assume you're just pretending to be naïve, Inspector? Oh, she was great with the *children,* or so I understand. It was the daddies that were the problem. I heard on the grapevine that she had real problems there. Never stayed in any one job more than six months.'

'Because of this mysterious attraction for the opposite sex.'

'Precisely. Galling, isn't it? The rest of us spend a fortune on clothes, make-up and hairdos trying to make the best of what Mother Nature gave us, and Perdita did it without lifting a little finger. She really didn't give a damn and yet they all came running.'

Including your husband, thought Thanet. And I can imagine how you felt about that.

'You really didn't like her very much, did you?'

'I don't go around murdering people I don't like, Inspector. Otherwise I'd have been put behind bars years ago.'

Maybe. But it was time, now, to put the all-important question. 'Nevertheless . . . Perhaps you could now give us an account of your movements last night?'

11

Mrs Swain smiled that slow, lazy smile again. 'Last night? Why, I was at home with my husband of course, Inspector. Like a good little wife.'

'Little' was scarcely the word he would apply to Mrs Swain. This was precisely the answer he had expected, of course. She must have realised that she would come under suspicion, in the circumstances. And there had been plenty of time for Swain to ring and warn her that they had been around to the house asking questions and to arrange that he and his wife should alibi each other. 'Could you be a little more specific?'

'Well, let me see. We had supper about 7.30, as usual. Pork and apple casserole, in case you're interested, followed by gooseberry fool. After-wards we watched television for a while, then I did some work. Then we went to bed.'

Pointless to ask which programmes she had watched. Working in TVS she would be certain to own a video. Gone were the days when people could be caught out because they had lied about their viewing habits.

'Did you know that Mrs Master was staying at Mrs Broxton's house?'

'Not until your men came around this morning. My husband would hardly have been likely to tell me where his mistress had flown to, would he?' Her voice suddenly deepened in a passable imitation of her husband's. ' "Oh, by the way, darling, Perdita's gone to stay with Va-nessa Broxton for a few days." '

'Perhaps not.' He rose. 'Well, I think that's all for the moment, Mrs Swain. But we might need to see you again.'

She stood up, grinned. 'Is that a threat or a promise, Inspector?'

'You're not planning any trips in connection with your work?'

'No. And if I do, I promise I'll let you know in advance, like the dutiful citizen I am. Cross my heart.'

'Thank you.' At the door he paused. 'Do you see much of Mrs Broxton these days?'

She grimaced. 'Vanessa? No. We were never particularly friendly, as I said, and anyway she's far too busy with her children, her work and her husband, in that order, to have much time to nurture friendships.'

'In that order? You surprise me.'

'Oh, make no mistake about it, her children come first with Vanessa. She's got all sorts of problems looming, I'm afraid, when they start going to school and want her to watch their Christmas plays and egg and spoon races.'

'Perhaps they'll go to boarding school.'

'Is that a dig at me, Inspector? If so, I suppose it's justified. Yes, I did take the easy way out. I couldn't stand all that guilt, you see, it's not my style. But Vanessa is a different matter. Funny, I'd never have thought she was the maternal type, but I've seen it happen before, especially in career women who leave it late to have a baby. They just fall in love with the child, and find themselves in an impossible position, torn between work and missing those few, short years of infancy. And of course, even when the children start school it's always the woman who has the ultimate responsibility for them. No one expects the father to take time off from work if a child is sick, it's always the mother who has to make excuses or frantically look around for someone to sit in. I tried it for a few years when my children were young. My husband wasn't working at home then and believe me, it was hell. It's the one area in which women will never achieve equality. It's choices, choices all the way, and compromise most of the time. And then more often than not you end up by pleasing nobody.'

This was true. Thanet had often heard Joan bemoaning the fact. And he had sympathised with her. But he didn't really see that there was much that could be done about it. He knew that in some households, where the man worked at home or in a job where flexible hours were possible, he would occasionally assume responsibility for the children. But this was rare and it was generally the woman who had the unenviable task of juggling the demands of home, children and career against each other. Vanessa Broxton's dilemma when her children's nanny had been rushed into hospital was typical, and had in a way led directly to Perdita's death. If she hadn't been desperate to find someone to look after them, if Perdita hadn't been looking for a sanctuary, if she and Vanessa hadn't met on the steps of the hospital . . . If, if, if, he told himself irritably as they walked back to the car. Always a pointless exercise.

'Cool customer,' said Lineham.

'You didn't like her.'

'Did you, sir?'

'Not particularly, no.'

'Think she was telling the truth about last night?'

Thanet shrugged. 'Difficult to tell. I imagine she's a good liar. But I have a feeling that no, she wasn't.'

'You think she might have done it, then?'

'She has a motive. And the nerve. I can just imagine her going around to have it out with Perdita . . .'

'She's got the build, too. If they had an argument she could have knocked her flying quite easily.'

And yes, Thanet could imagine Mrs Swain coolly stooping to examine the unconscious woman, then grabbing a plastic bag and slipping it over Perdita's head.

Lineham had obviously been thinking along the same lines. 'Perhaps we'll find some nice juicy prints on that bag.'

'Mmm. Well, we'll have to wait and see. Meanwhile, we'll put Bentley on to questioning the other householders in Wheelwright's Lane. If either of the Swains did go out that night, someone might have seen them.'

Back at the office Thanet reported briefly on the day's findings to a still subdued Draco. There was no word from Mallard about the post mortem; presumably nothing unexpected had emerged. No doubt the written report would arrive tomorrow.

He and Joan had arranged that Ben should spend the evening at a friend's house, so Thanet went straight from work to the hospital. He found Joan sitting in the small waiting room near the intensive care unit, head back, eyes closed. She looked exhausted. He sat down beside her, laid his hand gently on her knee.

She opened her eyes and gave a weary smile.

'How is she?'

'So far, so good. I've been allowed to look in on her from time to time and they say that the more time that elapses without a second attack, the better the prospects.'

'Good. Excellent. Will I be able to see her?'

'Oh yes, I'm sure you will, shortly. The doctor's with her at the moment. Have you finished for today?'

'There's someone I have to see, here at the hospital, then yes, I have. Will you be coming home, soon?'

'Probably, yes, depending on what the doctor says.'

'You look tired.'

'Yes I am.' She rubbed her eyes and smoothed back her hair. 'If we can just get through today . . . How has your case been going?'

'So-so. I didn't have a chance to tell you, last night. Do you remember a Perdita Master—sorry, no, that's her married name. I don't know what her maiden name would have been. Her stepfather's name is Harrow, but she might well have kept her father's name . . . Anyway, a Perdita somebody, at school?'

'Perdita Bly?'

'Could be.'

'I only remember one Perdita. It's an unusual name. She's two or three years younger than me. Small, slight, with lovely fair hair. She's an artist, she's getting quite well known now.'

'Was, I'm afraid. *Was* two or three years younger than you.'

Joan's eyes opened wide in shock. 'Luke, you don't mean she's the one who's been killed?'

'I'm afraid so.'

'How *awful*. How dreadful.'

'I'm sorry, perhaps I shouldn't have told you yet. You've got enough on your plate at the moment.'

'No, it's all right. I mean, I was never particularly friendly with her. It's just that when it's someone you know . . .'

Thanet nodded, understanding.

'What happened?'

'Are you sure you want to hear all this just now?'

'Yes. It'll take my mind off Mother. Oh dear, that does sound callous, but you know what I mean.'

Thanet had always talked to Joan about his work. It made such heavy demands upon him and therefore upon his marriage that he had always felt it important to share it with her and she, he knew, appreciated the fact that he trusted her enough to confide in her. She listened intently as he talked, her clear grey eyes fixed on his, a small frown of concentration between her brows. He noted the spark of recognition as he mentioned Vanessa Broxton's name and then, when he came to Ms Edge/Swain, she interrupted for the first time.

'Does she work at TVS?'

'Yes. I'm not sure what she does, exactly. She's tall, heavily-built, fair . . .'

'Victoria Edge. How extraordinary, Luke! They were all in the same form, at school.'

'So I gathered. Can you tell me anything about them?'

Her eyes glazed in thought and she was silent for a minute or two. 'Not much that'll be of any help, I shouldn't think.'

'Tell me what you remember.'

But Joan was right. She couldn't tell him much that was new. Not having been in the same year she hadn't come into close contact with any of them. But she did remember them, partly because each of them had in her own way stood out from the crowd, and partly because none of them had moved away from Sturrenden as had so many of their contemporaries and inevitably Joan had run into them from time to time—Vanessa Broxton, especially, in Court. Vanessa, she said, had always been serious, had already, by the time Joan left school, been acquiring a reputation for intellectual ability; her name had always been prominent at prizegivings.

Victoria Edge had stood out by virtue of her size, but also because she had had a talent for getting herself into hot water and it had occasionally fallen to Joan, as a prefect, to reprimand her.

Joan grimaced. 'Not that she ever paid any attention. She was pretty much a law unto herself.'

Now that was an interesting comment, thought Thanet. 'A law unto herself.' Did this mean that Mrs Swain regarded it as her right to do as she pleased, even if it were outside the law? And if so, how far would she go, in applying this principle? To murder?

'And Perdita . . .' said Joan. 'Well, I remember Perdita because she was always by herself, usually in a corner with a sketchbook in her hand. I used to feel sorry for her. She missed so much, I felt, by cutting herself off from the others.'

'You think it was a conscious choice on her part? She was a loner because she wanted to be one, not because she had resigned herself to the inability to make friends?'

'I would say so, yes. I certainly never got the impression, as you do with some people, that she was hanging around wistfully on the edge of things, hoping to be asked to join in. She was very self-contained. And forever drawing, as I said. It always seemed to me that she was doing what she wanted to do. I could be wrong, of course. Maybe she gave that impression because it was less humiliating than admitting she couldn't make friends, but I didn't think so and neither did anyone else, to my knowledge.'

'I see. And you never thought that there was any connection between the three of them?'

'No more than there always is between members of the same form. They were so different, I wouldn't have said they had anything in common.'

But they did now, thought Thanet grimly. Perdita's death had linked them for ever. It was the nature of that link that intrigued him. Or was he trying to read too much into the situation? Perhaps it had been sheer coincidence, nothing more. There was one thing that still puzzled him, though, as it had puzzled other people. Perdita's mother had mentioned it and so had Victoria Swain. He had intended to discuss it with Lineham, but had forgotten. Why had Perdita, so engrossed in her painting and drawing that her career seemed a foregone conclusion, deliberately turned her back on art and chosen instead to train as a children's nanny? He put the question to Joan.

She frowned. 'I didn't know she had. I assumed she'd studied art. I lost sight of her for years, but then I began to notice her name cropping up in local exhibitions. Then a couple of years ago the *Kent Messenger* ran a feature on her. Apparently for several years running she'd managed to get a painting hung in the Royal Academy Summer Exhibition and was beginning to exhibit regularly in galleries in London.'

Thanet was nodding. 'I thought you'd have heard of her, even if you didn't remember her from school.' He knew that Joan, who was very interested in art, kept a close eye on what was going on in the area. 'She was becoming very successful and I'm not surprised, having seen her work.'

'Yes, it's really good, isn't it? I've been wishing for ages that I'd bought some of her paintings years ago, when she was still unknown. They're way out of our price range now, of course.'

'I'll say!' Thanet was hearing Lineham's voice. *'Two thousand quid for one painting!'*

'Anyway, to get back to what you were saying, yes, I am surprised that she didn't go on to study art. A children's nanny! It seems so . . . inappropriate, somehow, for someone like her. Not that there's anything wrong with being a children's nanny, it's just that . . . Well, I'm more than surprised, I'm astounded.'

'Her mother says that she was going through a rebellious stage, that perhaps it was because it was taken for granted that she would go to Art College that she had to go off and do something entirely different.'

'Mmm. Could be, I suppose. Were there any children by the second marriage?'

'Not at that stage. There is a stepsister, but she's only thirteen now, so Perdita would have been in her twenties when she was born. And according to the stepfather Perdita was very fond of her.'

'So at the point when she was having to make up her mind what she was going to do, she was still an only child . . . Were she and her mother close, do you think?'

'I would say so, yes. I think Mrs Harrow would have liked Perdita to have gone to Maidstone College of Art, or Medway.'

'Perhaps that's your answer. Perhaps Perdita felt that what her mother really wanted was for her to stay at home. And with two Art Colleges so close she might have felt her mother would have been hurt if she'd said yes, I want to study art but I want to leave home to do it. Perhaps she needed her independence and felt that the only way to get it without upsetting her mother was to choose a career where she would have to go away to do her training. Seems a bit drastic, though, doesn't it?'

'I don't know. Mrs Harrow is desperately ill at the moment and I understand her health has been poor for years. Perhaps Perdita has always felt protective towards her.'

'Could be. Anyway, I don't suppose you'll ever know, now. The only person who could really explain it would be Perdita herself.'

'Incidentally, talking about Mrs Harrow's illness reminded me . . . You know I said the Super has been somewhat subdued lately? He told us this morning that his wife is ill, that she has to go to London for treatment. And apparently Louise told Mike that Angharad Draco has leukaemia.'

'Yes, I know. It's terrible isn't it? I heard this morning. I ran into Louise when I went into the town to buy some odds and ends for Mother.'

Thanet remembered his promise to Lineham, to ask Joan to have a word with Louise. But Joan, it seemed, had preempted him. She was telling him now that Louise had seemed rather low herself, and that with only a little prompting she had confessed to feeling depressed and nervous about going back to nursing when Mandy started school.

'Had you told her about your mother?'

'Yes.'

It was typical of Louise, Thanet thought, to spill out her troubles during such a brief encounter when she must have realised Joan was pressed for time and anxious to get back to the hospital, and he experienced, not for the first time, a spurt of resentment against her self-centredness and insensitivity. He didn't know how Lineham managed to put up with it.

'Don't look like that, darling.' Joan knew how he felt about Louise and could read him only too well. 'I did rather bring it on myself, you know.'

And that too, he thought, was typical. Joan always seemed willing to attempt to carry the troubles of the world upon her shoulders.

'Anyway, I was surprised,' said Joan. 'I'd always thought she was raring to get back to work. I told her it was perfectly normal to feel like that, that I'd felt like that myself, that we all did after taking a long break to look after the children. I said I was sure that if she did a refresher course she'd get her confidence back in no time.'

'Good. That's exactly what I told Mike. D'you think it helped?'

'Well, she certainly seemed more cheerful when we parted . . . Ah, there's Doctor MacPherson.'

A tall, lanky Scot, with sandy hair and brows, the doctor had a reassuring air of authority. It was good news. He was increasingly confident now that Joan's mother would be all right. If all went well, in the morning she would be moved out of intensive care and there was even a chance that by afternoon she might be allowed home.

Joan was radiant. 'What a relief. Oh, thank you, doctor. Everyone here has been wonderful.'

'She was a lucky lass, that her neighbour found her almost immediately. Tomorrow we'll have a wee chat, and discuss the course of treatment she'll have to follow. It will mean changes in her life-style and of course it would be best if there were someone to keep a close eye on her for a few days, at least.'

'We can arrange something, I'm sure,' said Joan. 'I can take a few days' leave. She can come home to us, to begin with.'

'Excellent. The heart has tremendous powers of regeneration and there is no reason why she shouldn't get back to living a perfectly normal life.'

'That really is great news. Thank you so much. Can we see her again, now?'

'Just for a wee while. Then she should rest.'

Mrs Bolton was looking much more her usual self. She looked pale

and tired, of course, but that was to be expected. Her body was recover
ing from a major trauma.

Thanet took her hand. 'How are you, Margaret?'

She smiled. 'Fine, thank you.'

'You certainly look better than when I came in this morning. You
gave us all a few nasty moments there.'

'Me too!' She glanced at Joan. 'You really must go home, dear. You
look exhausted.'

'Don't worry about me!'

'Did the doctor tell you? He thinks I'm going to be all right.'

'I know. What a relief!'

'So you will go and get some rest now, won't you?'

'For goodness' sake, Mother, do stop worrying about other people
It's the last thing you should be doing. Just relax and concentrate on
getting better.'

'Don't worry, I shall. But—'

'Mum,' said Joan, taking her mother's other hand, 'if it'll stop you
fussing I'll go, very soon, I promise. But there's someone Luke has to
see, here in the hospital, so I'll just sit with you quietly until he's finished, OK?'

'All right. This a case you're working on, Luke?'

'Yes. I'll be back as soon as I can.'

Visiting time was not yet over and most of the beds in the women's
surgical ward were surrounded by small family groups. Unlike most of
the other patients, Angela Proven, Vanessa's nanny, looked remarkably
bright and cheerful. She had just one visitor, a young woman of her own
age.

'I'll be off then, Ange,' said the girl, when Thanet introduced himself.
'I'll try and get in again tomorrow.'

'OK, Ros, thanks.'

Curtains were drawn around the bed and they were left alone.

12

'I think you're here under false pretences,' said Thanet, smiling, as he sat down.

'What do you mean?'

'You look much too healthy to be in hospital. Positively blooming, in fact.'

She grinned. 'I didn't know police officers were allowed to pay compliments.'

She was solidly built, verging on plumpness, with a mop of dark curly hair, round face and bright dark eyes. She was wearing a nightshirt with rows of ladybirds marching across the front. She would be good with children, Thanet thought, practical, reliable, but with a sense of fun.

Her eyes clouded. 'I suppose you're here about that poor woman.' She shivered and rubbed her arms, where gooseflesh had suddenly appeared. 'To think it might have been me . . .'

'I think we have to reserve judgement on that, for the moment, Miss Proven—'

'Angela,' she cut in.

'—Angela.'

'But why? It was a burglar, surely?'

'That is a possibility, yes. Though nothing was taken.'

'Only a possibility? You mean, it might have been someone she knew? That it was *deliberate?*' She shivered again. 'That's even worse.'

'We really don't know yet. That's what I'm trying to find out.'

'I don't see how I can help. I never even met her.'

'I'm aware of that. But part of my job is to talk to everybody who is even remotely connected with the crime. And as it took place in Mrs Broxton's house and that is where you work . . .'

She shrugged. 'Go ahead, if it'll do any good.'

Thanet sat back in his chair. It was important to look relaxed, somewhat difficult in the circumstances. Despite the spurious air of privacy induced by the curtain this interview was in fact taking place in public and within the hearing of anybody who cared to listen. His tone was casual as he said quietly, 'You've worked for Mrs Broxton for some time, I believe?'

'For nearly two years—well, twenty months, to be precise. I came when Henry was born.'

'You obviously get on well with her—with them.'

'She's pretty good to me. Treats me fairly—sees I don't get landed with all the housework, for example, makes sure I get my time off. And they've provided me with a Mini. I know it's so that I can go shopping with the children and take them out, but even so, I have the use of it in my spare time, and that's great. Especially living where we do. Some employers never think you might not like being stuck out in the country with no means of transport. And she doesn't try to undermine my authority with the children, that's another thing. You wouldn't believe how some mothers carry on.'

'She's very fond of the children, I understand.'

'Potty about them. She absolutely hated having to leave Henry, when she went back to work after having him. "Angela," she said to me, "for two pins I'd chuck it all in." '

'But she didn't.'

'Well, it's difficult for someone in her position, isn't it? I mean, you spend years building up your career and then you have children and you've got to decide whether to stop altogether or try to keep things ticking over. I think she knew that if she opted out she'd be very bored later on, when they didn't need her so much. But it wasn't easy for her, I can tell you.'

A bell rang and at once there was a scraping of chairs, a sudden heightening in the buzz of conversation up and down the ward. Goodbyes were said, footsteps receded, silence seeped back.

Thanet lowered his voice still further. 'How did Mr Broxton feel about this?'

She frowned. 'I really can't see where all this is leading.'

Thanet grinned. 'To be honest, neither can I. But can you bear with me? Believe me, the only way to proceed in a case like this is to gather as much information as possible and keep sifting it through. Most of it is irrelevant, but you never know.'

She grinned back. 'OK, you've convinced me. As long as you don't expect me to gossip about my employers . . .'

'Not gossip, no. What I would value is straightforward information, or conclusions based on your own observation. If you really feel you don't want to answer a question then fine, that's all right by me.'

'You mean that?'

'I wouldn't say it if I didn't.'

'OK, then. Not that there's anything to hide, but . . .'

The curtain suddenly swished back and there was some confusion while Thanet explained to a startled nurse that no, he was not a visitor trying to get away with extending visiting hours and the Sister came bustling up to clarify the situation. Those patients who were not comatose watched with interest. What was going on?

Finally they were left in peace again.

'You were saying, Angela, about Mr Broxton . . .'

A teasing look. 'You were asking, you mean . . . Well, Mr Broxton is a busy man. He really doesn't have much to do with the children. A lot of men aren't very interested in infants. Later on, when they're older, he'll probably find them much more rewarding. But I think he was quite keen for Vanessa to resume her career. I think he realises that she's the sort of woman who needs to use her brain.' Angela grinned. 'Not like me.'

'Now here's a question you might take exception to.' And if you do, thought Thanet, you'll have answered it just the same. 'Is everything all right between Mr and Mrs Broxton?'

'You mean, does he have a bit on the side? Not to my knowledge. No, they get on pretty well, really. They have the occasional argument, but no monumental rows or anything like that. He's very fond of her I think, in his own way.'

But Angela evidently wasn't as taken with Guy Broxton as with his wife, thought Thanet. Her tone was definitely lukewarm. Relevant? Most unlikely, he thought.

'Was Mrs Broxton friendly with Perdita Master?'

The mop of hair swayed to and fro as Angela shook her head. 'Not so far as I know.'

'So Mrs Master never rang up, came to the house . . . ?'

'No.' She hesitated.

'What?' Thanet prompted.

'I did hear Vanessa mention her once, though. She and Mr Broxton were discussing some exhibition they'd been to. Vanessa had wanted to buy one of Mrs Master's paintings, but Mr Broxton hadn't liked it.'

'*It just isn't to my taste, that's all.*'

'*Well I thought it was excellent.*'

'*I'm not disputing its quality. I agree, it was a very fine painting. I just don't want to have it hanging on my wall.*'

'*But why not?*'

'*It was too . . . dark.*'

'*How can you say that? There was a lot of colour in it.*'

'*I didn't mean visually. I meant in mood. Perhaps "dark" wasn't the right word. "Sombre", then.*'

'*I just think we ought to buy one soon. She's getting so well known, the prices will go sky-high and we'll be kicking ourselves for not buying earlier.*'

'*I thought we agreed we'd never buy anything for the house just because it's a good investment.*'

'*But if we like it* and *it's a good investment, that's a bonus, isn't it?*'

'*Yes. If. But that doesn't apply here. Perdita Master is, I grant you, a very talented artist, and her work may well, as you say, appreciate in value. But I find it depressing, not uplifting, and I don't want to have to look at it every morning when I come down to breakfast. Now if you want to buy that painting and hang it in your study then go ahead, that's fine by me.*'

'And did she?' said Thanet.

Angela shook her head. 'No.'

'And that was the only time you heard either of the Broxtons mention her name?'

'Until yesterday, yes. It stuck in my mind because we read *A Winter's Tale* at school, and I always thought Perdita such a sad name. Lost. The lost one.' The corners of Angela's mouth tugged down at the corners. 'And now she is, isn't she? Poor woman.' She looked on the point of tears.

Thanet was surprised, but reminded himself that robust as she may appear Angela had not only just undergone surgery but had sustained a nasty shock. She must have felt that she had had a narrow escape when the woman who replaced her had been murdered in the kitchen which by now must feel as familiar to Angela as that in her own home. He hurried to reintroduce a brisk note of common-sense back into the conversation. 'Mrs Broxton never mentioned that she had a friend who trained as a nanny?'

'No.' Angela shrugged. 'There was no reason why she should. It's not as though we ever met.'

There was no more to be learnt here, it seemed.

At the intensive care unit Joan was back in the waiting room. She stood up when she saw him. 'She's asleep now. It's what she needs most of all, they say. Rest.'

'Good. You're ready now, then?'

He helped her on with her coat. 'An early night for you, love. We'll pick up something to eat on the way home.' He held the door open. 'Do you think you'll be able to arrange a few days' leave?'

'Oh yes, I've already made tentative arrangements.' Joan tucked her arm into his as they set off along the corridor. Now that all the visitors had gone the place seemed virtually deserted. 'There's nothing the others can't deal with.' She pulled a face. 'Except, I suppose, Sharon. It's taken so much hard work to get her into the right frame of mind to make a real effort to kick the habit of shoplifting, I'm afraid she might revert if she feels I've let her down, walked out on her.'

'She'll understand, surely, if you tell her why.'

'With her head, yes. But not with her heart. By now her reaction to rejection is automatic, virtually outside her control. People have been walking out on her all her life—mother, father, boyfriends, husband . . . It's really tough being a single parent. It's difficult enough trying to work with two young children if you have the support of a husband, but when you're on your own . . . It must seem so much easier to her just to go out and steal the things she needs, especially when there they are, spread out all around her every time she walks into a shop. And she's offended four times already. It was only because of the children that she was given probation last time. I've got a nasty feeling that next time she might get six or nine months inside. And the children will be taken into care.'

'Yes, I can see that. What time are you seeing Dr MacPherson tomorrow?'

'Eleven o'clock. After he's finished his rounds.'

'In that case, couldn't you fit in one visit to Sharon tomorrow morning, first? Then if you arranged another appointment for, say, Friday, that would probably see her through the week. I'm sure we could find someone to sit with your mother for an hour or so on Friday.'

A door they were passing opened and a man stepped out without looking where he was going, bumping into Thanet. Thanet put out a hand. 'Look out . . . Oh, it's Mr Harrow, isn't it?'

Perdita's stepfather was almost unrecognisable in heavy tweed overcoat and fur hat pulled down over his ears. Presumably years of living in a hothouse had made him especially vulnerable to chills when he went out. He looked dazed, disorientated, and looked at Thanet without recognition.

'Inspector Thanet. We met this morning . . . And this is my wife.'

Harrow looked at him for a moment longer before his eyes cleared. 'Ah, yes. Of course. I'm sorry, I . . .'

'Are you all right?'

Harrow frowned. 'It's hot, isn't it?'

He put his hand up to his head and tugged his hat off, looked at it as though he'd never seen it before. His face was red and his forehead wet with perspiration. 'Sorry, Mrs Thanet, you must think me very rude. How do you do?'

Joan smiled as they shook hands.

They all began to move along the corridor.

'I've just been having a word with Sister, about my wife . . . Are you here visiting someone too, Inspector?'

'Yes. How is Mrs Harrow?'

Harrow frowned. 'If only they could find out what's the matter with her . . . Ah, there's Stephanie.'

So this was the Harrows' daughter, Perdita's young step-sister. The corridor had widened out into a waiting area and the girl sat there alone in an attitude of dejection, head bent, thin shoulders bowed. She looked up as they came into view and Thanet was disturbed by her expression. She's afraid, he thought. Terrified, in fact.

Harrow advanced on her, smiling. 'Sorry I was so long, Steph.'

The girl stood up. Small, slight, with a froth of frizzy fair hair, she looked disturbingly like her dead sister. She glanced at the Thanets, dismissed them as of no importance. 'What did she say?' Her tone was urgent.

That, no doubt was the reason for her fear. She thought her mother was going to die.

And, thought Thanet sadly, remembering the pitiful state that Mrs Harrow was in, she was probably right.

Harrow shook his head. 'She had nothing new to tell us. We've just got to be patient, that's all. Steph, this is—'

'Patient!' Stephanie looked frantic. 'How long do we have to go on being patient? Until Mum is . . .' But she couldn't bring out the word, choked on it. 'All this stuff about advances in medical science! It's been months now, and they can't even tell us what's wrong with her!'

'I know. Hush.' Harrow put his arm around her but she flung it off, grabbed up her anorak and began putting it on. 'Let's get out of here!'

She marched off along the corridor still struggling to get her arms into the jacket. With an apologetic glance at the Thanets Harrow followed her.

Thanet watched them go. He felt desperately sorry for both of them, sorry most of all, perhaps, that they didn't seem able to turn to each other for comfort.

'Poor girl,' said Joan, looking after them. 'It's not surprising she's in such a state. Her sister murdered, her mother . . . Is there really a possibility that Mrs Harrow might die?'

'More than likely, I should think.' Thanet was grim. He had encountered enough misery for one day. He put an arm round Joan's shoulders. 'Come on. Home,' he said.

13

When Thanet looked out of the window next morning he thought for a moment that it had been snowing. Trees, shrubs, lawn were all covered with a filmy blanket of white. Then he saw that it was merely an exceptionally heavy frost. Although it was warm in the bedroom he shivered at the prospect of going out. He hated the cold. Winter could never pass too quickly for him.

Lineham invariably arrived at the office first, Thanet was never quite sure why. Was the sergeant an insomniac, or an early bird by nature? Was it simply that he loved his work (true) and couldn't wait to get to his desk each morning? Or was it a need to get away from his family that drove him out of the house betimes each day?

In any case, whenever Thanet arrived first as he did this morning he felt quite smug. Should he as a reward indulge himself in a pipe before Lineham arrived? Perhaps not. He had been trying to cut down lately and, besides, the sergeant hated pipe smoke. Lineham was bound to be upset at being—Thanet consulted his watch—yes, a good ten minutes late, without having to suffer what he claimed was near-asphyxiation.

Thanet sat down and hunted through the stack of reports on his desk for the one on the PM. It wasn't there. Perhaps Mallard intended to bring it up himself, later. There was nothing from forensic yet, either. He must remember to give them a ring.

The door burst open.

'What a moron!' Lineham exploded. 'Idiots like that should be put off the road, banned from driving!'

'What's the matter, Mike?' Thanet could guess, in view of the weather conditions this morning. He himself had seen three cars at the side of the road with smashed wings and dented bumpers.

'Why on earth can't people keep their distance when the roads are cy? I could see this . . . this . . .' Words failed him. Lineham hated swearing. '. . . this IDIOT behind me, driving much too close, but there's nothing you can do except let cretins like that go past, and we were in a line of traffic, so I couldn't. And of course, the car in front of me braked unexpectedly . . . I was all right, I was far enough away to slow down in time, but this moron . . .' Lineham dropped into his chair and thumped his desk so hard with a clenched fist that the various objects on it jigged and rattled. 'I could kill him!'

Lineham had always been keen on cars and his Ford Escort was dear to his heart.

'How much damage is there?'

Thanet let him talk the incident out of his system. He knew he wouldn't get much sense out of him otherwise. Eventually the sergeant wound down. 'Sorry, I should have asked. How's your mother-in-law?'

'Better. They're moving her out of intensive care and say the risk of a second attack should now be past.'

'When'll she be allowed home?'

'Might even be today. We won't know for certain until the doctor's seen her this morning. She's coming to us for a while. Joan's going to take a few days' leave.'

'By the way, thank Joan for having that word with Louise, will you? She seems happier about things now.'

'Actually, that was purely fortuitous. I hadn't actually spoken to Joan about it.'

'Well I'm grateful, anyway. It really helped her to know that someone like Joan had felt exactly the same. She's already decided to take her advice and do some refresher courses.' Lineham shook his head in mock despair. 'I don't know. Women! You can tell them things till you're blue in the face and they don't take a blind bit of notice. Then along comes some outsider—no offence meant, of course, sir—and there they are falling over themselves to do precisely what you were suggesting in the first place . . . Anything interesting come in over-night?'

'Haven't had a chance to find out yet.'

A sheepish grin indicated that Lineham was back to normal. 'I did get a bit carried away there. Sorry. But honestly . . .'

Lineham looked all set to start sounding off all over again and Thanet had no compunction in interrupting.

'Mike!' He glanced at his watch. Eight-forty. 'Look, it's time to go down to the morning meeting.' He handed the reports over to Lineham.

'You'd better make a start on these, or we're never going to get any where today. And give forensic a ring, find out what's happening.'

But the meeting was quickly over. Draco had rung to say he couldn' make it and Tody took his place. It wasn't until Draco was absent. Thanet thought, that you realised what a difference his presence made Irritating he might be—infuriating, occasionally—but he did make the place hum, there was no doubt about that.

Mallard arrived soon after he got back to the office. 'What happened to your car, Lineham?'

Lineham opened his mouth but Thanet held up his hand. 'No. I absolutely refuse to hear it all again. Let's just say someone ran into the back of it.'

'Oh, bad luck.' Mallard peered at Lineham over his half-moons. 'You're all right, though?'

'Yes, *I'm* fine. Wish I could say the same about my car.'

'Good.' Mallard turned back to Thanet. 'Thought I'd just pop up with this.' He handed over the report. 'Not that there's anything very startling in it. Asphyxiation, following a blow on the head, just as we thought.'

'No ifs or buts?'

'Perfectly straightforward.'

'Not one single, minute revelation?'

'None. Sorry. I heard about your mother-in-law, by the way, Luke. How is she?'

Thanet once again gave a brief account of the situation.

'If she's over the first twenty-four hours the imminent danger should have passed. But I expect she'll have to make some changes, as far as diet and exercise are concerned.'

'So we gather. Doctor MacPherson's going to have a chat with her and Joan this morning.'

'Good. You make sure she follows his advice. The most important thing is that she shouldn't regard herself as a permanent invalid.'

'Not much likelihood of that, I shouldn't think.'

'And make sure you don't treat her like one, either. So many people still think that if they've had a heart attack they've got to languish the rest of their lives away in an armchair.' Mallard snorted. 'Lot of nonsense. The more they keep their circulation going the better. Exercise is the answer, Luke, and you make sure she gets it. Plenty of exercise. When she's had two or three weeks to recuperate, of course. But it's important to start in a small way as soon as possible, and build up the programme.'

'Don't worry. We'll see she does as she's told.'

'Good. Anyway, how's the case going?'

'Slowly, as usual.'

Mallard grinned and slapped Thanet on the shoulder. 'Patience, Luke. Patience. The older you get the more you realise how important it is to cultivate it.'

Thanet smiled back, remembering the years when Mallard's short fuse had been notorious. 'You're an example to us all, Doc.'

When Mallard had gone Thanet read through the post mortem report before handing it to Lineham. 'He's right. Doesn't help at all. Did you get anywhere with forensic?'

Lineham shook his head. ' "Soon", that's all.'

'I'll believe that when I see it. Anything interesting in the other reports?'

'Not really. The landlord of the Green Man confirms Mr Master's story. He and Mrs Master arrived there at a quarter or ten to nine, stayed half an hour or so. He remembers them because they spent the whole time arguing. In the end she walked out, and he followed.'

'Hmm.' Nothing new there. 'What about that supper safari the Broxtons' neighbour suggested might be going on that night, to account for all the cars she heard?'

'Not a whisper about that. I think we can take it there wasn't one.'

'So whose cars were they, I wonder? Anything else?'

'Routine stuff, that's all.'

'Have you gone right through them?'

'Just a few more.'

'Pass a couple over.'

A few minutes later Lineham said, 'Mrs Broxton's cleaning woman confirms the phone call Mr Master told us about. And . . .' His tone suddenly changed and he sat up. 'Listen to this. At around 9.15 on Monday morning she heard Mrs Master talking to someone called Howard on the telephone. She was arranging to meet him that evening.'

The night she died. Swain had denied any such meeting.

Thanet held out his hand. 'Let me see.'

He skimmed the report. *I heard Mrs Master say, 'See you tonight, then. Soon after nine.'*

'He was lying,' said Lineham with satisfaction. 'I knew it.'

And, as they had suspected, so was Mrs Swain. No doubt she and Swain had cooked up their mutual alibi between them.

It was what they needed, the first discrepancy, their first break. It was only a small matter but enough to open up new lines of enquiry. If a case was static, it was dead. All the same, Thanet knew it was important not to get carried away. 'Don't read too much into it, Mike.'

The phone rang. Bentley, who was doing the house-to-house enquiries in Wheelwright's Lane.

'Thought you'd want to know right away, sir. I've just interviewed a Mrs Marsh. She lives in one of the semi-detached cottages opposite where Mr Master and the Swains live. Her neighbour, an old lady, is away visiting her son, but Mrs Marsh has got a baby who's teething and she spent most of Monday evening in his bedroom walking about with him or sitting in the chair by the window, rocking him to try and get him off to sleep—'

'The bedroom's at the front?'

'Yes. There was no light on in the room, she'd just left the door from the landing open, and she drew the curtains back because she was bored stiff. So she had a good view of the houses opposite.'

'And?' Thanet knew he was being impatient but couldn't help himself. With any luck . . .

'She says they *all* went out during the evening—Mr Master, Mr Swain and Mrs Swain.'

'The Swains were together?'

'No, they left separately. Mr Master left some time before them, between eight and half past, she thinks, and then Mr Swain, around nine. Mrs Swain followed immediately afterwards.'

'Followed? You mean she got the impression that Mrs Swain was actually following her husband?'

'Yes. She says that as soon as Mr Swain's car had driven out, his wife came out immediately and went off in the same direction. Towards the village.'

And thence to Melton? 'If it was dark, how did she know which of them left first?'

'She knows the cars and both the houses opposite have security lights which come on automatically as soon as anyone comes out of the front door and crosses the drive. She saw them quite clearly, she says.'

'Did she see any of them come back?'

'Mr Master got back at around 9.30. Then a bit later, around a quarter to ten she thinks, Mrs Swain got back.'

'Before her husband?'

'Yes.'

'She's certain of that?'

'Seems to be. Says Mr Swain arrived home about half an hour after his wife. Says all the coming and going livened up her evening no end.'

Thanet could hear the smile in Bentley's voice. 'Well done, Bentley. Thanks for ringing in right away.'

'I thought you'd want to know.'

Thanet put the receiver down. 'Did you hear all that?' He recounted the conversation to Lineham.

'A witness!' said Lineham. 'Terrific! It's obvious, isn't it? Mr Swain arranges to go over to Melton to see Mrs Master soon after nine. Mrs Swain guesses that's where he's going—where else would he be going at nine o'clock in the evening?—'

'The pub?' said Thanet.

Lineham glared at him.

'All right, sorry, Mike. Go on.'

'—and decides to follow him.'

'Why?'

'Because she's curious to know where Mrs Master is? She's a pretty forceful type isn't she, Mrs Swain. Maybe she decided she wasn't just going to sit back and let Mrs Master take her husband away without a fight. So she decides she's going to tackle her. But she can't if she doesn't know where she is. She may even have asked her husband, but he refused to tell her. Anyway, the moment Mr Swain's car has driven off she's after him.'

'And then?'

Lineham paused. 'I haven't had time to think it through yet.'

'So think it through now. Go back to the point when Master arrives at the Broxtons'.'

'Well, let's see. Mr Master claims he got there at 8.30. After the argument about whether his wife will go with him or not, he drags her into the car and then drives off. He blackmails her into agreeing to have a drink with him, on the basis that if she won't he'll just keep on driving and the children will be left alone for hours. They arrive at the Green Man in Melton around 8.45. At around nine Mr Swain leaves Nettleton, followed by his wife—'

'If she did follow him, it would have been a bit tricky to avoid being spotted. The lanes around Melton aren't exactly thronged with traffic at that time of night.'

'That would have made it all the easier for her!' said Lineham trium-phantly. 'She could have kept her distance, she'd have been able to see the glare of his headlights some way ahead. And if she didn't actually get close enough for him to recognise the car—and as you pointed out earlier, it was dark—then she'd have been in no danger of him spotting her. After all, he'd have no reason to suspect he was being followed. I don't suppose she made a habit of it.'

'All right. So they're both in Melton. He turns into the oast house, she presumably hangs back or drives past.'

'Right. He knocks at the door, but Mrs Master is out at the pub with her husband, so he gets no reply.' Lineham stopped, frowned. 'This is where it gets complicated.'

'Yes. Because if he did it, it must mean that he hung around until after she and Mr Master got back at—9.20, was it?'

Lineham was consulting his notebook. 'Yes. Nine-twenty.'

'Well, let's say, for the sake of argument, that Master did exactly what he claims to have done, brought his wife back and then left. And let's say Swain did hang about waiting in case she came back. He sees them arrive, watches Master leave, then knocks on the door . . .'

Thanet paused, indicating that Lineham should continue the sce-nario.

'She takes him into the kitchen,' said the sergeant, 'and, for whatever reason, they have an argument, some sort of scuffle and she slips, bangs her head on the corner of the table, passes out.' He stopped, looking rueful. 'And that's where we come unstuck, isn't it, sir? I agree, I just can't see him putting that polythene bag over her head.'

Thanet was shaking his head. 'No, it just won't work, will it? For one thing, I can't really see why Perdita and Swain should have had an argument at all. Anyway, I don't think he did go into the house.'

'Why not?'

'Think, Mike! He's her lover. They've arranged to meet. He's hung around in the hope of seeing her and finally she gets back and he waits until her husband's gone then she lets him in. Even if, for the sake of argument, we say he did kill her, I can't see a disagreement blowing up to murderous proportions between them *and* his getting away, all in the space of ten minutes.'

'Why ten minutes?'

'Because that's when Mrs Broxton gets home.'

'But she didn't go straight into the kitchen!' said Lineham trium-phantly. 'She went upstairs because Henry was screaming.'

Thanet frowned. 'I'd forgotten that.'

'She didn't ring in to report finding the body until 9.40. So he would have had twenty minutes.'

Thanet waved his hand irritably. 'Ten minutes, twenty minutes, what's the difference? It's still not long enough. No, I don't think he went in at all.'

'But his wife might have!' said Lineham. 'Say Swain didn't wait, say he gave up and left before the Masters arrived back. *But say his wife didn't.*'

'You mean she might have been so geared up to having it out with Mrs Master that now she'd found out where she was staying she was determined to sit it out, no matter how long she had to wait.'

'Well, it would be quite in character, don't you think, sir?'

'Right. Say she did. Go on.'

'Mrs Master arrives home. Henry couldn't have been crying at that stage because if so she'd probably have picked him up and been carrying him when she answered the door to Mrs Swain. And she'd hardly then have taken him back up and plonked him in his cot while she talked to her, would she?'

'No.'

'So when she came in she probably either popped up to reassure herself that the children were all right or went to the foot of the stairs and listened to see if either of them was crying. In any case, she then went into the kitchen to make herself a drink of Horlicks or something. She puts the milk on the stove and then hears someone knocking at the front door. Mrs Swain knows that Mrs Master is in because she saw her arrive back and she's not going to give up easily. When she doesn't get any response from ringing the bell she hammers on the door—that's probably what woke Henry up, come to think of it. He might not have started crying immediately, so Mrs Master has taken her into the kitchen by the time he starts, and doesn't hear him. Then they have the argument and everything happens just as we've suggested.' Lineham looked at Thanet hopefully. 'What d'you think, sir?'

Thanet was looking for loopholes. 'What about Mrs Broxton?'

'It could all have been over by then. An awful lot can happen in ten minutes, or even five. Oh, I know what you said about ten or even twenty minutes not being long enough for a quarrel of these proportions to have blown up between Mr Swain and Mrs Master, and I tend to agree with you. They were lovers, after all. If she was going to break off with him she'd do it gently, lead up to it . . . But Mrs Swain is a different matter. She isn't going to hang around making polite conversation, is she? So it happens just as we've said and then, just as it's all over, Mrs Swain hears the front door slam. She realises she's got to get away fast, and lets herself out through the back door . . . Of course! That would explain why it was unlocked!'

'Could be . . . And it's only a ten-minute drive to Nettleton, she could still have been home by a quarter to ten . . . But if it did happen like that, why did she get back before her husband?'

'Perhaps he didn't feel like going home straight away, went to a pub, had a few drinks?'

'Possible, I suppose. Well, we mustn't get carried away by all this but it's certainly the most likely scenario we've come up with so far.' Thanet had jumped up, begun putting on his overcoat as he talked. He was eager now to tackle the Swains again, put this new theory to the test. 'Come on, Mike, let's go.'

14

The mid-morning traffic was light and they were soon clear of the town. They had decided to talk to Swain first, see if they could get anything more out of him before driving to TVS at Maidstone. Thanet's spirits rose. He was looking forward to the interview with Mrs Swain. She was a formidable opponent and he enjoyed a challenge. Interviewing was the part of his work that he enjoyed most, when mind and intuition were stretched to the limit and the skills he had built up through years of experience were fully employed.

Although the sun was high in the sky the temperature had still not risen much above freezing, and in the shade of trees and hedges frost still crisped the grass. The ground, Thanet guessed, would still be rock-hard, furrowed ridges in ploughed fields only just beginning to soften as the warmth began to penetrate. Persuaded by these early frosts that winter was upon them, soon now the trees would shed their remaining leaves, the glorious autumn colour would melt away and the woods become no more than dark smudges delineating the graceful curves of fields and Downs.

For a while both men were silent, thinking. Then, picking up the conversation where they had left it, Thanet said, 'I bet he doesn't even know she went out that night. She left after him and came back before him.'

Lineham grinned. 'I can't see she'd have told him she followed him.'

'No. In which case, if it was her suggestion, when they heard about the murder, that it might be a good idea to say they'd both been home all evening, he'd assume she was trying to protect him rather than herself.'

Lineham gave a cynical grunt. 'Typical, I should think.'

'You really don't like her, do you, Mike?'

'You said you weren't too keen on her either.'

'That's true. But I do find her stimulating. Pity she's at work. I'd like to have interviewed them together, seen how they interact.' Thanet was always fascinated by the way in which people can change in the presence of their partners. The bold become muted, the shy can blossom, the strong become weak and the weak strong, as if the chemistry which attracted them to each other in the first place is most evident when they are together.

Nettleton, as usual, seemed asleep. Thanet wondered if it ever woke up. They turned into Wheelwright's Lane and a minute or two later Lineham slowed down as they approached the cluster of houses. Thanet glanced at the cottage where Mrs Marsh their witness lived.

'Stop short of the Swains' drive, Mike.'

Lineham pulled up and they both got out of the car. It was immediately obvious that anyone in the front bedroom of either cottage would have an excellent view of the Swains' front drive directly opposite. The cottages were close to the road, the front gardens tiny, and there were no trees to obscure the view.

'Can't be much more than fifty, seventy-five yards to the Swains' front door,' said Lineham. 'And with security lights on . . .'

'The sightlines into the Masters' drive aren't as good, though. That tall beech hedge gets in the way.'

'True. But that really doesn't matter so much, does it, sir? He's already admitted going to see his wife, and the times tally with Mrs Marsh's statement.'

'Quite. Might as well leave the car here. There's plenty of room to pass.'

The neatly clipped yew hedges on either side of the five-barred gate had obscured their view of the garden and it was not until they were halfway to the front door that Thanet spotted Swain working in one of the flower borders over to the left, at the far side of the lawn. He was bent double cutting down spent herbaceous plants and the wheelbarrow beside him was piled high with autumn debris.

Thanet called his name and Swain straightened up, secateurs in one hand, a clump of dead flower stalks in the other. When he saw who it was he laid the stems on top of the heaped barrow and began to walk towards the two policemen, stripping off his gardening gloves as he came. He was wearing ancient corduroys, an old anorak and wellington boots. The picture of a healthy countryman was belied as he came closer by the pallor of his face, the dark smudges beneath his eyes. He obviously hadn't been getting much sleep lately. Guilty or innocent, not surprising in the circumstances.

'Sorry to trouble you. I wonder if we could have another word?'

Shoulders drooping with resignation Swain turned and led them along the narrow paved path at the side of the house around to the back door. Here he stopped, pushed it open and paused to lever off his boots, stepping in stockinged feet on to the doormat inside. Thanet and Lineham followed him in. Swain pulled out a chair and sat down, indicating that they should do likewise.

Thanet waited until Lineham was settled, notebook at the ready, then folding his hands together on the table leaned forward. 'We don't take very kindly to people who lie to us in murder enquiries, Mr Swain.'

Swain's response puzzled him. First there was what Thanet could have sworn was a genuine look of surprise, almost immediately overlaid by comprehension. But Swain's tone was firm. 'I haven't lied to you, Inspector.'

'There are, shall we say, sins of omission as well as commission.'

Swain hesitated. You could almost see him thinking, *How much do they know?*

'Mr Swain, when I asked you if you had seen Mrs Master on Monday night you said no. What would you have said, I wonder, if instead I had asked if you had *arranged* to see her on Monday night?'

Swain opened his mouth to reply and Thanet had to make a lightning decision: should he give Swain the opportunity to lie? If he did, time would be wasted and a tactical advantage lost. 'And before you say anything, I should warn you that we have a witness who overheard that arrangement being made.'

Once again Swain's reaction puzzled him. This time the look of comprehension in his eyes was immediate, but almost at once was overtaken by confusion. Why? If Perdita had told him that the cleaning woman had overheard the call, why should he now be feeling confused? Unless . . . Yes, that must be it. Perhaps Swain had first thought that his wife might have listened in on his conversation with Perdita, but had at once realised that it couldn't have been she who had told the police. It would have made nonsense of their agreed alibi.

As he watched Swain trying to make up his mind what to say he decided he would lose nothing by putting him out of his misery and might, perhaps, gain. Let off the hook, Swain would, as Lineham would have put it, owe him one. He explained about the cleaner, watching comprehension leach into the man's expressive eyes.

Swain made an embarrassed gesture. 'Yes, well, I'm sorry, Inspector, if I misled you. But I wasn't lying. I really didn't see her, you know.'

'Well, well . . .'

The unexpected, lazy drawl from the doorway startled Thanet, engrossed as he was in the way the interview was going.

'The third degree, and in my own kitchen! Who would have believed it?'

Victoria Swain stepped forward, moved indolently to stand behind her husband and rest her hands on his shoulders in a brief caress. Then she slid into a chair beside him. This morning she was wearing narrow black trousers, a silky pale blue blouse and a black knitted jacket with a design of huge pansies in shades of mauve and blue. Another Swain creation, Thanet presumed. Her blue eyes mocked him across the kitchen table.

Well, he thought, you wanted to interview them together, and here they are.

'Not at work today, Mrs Swain?'

'Sorry to disappoint you, but no, Inspector. As a matter of fact I'm working at home. I thought I heard voices, so . . .'

'I'm not in the least disappointed. In fact, I'm delighted. It will save us that tiresome journey through the M20 roadworks, to Maidstone. We were coming to see you next.'

'Really. How convenient.' She raised her hands, palms up. 'Well, here I am. Do your worst—or should I say, your best?'

Thanet saw Lineham shift slightly and guessed what the sergeant was thinking. *She really gets up my nose.*

Swain gave his wife an apologetic glance. 'It's no good, Vicky. They know.'

Know what? wondered Thanet.

'Know what?' said Mrs Swain. *Be careful,* her frown said. *Give nothing away unless you have to.*

'That I arranged to see Perdita on Monday night. The cleaning woman at Vanessa's house overheard Perdita on the telephone.'

'Oh dear, oh dear, what a calamity!' She raised an eyebrow at Thanet, inviting complicity. 'Servants have always been the bane of the middle classes, wouldn't you agree, Inspector? No privacy.'

'Well, now you're here, Mrs Swain, I will say to you what I said to your husband. We don't take very kindly to people who lie to us in murder enquiries.'

The blue eyes opened wide, baby-innocent. 'Lie to you, Inspector? Who's been lying to you?'

'As I also said to your husband, there are sins of omission as well as commission. He may have been guilty of the first, but you are most certainly guilty of the second.'

'Oh?' The innocence overlaid by wariness, now.

'Yes.' Thanet allowed the heavy monosyllable to hang on the air, the silence to stretch out. No harm in making her sweat a little. This wasn't a game and the sooner she realised it the better.

'All these tales of a cosy evening at home. Pork and apple casserole, wasn't it, as I recall? Followed by gooseberry fool. Then a little work, television and bed.'

'My, you have got a good memory, Inspector. Didn't even need to refer to your notebook . . . But, as a matter of fact, that was precisely what we did have for supper on Monday night. Down to the last detail.'

Thanet was tired of sparring. 'Was that before or after you both went out?'

Their expressions changed. Thanet was certain that it was the word 'both' which caused Swain's eyebrows to rise and the look of enquiry he turned on his wife.

Victoria Swain, however, did not even blink. 'I think you must be misinformed,' she said icily. The blue eyes were frosty now but Thanet thought that deep within them he detected the first flicker of unease.

'Reliably informed, as a matter of fact, and by a witness who could have no possible reason to lie.'

At the word 'witness' she tried to conceal her dismay, but failed. She shifted uneasily on her chair and Thanet could see that she was struggling against the temptation to look at her husband and gauge his reaction to all this.

'Witness, Inspector?' said Swain.

Thanet glanced at Lineham and nodded at the sergeant's notebook. Lineham obediently began to thumb through it. Both men knew that as Bentley had given the report by telephone there would be no written report in its pages. Thanet hoped the sergeant would make it sound good.

'Let me see . . . Here we are . . .' Lineham held the book up as if to see it more clearly. ' "On Monday evening Mr Swain drove off towards the village at about nine o'clock and Mrs Swain followed immediately afterwards . . ." '

Swain's head snapped around to look at his wife and Victoria Swain burst out, 'How could anyone possibly say that, even if it were true. It was pitch dark by then.'

' "I could see clearly because they have security lights which come on automatically as soon as anyone comes out of the front door and crosses the drive . . ." '

Mrs Swain simultaneously thumped the table in frustration and stood up. 'Must be that old biddy across the road, damn her eyes. Twitching her net curtains all day long, and nothing better to do than spy on her neighbours . . .' She marched across the room and stood with her back to them at the window, folding her arms tightly as if to hold her anger in, prevent it getting out of control. Her back was rigid and her head turned slightly to one side, so that from where he sat Thanet could see the muscles of her jaw working.

It was a tacit admission. But why so violent a reaction? he wondered. Was it because she had lost face, been caught out in a lie? Because she was going to have to bear the humiliation of admitting to her husband that she had followed him? Or was there a more sinister reason? Was she in truth the murderer, faced now by the fact that her alibi had crumbled?

She swung around to face him again. 'No!' she said, startling him. Had she read his mind?

But she was merely contradicting herself, it seemed. 'No, it couldn't have been her. She's away, isn't she? I saw her son carting her off plus suitcase on Saturday morning. So it must have been little Mrs butter-won't-melt-in-my-mouth Marsh.'

'Does it matter who saw you? The fact is, you were seen, both of you.'

'Of course it matters!' she said savagely. She glanced at her husband. 'For God's sake stop looking at me like that, Howard! I had a right to know where you were going, didn't I? I am your *wife.*'

'You mean, you actually *followed* me?'

Thanet saw her realise, too late, that she could have claimed to have gone somewhere else. It was unlike her to miss a trick. It could only be because the shock of being discovered had temporarily affected her judgement. He watched her collect herself and prepare to make the best of the situation. How would she do it? he wondered. And who would she tackle first? Himself, or her husband?

She glanced at Thanet. 'I should like to speak to my husband alone.'

He shook his head. 'You've had plenty of time to talk to him, if you wished, and there'll be plenty of time after we've gone.'

The blue eyes flashed ice at him but she did not hesitate. Swiftly she crossed to sit once more beside Swain, half turning her back on the two policemen as if to shut them out.

So her husband took priority. That was interesting. Had he in fact been mistaken? If Mrs Swain had truly felt herself to be in danger, would she not have tried to save her own skin, first? Was she innocent after all?

Thanet glanced at Lineham. The sergeant's eyes were sparkling. He was enjoying this.

Victoria Swain laid her hand on her husband's arm. 'I just wanted to know what was happening,' she pleaded. 'You can't imagine what it's like, being left in the dark . . .'

No response.

'I just thought, if I could talk to her . . .'

Swain's eyes narrowed. 'You saw her?'

'No. How could I? You know yourself that she wasn't there.'

Swain glanced quickly at Thanet, then back at his wife. Calmly, deliberately, he shook her hand off his arm, a telling gesture of rejection.

She drew back as if stung. Anger sparked in her eyes and her tone changed. 'Well what did you expect me to do? Sit back and do nothing while you ran after that little—' With an effort she stopped herself, glowered at Thanet. *Now look what you've done.*

Thanet didn't mind being blamed if the results were so fruitful.

'Well,' he said pleasantly, 'I think we're beginning to get somewhere. Correct me if I'm wrong, won't you? On Monday evening you, Mr Swain, set off for Mrs Broxton's house to see Mrs Master and you, Mrs Swain, followed. What interests us is what happened when you got there.'

They looked at each other.

'Nothing,' they said simultaneously, united at least in this.

'Could you be a little more specific?'

Swain shrugged. 'I rang the bell several times, but there was no reply.'

Lineham was scribbling something. He held his notepad out for Thanet to see. *Bell out of order,* he had written. Thanet nodded. He hadn't forgotten.

'Did you knock?'

'Yes, but there's no knocker and it's a great big thick door, so I doubt that anyone would have heard.'

Unless, like Master, you had been determined to make as much noise as possible, thought Thanet.

'So what did you do then?'

'I didn't quite know what to do. I couldn't understand it. There were lights on in the house and anyway I knew the children would be in bed, so she couldn't have gone out. I thought she might be in the bathroom or something, and failed to hear. So I hung around for a few minutes more then tried again. When she still didn't open the door I gave up. I thought she might have fallen asleep or something, she'd had a pretty exhausting couple of days, but since then . . .' He faltered. 'I've wondered, since . . . Perhaps she was . . . Perhaps she'd already been . . .'

But he couldn't say it. He gave Thanet a beseeching look. 'D'you think that's possible? I couldn't bear it if I thought she was . . . if I could have helped her, and she . . .'

If the man was lying he was putting on a pretty good performance, thought Thanet. He shook his head. 'It's impossible to be precise about time of death, Mr Swain. What did you do then?'

'I . . .' Swain avoided looking at his wife. 'I went for a drink.'

'Where was that?'

'The Dog and Fiddle, in Barton.'

'How long did you stay there?'

A shrug. 'I'm not sure. I had a couple of drinks. Half an hour, perhaps.'

'And you got home when?'

'Around a quarter past ten, I think.' For the first time Swain looked at his wife. 'Something like that, wasn't it?'

As Mrs Marsh, prisoner at the nursery window, had confirmed.

Victoria Swain was nodding.

'So let me be quite clear about this. You left here around nine, arrived at Mrs Broxton's house some ten minutes later and stayed only five minutes or so. So you would have got to the pub at about . . . say, nine thirty, and left around ten. Is that right?'

'More or less.'

Thanet glanced at Lineham to check that he had got everything down, then turned his attention to Mrs Swain. 'And what about you?'

She shrugged. 'More or less the same.'

'I should like a little more detail, please.'

'Oh God, if you must have chapter and verse . . .' She took a deep breath and launched into her story, rattling it off without hesitation and without once glancing at Swain. 'I left here immediately after my husband. When we got to Melton and he turned into the Broxtons' drive, I realised that that must be where Perdita was hiding out. I was a bit surprised, she and Vanessa have never been particularly friendly, as I told you, but I couldn't think of any other reason why Howard should go there. So I drove past and parked at the entrance to a field just beyond the house next door. Then I walked back. When I got there Howard was still standing by the front door, ringing the bell. Eventually he gave up, got back into his car and drove off—past me, actually. I had to duck behind a hedge.'

Thanet had been beginning to wonder if Swain and Master might actually have passed each other in the lane between the pub in Melton and the Broxtons' house. The timing was very close. But here was the answer. When Swain left he had gone the other way.

'I was worried in case he'd recognise my car, but he didn't,' Victoria Swain was saying. 'I'd parked well back, of course, and turned off the lights. But by the time I'd got back to it and got it started I realised I'd probably lost him.' She shrugged. 'So I came home.'

'And what time did you get back?'

Another shrug. 'Twenty, a quarter to ten?'

'Why did it take you half an hour to do a ten-minute journey?'

'Ah. The sleuth moves in for the kill! Sorry to disappoint you, Inspector. I wasted a little time driving around trying to see if I could pick up my husband's tracks.' She gave Swain a shamefaced grin. 'I'd make a rotten detective. And it was the first and last time, I promise.' She put her hand on his and this time although he did not respond he did not cast it off but let it rest. A spark of hope kindled in her eyes.

She really does care about him, thought Thanet. And although one would never have guessed it, meeting them as individuals, he is the one with the power and she is the supplicant. The question is, how much does she care, and how far would she go to keep him? As far as eliminating her rival?

One thing was certain, as he said to Lineham on the way back to the car, Victoria Swain was still high on the list. She had motive and opportunity aplenty.

15

When they reached the gate Thanet paused. Of its own volition his hand had found its way into his pocket and come out holding his pipe. He realised how much he was longing to smoke it and Lineham hated him smoking in the car. Besides, a thought had just occurred to him. 'Let's walk along the lane a little way, Mike.'

He took out his pouch, fed tobacco into his pipe and lit it, hunching his shoulder and turning away from the slight breeze in order to shelter the flame.

Lineham waited patiently. He was used to this ritual.

'I was just thinking . . .' Thanet paused to strike another match. 'The way you described the murder happening . . . D'you realise that everything we've said about Mrs Swain could equally apply to Master? By the time they got back he must have been pretty angry and frustrated. He could have forced his way in when she opened the front door . . .'

'Or gone around the back, even. No, it's highly unlikely the back door would have been unlocked.'

'Oh, I don't know . . .'

'What, when she was out there in the country alone in the house at night with two small children?'

'Not for any length of time, I agree. But say, for instance, that once she had satisfied herself that the children were all right she went straight to the kitchen as you suggested to make herself a hot drink. She puts the milk on to heat, rinses out the bottle, and opens the back door to put it out. This could all have taken the same length of time as it would have taken Master to decide he wasn't going to let the matter rest and make his way around to the back door. So as she opens it, there he is, waiting . . .'

It seemed all wrong to be discussing murder out here in the peace of the countryside. Ahead of them the lane curved to the left, flanked by brown ribbons of dead leaves and hedges glowing with autumn colour. Here and there the bright red hips of the wild rose mingled with clusters of blackberries shrivelled by the frosts.

His pipe still wasn't drawing very well and he took it apart, blew through the mouthpiece and put it together again. That was better. 'For that matter, I suppose we could say exactly the same about his mother. You said yourself that if we were looking for someone who wanted Perdita dead, her mother-in-law certainly qualified.'

'And *you* said it couldn't have been her because there was just no reason why she should have gone to see her.'

Thanet shrugged. 'Say I was wrong. Say there was a reason, and we just don't know about it yet? She's admitted that she knew where Perdita was staying . . .'

'I can't imagine how we're ever going to find out what that reason was, if there is one. She's not exactly going to hand it to us on a plate, is she?'

'Mmm. That's a tricky one, I agree. Any bright ideas, Mike?'

'Not a glimmer.' Lineham grinned. 'You'll just have to play it by ear, as—'

'I know—as usual.' It was true, Thanet thought, he did play it by ear. It was all very well to plan a strategy, to know which points you wanted to cover in an interview, but it was equally important to listen to what was not being said, to try to work out what was going on beneath the surface. Call it intuition, empathy, whatever, it was a vital skill in the policeman's repertoire and the most difficult one to acquire.

'Fancy having a go yourself, Mike?'

'No thanks. I think I'll pass, on this one.'

'Oh come on! You like a challenge, you know you do.'

'I just think you'd be much more likely to get somewhere with her than I would. You're good at worming things out of people.'

'So are you, when you put your mind to it.'

Lineham said nothing, just compressed his lips and shook his head.

A battered old Mini came around the bend in the lane ahead much too fast and they both had to jump back almost into the hedge. Lineham scowled after it. 'Idiot!'

Thanet decided to stop teasing. He didn't want to make Lineham feel awkward about refusing. He knew quite well why the sergeant—usually very keen to take an active part in interviewing—was so reluctant to take on Master's mother: she reminded him too much of his own. 'It's OK, Mike. I was having you on. It's just the sort of problem I like to tackle, you know that.'

Lineham looked relieved. 'When are you going to have a go then, sir? She's round at Mr Master's house now. I saw her car in the drive as we passed, earlier. It's still there, I could just see it through the hedge.'

'Yes, I know.'

'So what are we waiting for?'

Lineham wheeled around and set off back down the lane at a brisk pace, leaning slightly forward like a tracker dog scenting its quarry. With an indulgent smile Thanet followed. Lineham's eagerness and enthusiasm were two of his most endearing traits.

When they reached the car Thanet stopped and looked at his watch. 'I think I'll just ring in and see if there's a message from Joan.'

He and Joan had arranged that, depending on the time at which her mother was discharged from hospital and whether or not she was transported by ambulance, Thanet would try to be at the house when they arrived in case help was needed.

It was just as well he'd rung. The message was that no ambulance was available and Joan would appreciate it if he could manage a brief visit home between 2 and 2.30. Probably to help get his mother-in-law up the stairs, Thanet thought. He could ask Lineham to give him a hand. He checked the time. Twenty past twelve. Plenty of time.

Lineham was standing by the gate to Master's house, waiting, and as Thanet approached he held up his hand. 'Listen.'

One of the windows in the sitting room was open and angry voices floated out across the drive.

'Mr Master and his mother,' said Lineham. 'They're really having a go at each other about something.'

'Are you thinking what I'm thinking, Mike?'

Lineham grinned. 'Be interesting to know what it was about, wouldn't it?'

Avoiding the gravelled drive they moved quietly alongside the hedge to the house and then across to the open window.

'. . . have expected you to understand.' Mrs Master's voice.

'Oh, for God's sake, Ma, why can't *you* understand? How can you expect me to be interested in what's happened to a piece of jewellery when I've lost my *wife*.'

'But it was my mother's! The loveliest thing she ever owned! I should never have let you talk me into giving it to Perdita. And now . . . You can't imagine how it upsets me, to think I might never see it again.'

'Don't talk nonsense, Ma. I keep telling you, it can't just have vanished into thin air. It'll turn up.'

'How? It's not here, I'm certain of that, I've been through her things half a dozen times to make sure. The police assure me she wasn't wearing it, and Vanessa Broxton swears it's not at her house—'

'Will you stop going on about it! I'm sick and tired of hearing about it. I just couldn't care less, is that clear? I simply don't want to know!'

A door slammed and there was silence. Master had obviously stormed out of the room and Thanet didn't blame him. Mrs Master senior wouldn't win any prizes for sensitivity, that was certain.

He raised his eyebrows at Lineham and nodded in the direction of the front door. They both crouched double to pass the open window before straightening up.

'Wonder what it is that's missing,' said Thanet.

'She said she'd asked the police . . .'

'So it would be legitimate for us to be asking for further details.'

They exchanged smiles. Things were looking up, thought Thanet. If Perdita had been given a piece of family jewellery to which Mrs Master senior was particularly attached, might her mother-in-law not have gone to see her on Monday night to try and get it back? It would be in character. Mrs Master struck him as being very much the sort of person to cling on to things as well as people. If Giles had told her Perdita had left him she might well have thought the piece would be lost to the family for ever if she didn't make an attempt to retrieve it. Then if Perdita had refused to hand it over . . . Thanet had anticipated a difficult time trying to winkle out of Mrs Master a possible reason why she might have gone to see Perdita on Monday. Now it looked as though it might have been handed to him on a plate.

When she opened the door it was obvious that she was still ruffled after the row with her son. Two bright spots of colour burned in her cheeks and her eyes glittered dangerously when she saw who it was.

'What do you want this time? We told you everything we knew yesterday. Can't you leave us in peace?'

Today she was wearing a grey, black and white pleated skirt, a crisply tailored white blouse and a black silk scarf with a paisley pattern in grey, white and red. Despite her evident agitation she looked as well groomed as ever, and certainly not a day over forty. How did she do it? Thanet wondered.

'I understand you were enquiring about a piece of jewellery that seems to have gone missing?'

'Ah.' Her expression changed. 'I'm sorry, I thought . . .' She stepped back. 'Come in, won't you?'

She led them into the blue and cream sitting room. Today, with the sun shining in, the room looked less cold, less forbidding, but it was still Perdita's painting which drew the eye like a magnet, the pure brilliant colours glowing, seeming almost to pulsate in their neutral setting.

'I know you must all think I'm making a terrible fuss about nothing,' she said as they sat down. 'Especially in the circumstances. But it's the sentimental value as much as its actual worth. It was my mother's, you see . . .'

'How much is it worth, exactly?' Not wishing to betray his ignorance by direct questions Thanet was banking on the fact that sooner or later he would learn what 'it' was.

'Around five thousand pounds, as I said when I reported its disappearance. But that's not the point. As I say, it's the sentimental value that's important. It's well insured and I could easily buy another one, but it just wouldn't be the engagement ring my father bought for my mother.'

So it was a ring. Thanet tried to think back. No, Perdita hadn't been wearing one, he was certain of that. He would have noticed it, especially if it was as spectacular as it sounded.

'Could you describe it for me?'

Mrs Master looked irritated. 'I gave a full description when I reported its loss.'

'I'm afraid I haven't actually read the report myself. I just . . . heard about it. So if you could bear with me . . .'

'It's a diamond cluster. Six perfectly matched diamonds. A really beautiful ring. I know you may think it terrible of me to be fussing about it at a time like this, but, well, it's such a desirable object . . . It could so easily go . . . well, go astray.'

'Are you questioning the honesty of my men?' said Thanet calmly.

'Oh no. No, of course not. It's just that . . .'

'Because I can assure you that Mrs Master was not wearing the ring when we examined her and that it was not in her room at Mrs Broxton's house.'

He glanced at Lineham for confirmation and the sergeant gave an emphatic nod.

'Oh. Yes. I see. Well then, where can it be?'

'I really don't know.' *Nor do I care,* his tone implied. 'She might have left it at her mother's house. She stayed there overnight on Saturday, I believe.'

'Of course!' said Mrs Master senior, her narrow features showing the first signs of animation since they arrived. 'How stupid of me! Why on earth didn't I think of that?'

'It's understandable that you were worried about it,' said Thanet. 'It's obviously a valuable piece. Was that why you went to see your daughter-in-law on Monday night?'

It was the brief euphoria of relief that brought about her unguarded response, Thanet was sure.

'Yes, of course,' she said. And stopped, trying to hide her dismay. 'I mean . . . Well, not on Monday, of course.'

So she hadn't given up hope of concealing the truth.

Thanet raised his eyebrows. 'When, then?'

'Sunday. It must have been Sunday.'

'Really? When, on Sunday?'

'Sunday evening.' She was beginning to get the trapped, panicky look of someone who feels that he is inexorably being driven into a corner and knows that he is going to be unable to get out.

'What time?'

'Er . . . somewhere around nine, I suppose.' She reached across to the soft black leather shoulder bag which lay in the far corner of the settee, took out a wisp of handkerchief and crumpled it in her hand.

'Who told you that she was at Mrs Broxton's house?'

'Why Giles did—my son. I told you that yesterday.' Briefly she was defiant again, almost scornful. But almost immediately her expression changed. She became very still and her eyes widened in shock as she realised the trap she had dug for herself.

Thanet allowed the silence to lengthen, gave her time to realise that there was no way to extricate herself. Then he said softly, 'Quite. Your son didn't know where his wife was himself until Monday morning, did he?' Abruptly his tone changed, his eyes became steely. 'You must realise that lying to the police during the course of a murder investigation is a serious matter. Apart from holding things up it's bound to make us wonder what you're trying to hide . . . So let's try again. What time on Monday evening did you go to see your daughter-in-law?'

She dabbed at her upper lip with the handkerchief. 'I told you, somewhere around nine.'

'You can't be more precise?'

She shrugged. 'It might have been a bit earlier than that.'

Thanet had to admire her resilience. Already her confidence wa
returning. It showed in the raised angle of her chin, the way sh
straightened her spine. Only the thumb and forefinger plucking at a
corner of the handkerchief betrayed her tension.

'So what happened?'

'I rang the bell, but no one came. So I left.'

'Did you hear anything, see anyone?'

'Not see anyone, no.' She hesitated.

Was she genuinely trying to remember, Thanet wondered, or was she
trying to think of something, anything, that would let her off the hook?

'I remember now. I could hear a child crying—well, screaming, actu
ally. He sounded pretty upset. Yes. That was why I didn't wait. I
thought Perdita would be trying to calm him down and it wasn't a good
time to see her. I decided I'd come back some time during the week.'

True or not? It was possible, of course. If Henry had been disturbed
by the commotion Giles had made ten or fifteen minutes earlier, he
could well have worked himself up into a state of hysteria by then. In
any case it was obvious that this time she was going to stick to her story
and until they had some concrete evidence which disproved it they
would have to accept it. He glanced at Lineham and stood up. The
sergeant snapped his notebook shut and followed suit.

'Very well, Mrs Master. We'll leave it there for now. But I hope
you've realised that there really is no point in lying to us. We always
find out in the end . . . You won't be going away at all, for the next
few days?'

A flash of alarm. 'No . . . But why . . . ?'

'Good.'

Outside he said, 'No harm in frightening her a little. Well Mike, what
d'you think?'

'If she was telling the truth, it means she was there while Mr Master
and his wife were out at the pub.'

'If, yes. But if she knew they'd been out, because her son told her
. . . Say she did in fact go there later, after the Swains had left and
before Mrs Broxton arrived home . . . She would have realised that if
ever she did have to confess to being there that night, it would be safest
to say that it was during the period her son and his wife were out.
Though what she said about the child crying sounded authentic
enough.'

'Only because it was credible in the circumstances,' said Lineham eagerly. 'I mean, if she knew Master and his wife were out, it would be a likely thing to happen, wouldn't it? For the little boy to wake up and start crying? She didn't mention the crying at first, did she? And didn't you notice the long pause before she told us about it?'

'Yes, I did . . . And another thing . . . If Henry was yelling his head off at nine o'clock, and was still crying at 9.30, when his mother got home, why didn't either of the Swains hear him—or Master, for that matter, when they were there between 9 and 9.30?'

'I suppose he could have cried himself to sleep briefly, then woken up and started again?'

'Possible, I suppose. What we need, of course, is a definite lead. Let's hope that forensic report'll come through soon as promised, and that when it does it'll give us something definite to go on.'

'No wonder the elderly neighbour said she'd heard several cars,' said Lineham. 'It must have been like Piccadilly Circus there that night!'

As if Perdita were a magnet to which they were all being drawn, thought Thanet.

'Well, where now?' said Lineham as they got into the car. He looked at his watch. 'It's just before one,' he added pointedly.

'Feeling peckish, Mike? All right, we'll get a bite to eat in the village.'

After an excellent ploughman's lunch in the Green Man ('Three sorts of pickle *and* pickled onions!' said Lineham) they rang in to find out if the forensic report had come through.

'No joy,' said Lineham, shaking his head. 'Wish they'd get the lead out of their boots.'

'We'll call in at my house then, see if Joan needs a hand.'

Lineham had willingly agreed to help.

Joan came into the hall as they let themselves in. 'Oh good, Mike's with you. I was wondering how we'd manage to get her upstairs.'

'How is she?' said Thanet.

Joan pulled a face. 'Pretty weak. They provided a wheelchair to get her to the car and said that it was all right for her to walk from the car to the house if it wasn't too far. They said it's important for her to have a little regular exercise every day, and that in another week or so it should be all right for her to come downstairs as long as she doesn't climb the stairs more than once a day, until she's stronger. If you hadn't managed to get home I was going to make up a bed for her on the settee.'

'Right. Let's see what we can do.'

They all went into the sitting room. Margaret Bolton was lying on the settee with her feet up, looking alarmingly pale and fragile. Thanet supposed that the doctors knew what they were doing, but for the first time he appreciated fully the responsibility Joan had taken on. His mother-in-law was going to need a great deal of care and attention for some time yet.

'How are you feeling, Margaret?'

She attempted a smile. 'Hullo, Luke, Mike. A bit limp, I'm afraid.'

'Still, it's good news, isn't it? They must be satisfied that you're going to be OK now or they wouldn't have discharged you.'

'And,' said Joan, smiling at her mother, 'they say that there's no reason why she shouldn't get back to leading her normal life again before too long, didn't they, Mum?'

Margaret Bolton nodded. 'The sooner the better, as far as I'm concerned. I don't want to be a burden on you, Joan. You've got your work to think of, as well as your family.'

'Nonsense. Of course you won't be a burden. How could you? My office is quite happy for me to take a few days' leave and after that I'm sure we'll be able to get some help, if necessary.'

'Anyway,' said Thanet, 'we certainly don't want you worrying about it. That would be the worst possible thing in the circumstances. Now, let's see about getting you upstairs.'

'I've prepared Bridget's room for her,' said Joan.

'I assumed you would.'

Between them Thanet and Lineham easily managed to carry Mrs Bolton up the stairs and into the bedroom. The bed was made up, its covers invitingly turned back and Thanet couldn't help feeling a pang of loss when he noticed that the familiar clutter of objects had been cleared from Bridget's dressing table and bedside table and replaced by the things which Joan had unpacked from her mother's suitcase.

They lowered Mrs Bolton gently on to the edge of the bed.

'Anything else we can do?'

Joan shook her head. 'I can manage now. Thanks, darling.'

'See you tonight, then.' Thanet kissed her and left her to help her mother undress.

'Doesn't look too good, does she?' said Lineham, when they were back in the car.

Thanet shook his head. 'I was thinking just a few minutes ago, I hope the doctors know what they're doing.'

'When I told Louise, last night, she said that this is the best way to treat heart attacks in the elderly. She says it's essential to keep the circulation going and this is why they now get them up so soon and insist on regular bouts of mild exercise. And the recovery rate, she says, is excellent, if they survive the first twenty-four hours.'

'That's what Doctor MacPherson said. Let's hope he's right . . . Anyway, we'd better get back to work. Give them another ring, see if that forensic report is in.'

It was.

'Good,' said Thanet. 'Back to the office, then, let's see what they have to say. Let's hope they give us something we can use.'

16

Superintendent Draco was just getting out of his car when Lineham pulled into the car park at Headquarters. Draco raised his hand in salute and waited for them.

Thanet thought that the Super looked terrible: all Draco's bounce had gone, the pouches beneath his eyes were soft and puffy and his sallow skin had an unhealthy pallor to it. Whereas he would once have bounded up the steps to the entrance door, now he plodded and Thanet and Lineham had to adjust their pace accordingly.

Thanet wondered whether to ask after Draco's wife, but couldn't bring himself to do so. He wasn't sure if he was being tactful or just plain cowardly.

'How's it going, Thanet?' Even Draco's voice lacked its usual vigour.

'Not too badly, sir. It's a bit complicated. Too many suspects, all with motive and opportunity. Trouble is, so far we haven't got a single piece of concrete evidence to tie any of them in with it.'

'Forensic report through yet?' But Draco didn't look as if he were really interested in the answer. Incredible for a man who had once told his team that if anyone so much as sneezed in his patch he wanted to hear about it.

'We haven't seen it yet, but it's just come in, sir.'

'Good.'

They parted in the foyer and on the way upstairs Lineham said, 'D'you think she's worse?'

'I couldn't pluck up the courage to ask.'

In the office Thanet eagerly skimmed the forensic report. He read it again more slowly, conscious of Lineham barely containing his impatience to hear what it said. Then he handed it to the sergeant and went to stand looking out of the window. Something was nagging at his memory. What was it?

Outside sun glinted off glass and chrome, leaves fluttered down from trees, people went about their business but Thanet saw it all only as a blur. His attention was wholly focussed elsewhere. What was it, that he was trying to remember?

Lineham's voice disturbed his concentration. 'Pretty disappointing, isn't it? Loads of smudged prints on the polythene bag but nothing clear enough to be of any use. Just one good print on that and we could have nailed him.'

'Not necessarily, Mike. Counsel would have argued that it could have been made at any time.'

'Maybe, but at least it would have pointed us in the right direction . . . What about this blue fluff?'

Blue woollen fibres had been found in the polythene bag.

'Perhaps we ought to concentrate on that, do you think, sir?'

'I should think only luck will help us there. Just think, Mike. Those fibres could have come from anywhere—from any piece of clothing or item of household goods, past or present, owned by any of the suspects or their families.'

Thanet became aware that he was massaging his right temple, that he had a slight headache—or perhaps not so much a headache as a build-up of pressure, as if the memory that was eluding him were physically trying to push its way out of his brain.

'Still, it's a starting point, isn't it, sir? If you don't mind me saying so, if we gave up before we began just because we didn't think we'd get anywhere, well, we never would get anywhere, would we?'

'Point made, Mike. So where do you suggest we begin?'

'We could systematically work through the wardrobes and cupboards of each suspect in turn.'

'Beginning with whom?'

Lineham shrugged. 'Mrs Swain?'

'That'll be fun when we get to Swain's workroom,' said Thanet, remembering his brief glimpse of the floor-to-ceiling shelves packed with cones of wool, the sample swatches trailing multi-coloured strands.

Lineham grinned. 'The lab boys'll go mad!'

'Anyway, perhaps it would be sensible to ask . . .' He stopped.

'What's the matter, sir?'

Thanet became aware of how he must look: dazed stare, mouth half open in astonishment.

'Mike! Just a minute.' Thanet sank down into the chair behind his desk. He needed a moment to readjust. It was as if he had been looking at the whole thing from the wrong end of a telescope.

'Are you all right?' Lineham's face loomed at him as the sergeant bent forward in concern and Thanet flapped him irritably away. 'Yes, yes! I just need to think, that's all.'

He watched Lineham retreat, trying unsuccessfully not to look hurt.

'Oh all right, Mike, I'm sorry. It's just that I suddenly realised . . .'

Lineham's face changed, became eager. 'What?'

Thanet leaned forward. 'We've been over and over the timing of all the suspects' movements on Monday night, trying to work out the sequence of events. We've queried all those timings, checking and cross-checking, believing or disbelieving. But there's one person whose statement we've never questioned.'

Lineham frowned. 'Whose?'

Thanet told him, and had the satisfaction of seeing the look of astonishment on his sergeant's face. 'Now you know why my jaw dropped just now.'

'Mrs Broxton?' Lineham was still looking incredulous.

Thanet nodded.

He recalled the image his memory had presented him with just now. As clearly as if she were sitting before him in his office he had remembered Vanessa Broxton as he had first seen her on Monday night. Huddled in a corner of one of the big sofas, feet tucked up beneath her, she had been wearing the clothes she must have worn in Court that day, a straight charcoal grey skirt and white blouse. And, slung loosely around her shoulders, a thick blue knitted jacket.

'Remember when we interviewed her on Monday? She was wearing a blue woollen jacket.'

'But that doesn't mean a thing. I mean, even if the fibres did turn out to be from that jacket, it wouldn't be any help to us. Counsel would argue that the bag in which the jacket had once been was lying around in the kitchen and the murderer just saw it and grabbed it.'

'Unlikely, Mike, with small children in the house. The danger of leaving plastic bags lying around is so well known by now . . . I bet you and Louise don't, do you?'

Lineham shook his head.

'Well, I can't imagine Mrs Broxton doing so either. But she is the one person who'd be able to find one in that house in a hurry, isn't she?'

'But why would she want to?'

'Ah well, now that's what I suddenly realised. She did have a reason,
a powerful one . . . Just think, Mike. She's devoted to those children.
Her nanny, Angela Proven, told me that she's "potty about them", that
she absolutely hated having to leave Henry when she went back to
work. That she'd even told her that for two pins she'd chuck it all in. I
quote. And you remember what Mrs Swain told us? That Vanessa's
children came first with her, that motherhood had overwhelmed her.
She said she'd seen it happen before, especially in career women who
leave it late to have a baby. They fall in love with the child, she
said . . .'

'So? I'm sorry, I still don't get it.'

'Well don't you see, the one thing that would arouse Vanessa
Broxton's fury is ill-treatment of her children. And Perdita leaving
them alone in the house at night would certainly count as that, wouldn't
you agree?'

Lineham nodded.

'So, just say Mrs Master senior was telling the truth. You remember
she said she heard a child screaming while she was ringing the bell just
before nine . . .'

The light had finally dawned, he could see it in Lineham's face.
Lineham raked his hand through his hair. He looked stunned. 'Draco's
going to love this.'

'So what? We've never treated her any differently from any of the
other witnesses. Why should we, just because of her position?'

'True. So, you mean, supposing Mrs Broxton didn't return at 9.30 as
she claimed, say she got back earlier, while Mr and Mrs Master were
still out . . .'

'Exactly!'

'And Henry was in a real state, practically hysterical . . . Yes, she
would have been livid, wouldn't she? No, hang on a minute. That won't
work. That means she would have been in the house when Mr Swain
came knocking.'

'Not knocking, Mike, *ringing*. And the doorbell was out of order.'

'He did say he knocked as well.'

'But he also said the door was so solid that unless he had really
hammered at it it would have been difficult to make much impact. And
I don't suppose he would have liked to do that, not like Master who was
determined to make as much noise as he could. No, if she was busy
trying to calm Henry down she might well not have heard him. It's a big
house and we've found this ourselves, haven't we, when we go to big

houses, even when the doorbell is working and there's a knocker too. How many times have you heard people say, "But I was in, all the time"?'

Lineham nodded, conceding the truth of this.

'So, say all these people have been telling the truth: Mrs Master senior came and went away just before Mrs Broxton arrived home; Mr Swain came and left soon afterwards; his wife did just what she said she did, followed him, watched him leave and set off again without coming near the house . . .'

'And then the Masters arrived home.'

Thanet nodded eagerly. 'Quite. Now, just visualise it: this was at twenty past nine. Mrs Broxton has probably just managed to calm Henry down—you know how long it takes when a child is in a real state. And all the time she's seething. Where is Perdita? She hasn't had time to look all over the house, probably just had a quick look in the kitchen and the bedroom before attending to Henry. And then she hears the front door slam. Until now it probably hasn't even occurred to her that Perdita could actually have gone out and left the children alone in the house, but now . . . She spends another minute or two making sure that Henry is thoroughly settled and then she races downstairs, absolutely furious. Meanwhile Perdita, reassured by the silence from upstairs, goes into the kitchen to make herself a hot drink . . . And from then on it happens just as we've suggested.'

Lineham had been nodding from time to time but now he stopped. 'OK, say it did happen like that, they had a row, Mrs Broxton is so angry she goes to grab her by the shoulders to shake her, Mrs Master steps back, slips and so on . . . I still can't buy Mrs Broxton looking around for a polythene bag and deliberately finishing her off.'

Thanet stared at him in silence. Carried along by the excitement and impetus of what had seemed a brilliant new explanation of what had happened he had chosen not to face that final stumbling block. He sat back in his chair and sighed. 'You're right, Mike. I can't see it either.'

'I think,' said Lineham, obviously determined to drive the point home, 'that she'd have been horrified when she saw Mrs Master lying there unconscious. She'd have been much more likely to rush to the telephone.'

'Yes, yes. You're right, you're right.' Thanet felt for his pipe. He was in need of consolation and for once he was going to ignore what Lineham felt about it. 'Ah well, back to the drawing board, as one

night say. Pass that report back, will you, Mike, let me have another
ook at it.'

While he was studying it he lit up.

Lineham got up to open the office door.

'I do wish you wouldn't make me feel such a pariah, Mike.'

'Sorry, sir.' Lineham glanced pointedly at the curls of smoke beginning to wreath their way towards him. 'It's just that . . .'

'I know, I know.' Disappointment was making Thanet unwontedly
irritable. 'Well, I suppose we'd better do as you suggest about the fibres, beginning with the Swains.' He sighed. This was going to take for
ever. 'Get a search warrant and put a team of four on to it. As you say,
the lab boys are going to love this. But if it's the only way . . .'

'Right, sir.' Lineham was already lifting the telephone.

Meanwhile, where did they go from here? Thanet looked at the reports stacked on both his and Lineham's desks and groaned inwardly.
He knew, really. They had reached the stage in a case that he disliked
most of all, the point where they needed to have a thorough reassess-
ment of everything that had come in. He and Lineham must now each
work his way systematically through every single report. It was surprising how often some hitherto disregarded scrap of information could
acquire a new significance in the light of subsequent findings, and it was
also the only way to get a clear overall view. Always, in the first day or
two, there was so much to try and assimilate, so many people to interview, that it was impossible to do anything but follow up one lead after
another. But there usually came a point when the pace slowed, even
ground to a standstill. And then . . .

He sighed, shuffled his chair closer to his desk, pulled the pile of
reports nearer to hand and took the first one off the top.

He wasn't even aware that Lineham had been out of the room until
the sergeant came back and said, 'Report time, I see.'

Thanet nodded.

Lineham pulled a face, sighed, sat down at his desk and was immediately engrossed.

For the next hour they worked steadily, the silence broken only by
the occasional comment. Thanet shifted position from time to time,
trying to ease the familiar dull ache which was the result of a back
injury many years before. He was just beginning to wonder how Draco
would react if he entered the room and found his Detective Inspector
stretched out on the floor doing back exercises when there was a knock
and Bentley put his head around the door. Thanet could tell at once

that there was something up. The DC's usually placid face was animated, his eyes sparkling with excitement. 'Someone asking to see you,
sir.'

'Who? Well come in, man, come in.'

'Mrs Broxton, sir. And her husband.' He paused, to give emphasis to
his next words. 'And her solicitor.'

The atmosphere in the room suddenly changed as Thanet and
Lineham exchanged glances. Had Thanet hit the nail on the head after
all?

His lethargy of a moment ago was gone, the ache in his back forgotten. His stomach clenched with excitement. 'Send them up.'

17

Vanessa Broxton wasted no time on preliminaries.

'I'll come straight to the point, Inspector.'

Superficially she looked as she always did in Court—well-groomed and confident. She was wearing a dark grey herringbone tweed suit with a black velvet collar, white blouse, high heels. Studying her more closely, though, Thanet could detect the signs of strain: the too rigid posture, the occasional tightening of her jaw muscles and the fear which lurked at the back of her eyes. Despite the latter, however, she looked —what was the word?—resolute, that was it. Yes, resolute.

The two men who flanked her were a complete contrast: her husband tall, fair, well built, striking; the solicitor short, dark, slight, nondescript. Thanet was not fooled by the man's appearance. Geoffrey Mordent was the senior partner in one of Maidstone's largest firms of solicitors, and widely respected for his ability as well as his humanity.

Vanessa Broxton was looking Thanet straight in the eye. *I have nothing to hide.*

Guy Broxton had been watching her. Now he turned an assessing eye on Thanet.

Mordent, too, had been looking at her. Now, as she glanced at him he gave a faint smile and nodded, encouraging her to continue.

'When you interviewed me on Monday night, Inspector, I'm afraid I was less than frank with you. No, to be blunt, I lied to you. I'll explain why in a minute, but for the moment suffice it to say that I now realise how very foolish I was. So I've come to tell you what really happened.'

She glanced at Mordent, who nodded again and said, 'Mrs Broxton is here entirely with my approval. I am in full agreement with her desire to be frank with you, and wish to make it clear that although I shall naturally protect her interests, I am present chiefly as a friend.'

Thanet nodded. 'Please continue, Mrs Broxton.'

She hesitated for a moment, then said, 'The first thing I lied to you about was the time. I said I arrived home at 9.30, but in fact it was half an hour earlier.'

Thanet restrained himself from casting a triumphant glance at Lineham. So he had been right.

'As I told you, the moment I opened the front door I heard Henry screaming—no, it was before that, even. I could hear him as I put my key in the lock. Then it happened just as I told you. In the hall I hesitated for a moment, calling Perdita, but I didn't wait to see if she was around, I rushed straight upstairs to Henry's room. As I said, he was practically hysterical, I'd never seen him in such a state before. So naturally I picked him up, walked about with him, did everything I could to soothe him, quieten him down. And all the time I was getting more and more angry, wondering where on earth Perdita was, wondering how she could possibly have let him get into such a state . . . Anyway, he had just calmed down and I on the point of putting him back to bed when I heard the front door slam. Up until then it had simply never occurred to me to think she could actually have gone out and left the children alone in the house . . .'

Her voice was beginning to rise in remembered outrage and she stopped, took a deep breath and waited a moment before continuing.

'I put Henry down in his cot, but of course this woke him up and he clung to me, started to cry again. Perdita must have heard him and she came straight upstairs and into the nursery. She looked pretty appalled to see me there, as you can imagine. She started to apologise, but I just hissed at her to go away, go downstairs and wait for me. It took a good five minutes longer to get Henry settled and all the while I was seething, thinking of what I was going to say to her when I saw her. Then suddenly Henry went out like a light. I suppose he was exhausted with all the crying. So I tiptoed out on to the landing, then ran downstairs.'

Thanet could visualise it all: Perdita truly appalled, as Vanessa Broxton had said, to find Henry in distress and Vanessa returned home unexpectedly. Still upset after her forced excursion to the pub with Giles, full of guilt, distress and self-justification, she would have been in a highly volatile state by the time Vanessa came down. Probably she had started to make a hot drink in an attempt to calm herself down by the familiar, soothing domestic task . . . And Vanessa, churning with fury, boiling up for a confrontation, flying down the stairs and bursting into the kitchen . . .

Vanessa Broxton's composure was slipping and her husband reached out and took her hand, clasped it tightly. 'It's all right, love. Keep going, the worst'll soon be over.'

She shook her head, her eyes bleak. *This will never be over, for me.*

'She was in the kitchen. She was holding a saucepan with milk in it. All I could think was, she goes out and leaves my babies alone and then calmly comes into the kitchen and makes herself cocoa!'

'What the hell d'you think you were doing?'

'It was . . .'

'I come home unexpectedly and what do I find? Henry hysterical and you're not even here! You'd gone out, for God's sake! Gone out and left my babies alone in the house!'

'It wasn't . . .'

'I don't care what you say, there can be no possible excuse, d'you hear me, no possible excuse!'

'But, Vanessa . . .'

'Don't Vanessa me! In fact, don't ever speak to me again. Get out of my house this minute, d'you hear me, get out!'

Vanessa Broxton buried her face in her hands.

Her husband put his arm around her and briefly she turned, rested her forehead against his shoulder. Then she looked back at Thanet. 'It was an accident, I swear,' she whispered. 'And even now, looking back, I can't really tell you what happened. I've thought and thought about it, and I've worked out what *must* have happened, but that's not the same, is it? I think I must have pushed her, but . . . All I really know is that one minute she was standing in front of me and the next she was . . . just lying there, on the floor. I vaguely remember hearing a crash, but apart from that . . . Her eyes were closed and her head was bleeding . . . I couldn't believe it. I knelt down beside her, calling her name. I felt for her pulse and it wasn't there . . . Dear God, it wasn't there . . .'

Vanessa Broxton shook her head in remembered disbelief. 'I realised she was dead and I'd killed her.' She bent her head in shame and contrition.

There was a moment's silence before Thanet said, 'And then what did you do?'

She looked up. 'I didn't mean to harm her, I swear it. It's just that . . . I'd never been so angry in my life before. I was beside myself.' She gave a wry smile. 'Never again will I disbelieve a client when he says he didn't know what he was doing.'

Thanet repeated his question. His calm acceptance of her account seemed to reassure her. Or perhaps she felt that she was now past the part of her story that was hardest for her to tell. In any case she made a visible effort to be brisk and matter-of-fact.

'Naturally I didn't know what to do. I was, well, stunned, I suppose, for the first minute or two. And then my first instinct was to call the police. Which is, of course, what I should have done. There's a phone in the kitchen and my hand was actually on the receiver when I thought, but if I do call them, and I'm arrested what will happen to the children? Angela was in hospital, my husband abroad . . . There were a couple of friends I could ring, but that would have involved getting Henry and Alice up out of bed and transferring them and I wasn't sure, if I were arrested, if the police would allow me to do that. And after the upset Henry had already had that night I certainly wasn't going to allow him to be frightened out of his wits by having a complete stranger do it.' She gave an apologetic smile. 'I wasn't thinking ahead at all, as you see. I was in a panic, I suppose. I knew I'd have to call the police eventually, but I just couldn't think straight and I realised I had to have a little while to myself, first, to work out what I was going to say to them.

'I went into the drawing room. I was still shaking and I decided to allow myself just one drink—no more, because I knew I couldn't risk not being able to think clearly. So I poured myself a stiff whisky and drank it, telling myself that as soon as I'd finished it I'd ring you. But I kept thinking about the children and worrying about what would happen to them if I was arrested. Then there was my work . . . If this all came out, I was finished. Even if I were acquitted I couldn't imagine many solicitors would be anxious to employ me . . . Then I suddenly thought, why own up at all? I could just say I'd come home and found her like that. It would buy me some time, give me a chance to pull myself together and sort something out for the children . . .' Vanessa Broxton stopped, shook her head and gave a wry smile. 'I can't believe it really, can't believe I was so stupid! Me, of all people, with the sort of work I do! It was a sort of madness and I'm deeply ashamed of myself, I assure you . . . Anyway, that was what I decided to do. But I knew I'd have to make sure an intruder would have been able to get in, so I steeled myself to go back into the kitchen and unlock the door. Then I returned to the drawing room and tried to think calmly, work out exactly what I was going to tell the police when they arrived. Then I dialled 999 and reported the murder.'

There was a long silence. Thanet was aware that they were all looking at him expectantly, awaiting his reaction, but he was thinking furiously. Had Vanessa Broxton told him the whole story, or not? She had said nothing about the plastic bag and Thanet was inclined to believe her. Her story had the ring of truth to it. He could imagine it all happening as she had said, what he could not swallow was the possibility that she had then decided to finish Perdita off. Because if she had, it would have been a conscious, deliberate act, and he really didn't think her capable of calculated murder, however upset she might have been at the time. But if she hadn't . . .

Light suddenly dawned.

Of course!

How stupid, how blind he had been!

All along, as Lineham had said, that polythene bag had been the stumbling block. But if not one, but *two* people had been involved, the whole thing became comprehensible.

He could see it all: the murderer—faceless as yet—looking in through the kitchen window, seeing Perdita lying unconscious on the floor, trying the door and finding it unlocked and then, seeing his—or her—golden opportunity, seizing his chance . . . It would have taken no time at all.

Lineham was frowning. He hadn't seen it yet, then. The sergeant glanced up, caught Thanet's eye, his gaze sharpening as Thanet's excitement communicated itself to him.

The silence in the room had become uncomfortably protracted. Broxton stirred, cleared his throat as if to remind Thanet that they were waiting.

'Mrs Broxton,' said Thanet, picking his words with care. 'Are you sure you have told us the whole story? I want you to think back now, and make sure that you have omitted nothing.'

There, he had given her one last chance to mention of her own free will that final act if she had indeed committed it.

She was frowning, puzzled, obviously aware that he had something specific in mind. She shook her head. 'Not to my knowledge, no. If there is something it's because I've just forgotten about it.'

'This is scarcely something you could have forgotten.' Thanet's tone was dry. If she were innocent, it was time to put her out of her misery.

The three of them were staring at him intently, trying to read his mind.

'Well?' said Broxton impatiently. 'Are you going to tell us what it is?'

'Mrs Master did not die from that fall. As she fell she did bang her head hard against the corner of the kitchen table, yes, and this knocked her out. But she died of asphyxiation.'

The astonishment on their faces—including Vanessa Broxton's—was, he would swear, genuine.

Then they all spoke together.

'Asphyxiation?'

'But . . .'

'I don't understand.'

'Someone,' said Thanet, 'took a polythene bag and pulled it over her head as she was lying there unconscious, and smothered her.'

He was watching Vanessa Broxton as he spoke. Her eyes opened wide in horror, the whites showing clear around the irises. One hand went up to her mouth and the other raked through her hair.

Her husband and Geoffrey Mordent had turned to look at her.

'But . . . But that's impossible!' she whispered.

Thanet shook his head. 'I've read the post mortem report and I'm satisfied that that was the cause of death. And of course I saw the polythene bag over her head myself.' He glanced at Lineham. 'We all did.'

Lineham nodded.

Suddenly Broxton was on his feet. 'Now look here, Thanet, are you implying that my wife cold-bloodedly murdered that woman? Because if you are—'

Geoffrey Mordent reached across Vanessa and tugged at Broxton's sleeve. 'Sit down, Guy. We both know she would have done no such thing. And I don't believe that Inspector Thanet is implying anything, he's simply informing us. Besides, don't you see? As far as Vanessa is concerned, this alters the whole thing? *Someone else killed her.*'

'But I felt for her pulse,' whispered Vanessa. 'It wasn't there. She was dead, I tell you . . .'

Thanet shook his head decisively. 'No. It's an easy mistake to make, one that's been made many times before, I assure you. The shock of it all would have blunted your perception.'

'But then, how . . . who . . . ?'

'That, obviously, is what we yet have to discover. Tell me, when you arrived home, did you put your car in the garage before going into the house?'

She nodded. 'Yes, of course.'

So no one would have known she was there, thought Thanet. To all intents and purposes the place was deserted.

'Did you hear anyone knock at the front door?'

'No. No one. The doorbell isn't working, of course, and the door is so thick and heavy it's very difficult to make anyone hear just by knocking on it, unless you really hammer at it. And I was upstairs with Henry and he was crying most of the time. Even if he hadn't been, I don't suppose I would have heard, it's not as though I was expecting anyone and listening out for them. You mean . . . ?'

'Did you hear any cars outside?'

Again she shook her head. 'I was too preoccupied with Henry to have noticed . . .'

'And when you were downstairs, in the drawing room, after the incident?'

'No. I was in such a state I don't suppose I'd have noticed if a herd of elephants had thundered through the front garden.' For the first time she managed a faint, rueful smile.

Thanet was working it out. If Perdita arrived back at 9.20 it would have been 9.25 before Vanessa went down to the kitchen. The brief confrontation with Perdita would have taken only a minute or two, say until 9.30 at the latest. Vanessa had rung the police at 9.40 and they had taken a further ten minutes to arrive . . .

'You must have been in the drawing room for at least twenty minutes before the police arrived?'

She frowned, paused to work it out. 'I suppose so, yes.'

'And how long was it before you went back into the kitchen to unlock the back door?'

'Five, ten minutes? It's difficult to tell.'

So the murderer could have slipped into the kitchen either before or after that.

'Now think carefully: did you on that occasion look at Mrs Master's body?'

'You're suggesting that the murderer might already have come in by then?' She shook her head. 'I'm sorry, I can't help you there. I'm afraid I studiously avoided looking at her. I was aware of her lying there, of course, out of the corner of my eye, but I certainly didn't notice a polythene bag over her head, or obviously all this wouldn't have been such a shock to me.'

'That polythene bag . . . Might it have been lying around some-where, in the kitchen?'

She shook her head emphatically. 'Absolutely not. Angela and I have always been very careful not to leave plastic bags lying around, and I'm sure Perdita would have done the same.' She frowned. 'Though until all this happened I would have sworn that she would never have left young children alone in the house . . . I still can't believe that she did.'

Lineham shifted position and Thanet knew what he was thinking: why don't you tell her that Master forced his wife into the car, black-mailed her into staying with him?

Thanet said nothing. He had his reasons.

'Anyway,' said Broxton to his wife, 'you can now stop tormenting yourself. Someone else killed her.' He glanced at Thanet. 'You can't imagine what a relief it is, to know that.'

'But that's not true!' said Vanessa. 'Don't you see that, Guy? I killed her just as surely as if I had put that bag over her head!'

Broxton took her hand. 'Darling, don't be ridiculous! How can you say that?'

She was shaking her head vehemently. 'And how can you say I'm innocent? If I'd called an ambulance immediately, as I should have, and stayed with her until it arrived, Perdita would still be alive . . . Don't you *see?*' she repeated. 'I helped him, didn't I? First I made her uncon-scious so she was helpless, didn't have a chance . . . Then I unlocked the door to let him in and finally I left her alone and defenceless! I made it so easy for him!'

'Not intentionally!'

'That doesn't make any difference. Oh, it might make a difference legally, but morally, emotionally . . . No, I'm as guilty as he is.'

Broxton cast a look of helpless frustration at Thanet. *Can't you make her see how wrong she is?*

But Thanet knew that nothing he could say would make any differ-ence. Somehow Vanessa Broxton was going to have to come to terms with what had happened, but it would take time, a long time. Perhaps she never would get over it. He had seen this coming. This was why he had said nothing as yet about Perdita having been forced into accompa-nying her husband. It was, he knew, unfair to the dead woman to go on allowing Vanessa Broxton to think so badly of her, but if Vanessa knew she had misjudged Perdita, that if only she had allowed her to explain

Perdita would still be alive, she would be feeling even more guilty. Assuming the murderer were caught she would have to find out eventually, of course, at the trial if not before, but perhaps by then she would be less raw, less in shock. No, the best course would be to take her husband quietly aside at some point, tell him the truth, and suggest he tell his wife if and when the time was right to do so.

Geoffrey Mordent was also trying to comfort her. He patted her arm. 'Guy is right, Vanessa. You didn't intend to harm her. As we've said all along, it was an accident, you must hang on to that. At least you now know that it wasn't you who killed her.'

'I know you're trying to be kind, Geoff, but it won't work. I know how I feel and nothing is going to change that.' She looked at Thanet. 'If you want me to make that statement, Inspector . . .'

She stood up.

'Sergeant Lineham will go with you. Thank you for being so frank with us.'

'What will happen now, Inspector?' said Broxton.

'At the moment, nothing. But we might well have to talk to you again, Mrs Broxton, so please don't go away without letting us know.'

Lineham opened the door and Vanessa Broxton led the way out, grim-faced, her burden of guilt only marginally lighter than when she had arrived.

18

When Thanet let himself into the house that evening Joan was just putting the telephone down. She snatched it up again, listened, then pulled a face before replacing it.

'Oh, what a shame, I've been talking to Bridget, you've just missed her. I didn't want to upset her, when she's just settling in, but I thought she'd be furious if I didn't let her know about Mum.'

Bridget was very fond of her grandmother.

'She wanted to come home right away, but I said no. I thought it would be too unsettling for her, and now that the worst of the danger is past . . . You do think that was the right thing to do?' she asked anxiously.

'Yes, I'm sure that was best. It would be pointless for her to come home at this stage. And I agree, if you hadn't said a word about your mother she'd be furious when she found out, later . . . Your mother's still all right, then?'

Joan nodded.

'Good. How about Bridget?'

Joan wrinkled her nose. 'I'm not sure. We chatted for a while before I told her, and although she *says* everything's fine, I suspect she was just trying to reassure me.'

They went into the kitchen, where Joan had supper under way. She began peering into saucepans, stirring things.

'I wonder what's wrong,' said Thanet. He trusted Joan's intuition in such matters.

'Just the strangeness of it, that's all, I should think. We thought she'd be a bit homesick at first.'

'You think I ought to give her another ring? No, I suppose not. She'd realise why.'

'Or think we're fussing. No, best to leave it for the moment. Anyway, she said she might be going out.'

Out. Thanet blanked out alarming visions of smoke-filled pubs crowded with undesirable young men, of frenzied discos where drug-pushers and pimps lurked in the shadows on the look-out for just such tender prey as Bridget.

'Did she say who with?'

Joan shrugged, straining the water off the potatoes. 'Some of the other girls, I imagine. I didn't ask.'

Far better not to, they had discovered. Bridget was happy to volunteer information unprompted but presented with questions she became the proverbial clam. Most teenagers were the same, Thanet assumed. He would just have to get used to the idea that she was now out of his orbit, that the people with whom she was in daily contact were strangers to him, the places she frequented as unfamiliar as if she were in a foreign land.

Joan added margarine, black pepper and milk to the potatoes, plugged in the hand blender and switched it on. She raised her voice slightly above the noise. 'No point in worrying about it. She'll tell us soon enough if she wants to talk. She probably wants to feel she can cope with it by herself. And knowing her, she wouldn't want us to worry.'

'I suppose not.'

Joan glanced at his face, switched off the blender and put it down. Then she came to put her arms around him. 'She'll be all right, darling. Don't worry.'

Joan's hair was soft and silky against his cheek and smelt of summer meadows. 'I know.'

They kissed, a kiss of mutual reassurance. Their first chick had flown the nest and it was hard to accept that she was on her own now. They could only hope that they had equipped her well enough to face whatever problems came along without too much heartache.

Joan turned back to her preparations.

'I'll lay the table,' said Thanet.

'It's done.'

'Ben in?'

'He ate earlier, it's Judo night.'

'Of course. I'd forgotten it was Wednesday. Well, I'll just pop up and see your mother, then.'

'Right. You might well find she's asleep. I made some soup and gave it to her about half an hour ago, I thought it would be the best thing for her at the moment.'

Upstairs all was silent. Joan had left a small table lamp alight in Bridget's room and Thanet tiptoed in, suppressing the familiar sensation of loss that gripped him whenever he was reminded of her absence. Mrs Bolton was asleep, curled up on her side, only the top of her head visible above the duvet cover. Her breathing was shallow but regular. Reassured, Thanet moved quietly back across the room and down the stairs.

'Fast asleep,' he announced.

'Good. We'll eat, then.'

Supper was unusually good. Joan was an excellent cook, but with a full-time job she had neither the time nor the energy to spend on preparing food during the week. That was another way in which they were going to miss Bridget, Thanet realised. On her evenings off from the restaurant where she had been working for the past year, if she wasn't going out Bridget had often cooked the evening meal for the family, frequently experimenting with recipes she had gleaned at work. But today, despite the fact that Joan had had her mother to look after, she had obviously made a special effort and Thanet made appreciative noises as they ate the cream of celery soup (made with skimmed milk, as Joan was quick to point out) and chicken breasts cooked with a ragout of peppers, courgettes, onions and tomatoes. For pudding there was a selection of fresh fruit.

As they ate Thanet told her about the latest developments in the Perdita Master case.

'Poor woman,' said Joan, when he had finished telling her about the interview with Vanessa Broxton. 'How is she going to feel when she finds out that Perdita hadn't been neglectful of the children after all . . . ? She must feel bad enough already. But to learn that it really wasn't Perdita's fault, that if only she'd given her a chance to explain none of this need have happened . . .'

'I know.'

'It's terrible to think your life can change so dramatically for the worse in such a short space of time. There she was, with everything any woman could wish for and then suddenly there comes this bolt from the blue . . . You know, I'm really surprised that she didn't give Perdita an opportunity to explain. She did know her, after all, knew that she just wasn't the kind of woman to walk out on two babies without some pretty compelling reason.'

'I think that half the problem was that when she got home she was feeling pretty fragile. For a start, she must have been disappointed that her first decent case for many months had gone short on the first day. Then she broke down on the motorway and had to wait ages for the RAC to arrive. To find Henry in such a state and then to discover that Perdita had apparently just walked out on them . . . It must have been the last straw.'

'Yes, I can see that.'

'At least her account helped me to understand what really happened. Until then I just couldn't seem to get it clear in my mind. Anyone can lose his temper, have an argument, and it was easy to see how Perdita had slipped in the spilt milk . . . But there's such a divide between something that happens in the heat of the moment and the deliberate act of killing someone with a plastic bag. The second I realised that two people must have been involved it all made sense. I can't think why I didn't see it before. I was just being particularly dense . . .'

They had finished eating and Joan began to gather up the dishes.

'Leave that,' said Thanet, taking them from her. 'I'll do the washing-up—no, no argument,' he said firmly as Joan began to protest. 'You go and put your feet up. Coffee?'

'D'you mind having tea?'

'Tea it shall be.'

'I'll just pop up and take another look at Mum. No, I must, really. Then I'll sit down, I promise.'

But Thanet had almost finished the washing-up before Joan came back downstairs. He could understand her need to keep checking on her mother, but he was concerned about her. She was looking very tired. The strain and anxiety of the last two days had taken their toll and he hoped she wasn't going to exhaust herself by over-zealous nursing.

When he took the tea in she was looking thoughtful. She accepted her cup with a word of thanks and then said, 'So who d'you think could have done it?'

Thanet sat down, adjusting a cushion in the small of his still-aching back. He lit his pipe. 'Ah, well that's the problem. There are several possibilities. But to be frank, I don't think it was either Master or Swain. Mike says he can imagine Master saying to himself, Well, if I can't have her no one will, and I suppose to some degree I can agree with that if the act of smothering her with that bag were done in the heat of the moment. But if Vanessa Broxton caused the fall, I can't imagine Master coming into the kitchen and cold-bloodedly murdering his wife. If he had seen her lying there on the floor I think he'd have been much more likely to get into a panic, ring for an ambulance, and try to revive her. And the same goes for Swain. No, as I said to Mike, whoever killed her really wanted her dead.'

'So that leaves her mother-in-law or Swain's wife. Your back's playing up tonight, isn't it? Why don't you stretch out on the floor?'

'Perhaps I will, when I finish my pipe.' Thanet grinned. 'I was tempted to this afternoon, but I didn't think Draco would approve. He's been looking pretty grim today, by the way.'

'New developments?'

'I didn't like to ask.'

They were silent for a few moments, thinking of the Dracos. Joan sighed and then returned to their discussion. 'What's Mrs Master senior like?'

Thanet grimaced. 'Let's just say I'm glad she isn't my mother-in-law.'

'Which reminds me.' Joan put her cup down and started to get up. 'I'd better just . . .'

Thanet put his hand on her arm and gently restrained her. 'It's not ten minutes since you last went up.'

'I know, but I must. It won't take a minute . . .'

Thanet laid his pipe in the ashtray. 'I'll go this time.'

When he got down again his pipe had gone out and he decided to take Joan's advice, stretch out on the floor. Tired muscles protested at first as they came into contact with the unyielding surface and then, miraculously, as Thanet relaxed, the pain began to ease. 'Lovely,' he said, with a beatific smile.

Joan nudged him with her toe. 'Don't go to sleep. You still haven't told me. Why don't you like her? Perdita's mother-in-law, I mean? What's she like?'

'Well, I told you about the fuss she's making over the ring, so that gives you some idea . . . Let me see, she's slim, elegant, looks a good ten years younger than she must be. Sharp, forceful, likes to get her own way, arrange the world as she wants it. Which includes having a firm grip on her son.'

'Poor man. A bit like Mike's mother in that respect, then.'

'Yes, Mike didn't like her, I can tell you. But Mrs Lineham is only a mild version of Mrs Master, I assure you.'

'And Mrs Master hated Perdita, you say?'

'The general opinion is that she would have hated whoever her son married. Apparently she never showed her dislike openly, presumably for fear of alienating Giles, but everyone agrees that she never missed a chance of getting at Perdita, making her feel inferior.'

'D'you think he really was unaware of what was going on?'

'No. That was obvious, from various things he said to his mother when we interviewed him yesterday. But I suspect he'd never actually brought it out into the open before.'

'So she's a real possibility, you think?'

'Yes. Though if she was telling the truth, she's in the clear. She says she arrived there somewhere around nine, perhaps a little earlier.'

'But you don't believe her?'

'Well, that's the trouble. There's one detail in her story which seems to bear it out. She says she could hear a child screaming, so she left, didn't bother to wait because she thought Perdita would be occupied with trying to calm him down.'

'So that would have been just before Vanessa arrived home.'

'That's right. Wait a minute, though!' Thanet rolled over on to his side then sat up, wincing. 'Just say all that was true, but that on the way home Mrs Master changed her mind. She desperately wants that ring back, you know. Perhaps she thought she'd been too hasty, should have waited. So she went back, arriving after Perdita's return. She couldn't make anyone hear, so she went around the back, looked in through the kitchen window, saw Perdita lying there, found the door unlocked and saw her chance . . .'

'You really think she'd be capable of that?'

Thanet thought for a minute or two before answering. 'Yes, I do.' He eased himself down on to the floor again.

Joan shivered. 'She doesn't sound my idea of the ideal mother-in-law either! What about Vicky? Victoria Swain,' she added to his uncomprehending look. 'She was usually called Vicky at school.'

'Yes, well, I'd say the same about her. It's interesting, really. To meet the Swains individually you'd say she's the one who wears the trousers, but when you see them together you soon realise that he does. She tries to hide it under that flippant devil-may-care attitude, but it's obvious that she adores him and would, I imagine, do anything to keep him. And the other thing is that her image is obviously very important to her. I should think she'd go to any lengths to preserve it. She sees herself as strong, successful, independent. She wouldn't enjoy being made a laughing stock in front of her colleagues, seen as a woman who couldn't keep her husband.'

'Well, as I told you, she was certainly a law unto herself at school. If she wanted to do something she did it, and if it got her into trouble then that was just too bad.' Joan grinned. 'I used to dread her doing something wrong while I was on duty. She'd just stand there with a mocking smile on her face and apologise sweetly while it was obvious to anyone watching that she was just making fun of you.'

Thanet shook his head and tutted. 'Oh dear oh dear! Very undermining of one's authority, that!'

Joan picked up a cushion and swiped him with it. 'You're supposed to be sympathetic!'

Thanet put up his arms to fend her off. 'I call this taking unfair advantage of a man while he's down. I was only joking!'

'Precisely!' But she put the cushion down, got up. 'I won't be a minute.'

'But . . .'

But she was already gone. She couldn't go on like this, she'd wear herself out. He'd have to talk to her about it and she wouldn't like that. He sighed. Joan could be pretty stubborn when she chose. He rolled over and eased himself to his feet. He couldn't argue with her from the disadvantage of a supine position.

When she came back down he was sitting on the settee.

'I thought you were supposed to be resting your back.'

'It's much better, honestly. Besides, this is more important. Listen, love, you simply cannot go on running up and downstairs every ten minutes.'

Joan was immediately on the defensive. 'I didn't while we were eating, did I?'

Thanet shook his head in exasperation. 'That's beside the point. You know what I mean.'

'I can't help it, Luke.'

'But you can. You must. I'm only thinking of you.'

'I realise that, but it won't go on indefinitely, you know. Once the first couple of days are over I'll feel better about leaving her alone for longer periods. I just have to keep on making sure she's all right, that's all. I keep thinking, if she had another attack and I didn't know . . . It was different while she was in hospital. I knew then that someone was keeping an eye on her all the time. But here, there's only me. I'm the one who's responsible.'

Thanet could understand all too well how she felt. And knowing Joan, if he extracted from her some kind of promise which was against her conscience, that would worry her so much she'd be even worse off. Reluctantly, he conceded. 'I can see that. All right. But do try not to overdo it, love.'

'I will try. But it's true, what I said. I can't seem to help it. It's an inner compulsion which says Go and look, go and check, and I just can't not do it.'

'Well, I hope you're not going to worry yourself sick when we have to leave someone else in charge.'

'I don't think I will. I honestly believe I'll feel better about it with every day that passes.'

'We'll have to try and fix up some kind of rota for next week.'

Doctor MacPherson had apparently said that Joan's mother ought to have someone around for the next week or two, and Joan had volunteered to keep her with them for that period. Joan had been given a few days' leave, but next week would be difficult. There were various things arranged at work, including a three-day course at Canterbury which Joan was running. It had been fixed for months and she really didn't feel that she could back out at the last minute.

They discussed possible arrangements for a while and then Joan said, 'It's all very well talking about the next couple of weeks, but it's what happens afterwards that's worrying me. I know Doctor MacPherson says that she will quickly get back to normal, but I keep thinking about what happened this time because she was living alone. What if they hadn't happened to be going shopping and Mrs Parker hadn't found her when she did? Mum'd be dead by now. It doesn't bear thinking about.'

'What are you saying, love?' Though Thanet could guess.

She hesitated, flickered a brief, assessing glance at him. 'I was wondering how you'd feel if I suggested she come and live with us.'

Now it was Thanet's turn to hesitate. He should have seen this coming, earlier, have given it some thought. But he'd been so busy today, there really hadn't been time . . . 'I certainly don't think it's something we ought to rush into.'

'Well we wouldn't, obviously. But that's not telling me how you *feel* about the idea.'

Thanet considered. 'It certainly doesn't fill me with dismay, if that's what you mean. I'm very fond of your mother, as you know, we've always got on very well together. I think that what I'd find hardest is the lack of privacy. There'd always be someone else around. I know that Ben still is, at the moment, but in a few years he'll be gone too, no doubt, and I must admit that for me the only consolation for losing both the children would be that we'd have more time to be together again just the two of us. That's pretty selfish, I suppose . . .'

'No, I feel the same. But we wouldn't have to sacrifice that, you know. I was thinking . . . We could always sell both houses, ours and hers, and buy a larger one, with a separate granny annexe.'

'You have been putting your mind to this, haven't you? Yes, that would be a possibility. But would it be the answer?'

'What d'you mean?'

'Well, consider. We're not talking about having your mother to live with us because she's lonely, or because she can't look after herself. She has plenty of friends, leads a very active, busy life, and until now her health has been good. And the doctor says she'll get back to normal quite quickly. The only reason for having her live either close to us or with us is that there'd be someone to keep an eye on her all the time, so that in an emergency help would be close at hand. But it wouldn't be, would it? She'd be alone all day during the week, and without the advantage of neighbours who know her and care about her.'

Joan sighed. 'I hadn't thought of it like that. That's true. And I wouldn't want to give up my job. Though that's pretty selfish, too.'

'Not at all! Can you imagine what your mother would say if you even suggested it? She'd never agree, you know that.'

'True . . . What d'you think we ought to do then?'

'Wait,' said Thanet firmly. 'As I said, there's no need to rush into anything. Let's see how she is, in a month, three months, and then reconsider. I'm certainly not against the idea in principle, but I think that in any case we have to wait until she's well enough to discuss it with her, see how she feels. Because whatever we do, it's got to be a solution which is acceptable to her as well as to us.'

'You're right, of course. All right, that's what we'll do. Thanks.'

'For what?'

'For being prepared to consider the idea seriously. A lot of men would have been horrified at the prospect.'

'And a lot wouldn't. The reasonable ones, anyway.' He grinned. 'And I, of course, am a reasonable man.'

'Modest, too.'

'Of course.'

The phone rang. He got up, careful of his back. When he returned Joan took one look at his face and said, 'What is it, what's wrong? It's not Bridget . . . ?'

He shook his head. 'No. That was the hospital. I asked them to let me know if there was any radical change in the condition of Perdita's mother. She died an hour ago.'

He sat down and put his head in his hands. 'I knew I shouldn't have interviewed her yesterday morning. I told you how ill she looked, didn't I? When I saw the state she was in I should have left her alone.'

'But you said she insisted on going on with the interview.'

'I know, but . . .'

'Luke. Use your commonsense. You're not seriously suggesting that the fact that you interviewed her yesterday had anything to do with her death, are you? Because if so—'

'You didn't see how ill she was, Joan. If you had . . . Anyone in that condition should be left in peace.'

'I still don't think you can blame yourself. If you ask me the blame lies with her husband. In his position I think I'd have insisted that she wasn't even told about her daughter's death. She was in no fit state to hear news like that.'

'Maybe it's because he knew she was dying that he felt she should be told, that she had a right to know.'

'Oh, I don't know, it's so difficult . . . But in any case, I think he should have warned you just how ill she was. And he didn't, did he?'

'No.'

'And I suppose, if I'd been her . . . I think I'd have wanted to talk to you, to feel I'd done all I could to help you find out who'd killed my daughter. In fact, I think I'd have been pretty angry if I'd been prevented from seeing you, just because I was ill.'

'Terminally ill.'

'All right, terminally ill . . . Do you think she knew she was dying?'

Thanet sighed. 'I don't know. I wouldn't be surprised. And I suppose you're right. She was very determined to tell me everything I wanted to know.'

'Well there you are, then. Stop blaming yourself. You talk about my conscience, but yours is just as bad!' Joan stood up. 'Come on, it's time we went up. I've got to give Mother her last dose of pills and settle her for the night. And I think you ought to have a hot bath, for your back.'

She was right. A hot bath would help. Thanet ran the water as hot as he could stand it and relaxed, staring mindlessly at the ceiling through clouds of steam. Unbidden, an image of Perdita's body floated into his mind, that pathetic, almost child-like figure, the face disfigured by the unnatural sheen of plastic. He'd read a novel once called *Little Boy Lost*. That's what Perdita had been, despite her actual age. Little Girl

Lost. Although he could never recall seeing her in life he pictured her vividly now, a solitary figure in playground or classroom, bent over her sketchbook, absorbed in her drawing. Strange that she hadn't gone to Art School, had insisted instead on ignoring her abiding passion and following a completely different career. And sad that she had never had children of her own. Or perhaps not. Perhaps, together with the lack of joy in her marriage, it was her childlessness that had enabled her to channel all her creativity into her work and produce such haunting paintings, paintings with the power to imprint themselves on the mind of the beholder and linger in the memory. He could visualise them now, especially the one that hung in the Harrows' sitting room, the one of the garden of lilies at night. Why had it had such a powerful impact upon him? he wondered.

The water was cooling now and he sat up, ran some more hot, lay back again, still thinking about this. If the mind of an artist is revealed in his work, what did Perdita's tell him about her? What were the emotions which animated it? Anger, for a start, he realised, remembering the explosion of colour in the painting in the drawing room at her house. Anger against what, or whom? he wondered. And, of course, sadness. Sadness, melancholia, pessimism, whatever you chose to call it. But Perdita's pessimism had not been ill-founded. She had indeed died before her time, as she had always thought she would.

Doomed to die. It was almost as if she knew that she was doomed to die . . . Mrs Harrow's words wreathed and twisted their way through his thoughts like the wisps of steam which hovered just below the ceiling above him. Had Perdita known? Could she have known? Or was it possible that because of the strength of her conviction she had somehow, subconsciously, manoeuvred herself into the position where an early death was not only likely but inevitable?

He shook his head. No. He was becoming fanciful.

But the thought lodged in his brain, stayed with him. He had lain so long in the bath that by the time he got to bed Joan was already asleep. He yawned, stretched, relaxed. It shouldn't take long to get to sleep tonight. He was tired. So tired . . .

But perversely his brain refused to switch off. There had been so much to absorb over the last couple of days, so many people to see, so many assessments to make. Snatches of conversation kept swirling through his brain interspersed with fleeting, vivid images: Vanessa Broxton as he had first seen her on Monday night, huddled in a corner of the settee, then staring bleakly at her husband this afternoon: *Don't ou see? I made it so easy for him, I'm as guilty as he is;* Giles Master's mother grasping her son's arm, red talons digging into flesh: *Why did you have a fight?* And Master: *Perdita and Swain were having an affair. Perhaps now you'll be satisfied;* Victoria Swain: *for God's sake stop looking at me like that, Howard! I had a right to know where you were going, didn't I? I am your wife.* And Swain: *You mean, you actually followed me?* Then the Harrows: Stephanie, pale and frantic, sister dead, mother dying (dead, now, Thanet reminded himself. Poor kid): *How long do we have to go on being patient? Until Mum is . . .* Harrow himself: *My wife can't stand the cold.* And Mrs Harrow, her emaciated body encased in thick woollen dressing gown, woollen bedjacket draped around her shoulders: *It's almost as if she knew that she was doomed to die.*

Doomed to die . . .

The words echoed along the corridors of Thanet's brain. Desperate by now for sleep he turned over and snuggled up to Joan's comforting warmth, tried to fill his mind with soothing images of country walks, days at the seaside, anything to slow down his thought processes and take his mind off the case. Gradually it worked and he began to drift. Far far away at the end of a long tunnel was a tiny spot of light. He allowed himself to float towards it. When he got there he would, he knew, make an important discovery. Water suddenly began to flow through the tunnel towards him, carrying him backwards, away from his goal, and he began to swim, to strike out strongly. He had to get there, he had to. Water was getting in his eyes and his nose and his arms and legs were beginning to ache. But he couldn't give up, he couldn't, wouldn't. He was at the point of despair when suddenly the thrust of the water began to diminish, to ease. Suddenly he was on his feet staggering towards the end of the tunnel, the light increasing with every second, searing his eyeballs and zigzagging into his brain.

Someone was shaking him. 'Luke, wake up.'

He opened his eyes. Joan was leaning over him, her face full of concern. A gentle light from the bedside lamp played on her hair, outlined the soft curves of her breasts. 'You were having a nightmare.'

He smiled up at her, shook his head. 'Not a nightmare.' He put his arms around her and pulled her close.

He felt marvellous, invincible.

At last he knew why.

And who.

19

'So what d'you think, Mike?'

Thanet awaited Lineham's verdict with eagerness. He had just finished propounding his new theory. The sergeant had listened intently, frowning with concentration, fiddling with a paperclip which he had unbent and twisted until now it snapped in his fingers. He tossed it on to his desk and shook his head. 'It's a bit of a long shot, isn't it, sir?'

Thanet was disappointed. He had hoped for a more positive reaction than this.

'I don't think so, no, not particularly,' he said stiffly.

'But with respect, sir . . .'

'Oh, not again, Mike! I've said before, if you disagree with me, why not come straight out with it?'

Thanet was being unreasonable and he knew it. Another time he would simply have teased Lineham, as he often had on this particular subject.

At this point Lineham would usually look sheepish but now, stung perhaps by Thanet's tone he said, 'D'you really want to know, sir?'

Thanet had a feeling he wasn't going to like what he was about to hear, but if he wasn't to lose face he had no choice but to say, 'Of course.'

'It's because I know that if I do—come straight out with it, that is—I'll get my head bitten off.'

'That's not true!'

'Isn't it, sir? Be fair. You really don't like it when people disagree with you.'

It was true that he did like to be right. It was one of his major faults, Thanet knew. 'Oh come on, Mike. I'm always ready to listen to someone else's opinion, you know that.' He wasn't that unreasonable, was he? Surely not.

'Eventually, yes.' Lineham's grin took the sting out of his words and recognising the justice of them Thanet grinned back.

'All right, all right, so you've made your point. Can we now get back to what you were going to say. "With respect . . ."'

'Just that we've got no actual evidence. It's all, well, guess—er, surmise.'

'I'll ignore that attempt to be tactful, Mike. Yes, there is a certain amount of guesswork, I agree. Personally I'd prefer to call it intuition. But then, there always is, in police work, you know that as well as I do. The important thing is that it should always be based on fact and you have to admit that this theory does fit the facts as we know them.'

'Maybe.' Lineham still sounded doubtful. 'But as far as proving it is concerned, everything depends on matching that sample.'

'Exactly. So I want you to concentrate on that. Go and get hold of another sample to compare it with and then take it straight to Aldermaston. I'll give Bob Farley a ring, tell him how urgent it is that the tests are done immediately you get there, and he can get everything set up.'

Detective Sergeant Farley was the Police Liaison Officer at the Aldermaston lab and Thanet knew him well, having worked with him for several years.

'How long do you think it will take you?'

Lineham glanced at his watch. 'It's half-nine now. Say half an hour to collect the sample, an hour and a half to get there, half an hour to get the tests done, an hour and a half back . . . Four hours or so, I should think.'

'I'll expect you between 1.30 and 2, then. Fine.'

'I could always ring you from the lab with the result, then you needn't wait for me.'

Thanet knew how much it must have cost Lineham to make this offer and he appreciated his generosity. The sergeant would be bitterly disappointed not to accompany Thanet when he made the arrest. Provided, of course, that the tests came up with the expected result. But he wouldn't think about that. He was right, he knew it, he felt it in his bones.

'No, Mike, I'll wait. I expect—'

The telephone rang.

Thanet lifted the receiver, listened. 'Put her on.'

Lineham raised his eyebrows interrogatively, but Thanet did not respond. All his attention was directed at what he was hearing. It was some time before he spoke. 'Yes. Yes, I see . . . No, I'm not surprised, I suspected as much . . . No, you can leave it in my hands now, I'll make all the necessary arrangements . . . Yes, of course, we'll do our best . . . That's an exceptionally generous offer, I'll tell them that . . . I should think it will be late afternoon . . . Yes, I agree . . . Could you? That would be excellent . . . Yes, I think that would be best . . . Meanwhile, I'll ring you back later to let you know what's happening . . . Yes. Thank you. Goodbye.'

He replaced the receiver and sat gazing at it for a few moments deep in thought, his face sombre. Then he looked at Lineham. 'I was right, Mike. Not that it gives me much satisfaction.' He recounted the conversation to Lineham, watching the sergeant's face change, become as grim as his own. At the moment this vindication of his theory meant very little to him. It was one thing to have suspected, another to have those suspicions confirmed. So much suffering, past, present and future . . .

'So it's all the more urgent to get that confirmation on the sample.'

Lineham rose. 'I'm on my way. I'll give you a ring from the lab in any case, when we know the result.' He hesitated. 'What are you going to do meanwhile, sir?'

Thanet was already reaching for the telephone. 'Make some phone calls. I want to get all this sorted out before you get back, if I can, so that we know exactly what the position is. But I want you with me when I make the arrest, so I will wait for you, as I said.'

'Thanks. I'd hate to miss that.'

There was much to discuss, much to arrange, and the rest of the morning passed swiftly. By twelve Thanet was waiting for Lineham's call, satisfied that he had done everything that could possibly be done at this juncture.

Now all he needed was confirmation from the lab. With that evidence he should be home and dry. Without it—well, things would be very much more difficult. Surely they should have finished the tests by now? He stood up and began wandering restlessly about the office, picking things up and putting them down without really seeing them. He became aware that the sky had cleared and the sun was shining. He had been so preoccupied he hadn't even noticed. He was crossing to the window when the telephone rang. In his haste to answer it he banged his knee on the corner of his chair. He snatched the receiver up, rubbing his kneecap.

'Lineham here, sir. We got a match!'

The relief was overwhelming, the pain forgotten. 'Terrific! How soon are you leaving?'

'Right away.'

'Good. Don't break your neck on the way home. I won't go without you.'

'Thanks.'

Elated, Thanet replaced the receiver. Then he remembered what would follow the arrest and his heart sank. When you were working on a case you couldn't think any further than solving it. It was only when that hurdle was surmounted that you really became aware of the aftermath. An arrest was never the end. The lives of friends and relations of both murderer and victim are often blighted for years. And in this particular case one innocent victim might perhaps never recover.

His knee was still aching and he stood up, tested it. No real harm done. He would go to the canteen and have some lunch, get a sandwich for Lineham to eat in the car. They wouldn't want to linger once the sergeant arrived.

By two o'clock they were on their way, tense and silent. Thanet was preoccupied with planning the crucial interview ahead, trying to anticipate possible obstacles, to decide how to counter possible lines of resistance. Despite the fact that they now had concrete proof of the murderer's presence at the scene of the crime, he knew that this did not necessarily mean that he would get a confession. And a confession was what he was aiming for. He wanted it over, done with.

Apart from a young mother pushing a pram Wayside Crescent was deserted.

Lineham glanced at the house as they got out of the car. 'Think he'll be expecting us?'

Thanet shrugged. 'Who knows?' All the curtains were drawn, he noticed, an almost obsolete way of announcing a death in the family. Oh God, in concentrating upon the murder he had ceased to think of Harrow as a widower of less than twenty-four hours. He remembered Harrow's protectiveness towards his wife. Whatever else the man was guilty of, his concern for her had been genuine. Thanet hardened his heart. He wasn't going to allow sympathy to get in the way.

In silence they walked up to the front door, rang the bell. Already, Thanet noticed, minute signs of neglect were beginning to mar the pristine perfection so noticeable on their first visit. Empty crisp packets and sweet wrappers had blown on to the front drive and muddy footprints defaced the shining surface of the quarry tiles in the porch. Footsteps sounded within, the door was unlocked and a blast of warm air came out to meet them, as if the gates of Hell had briefly opened.

'Mr Harrow? We'd like a word.'

Harrow looked at him dully, without recognition. He was wearing the same dark grey suit and black tie as on the last occasion they had visited him. But last time it had been to mark a different death, Thanet reminded himself. And that death was the reason why they were here.

'Detective Inspector Thanet and Detective Sergeant Lineham.'

Harrow's expression changed, became impatient, faintly hostile. 'Does it have to be now, Inspector? I'm just off to the undertaker's. I don't know if you've heard, but my wife died last night.' *You ought not to be bothering me at a time like this.*

'Yes, I did hear. I'm sorry. All the same, I'm afraid I must insist . . .'

Harrow hesitated a moment longer, then shrugged, stood back and ushered them into the stifling semi-darkness of the sitting room. Thanet had a brief glimpse of the lilies and the moon in Perdita's painting gleaming ghost-white on the wall opposite the fireplace before Harrow switched on the electric light and the sickly yellow glow of artificial light in daytime robbed the picture of some of its magic.

Harrow sat on the very edge of his seat, an obvious hint that he expected the interview to be brief.

Shock tactics, Thanet had decided, would be best and as soon as they were settled he nodded at Lineham and watched Harrow as the sergeant delivered the caution. Harrow's hands were resting on his plump knees and now he rubbed them back and forth as if his palms had begun to sweat. Thanet saw the muscles of his throat move in an involuntary though silent gulp of fear. But the man's face remained impassive. He must have lived through this moment in his imagination so often over the years and especially since Monday night that he had managed to armour himself against self-betrayal.

'Is this some kind of bizarre joke, Inspector? If so, I don't find your sense of humour to my taste.'

Thanet shook his head. 'No joke, Mr Harrow, as you know only too well. I don't treat murder with levity, I assure you.' The temperature in the room was so high that already he was conscious of the prick of sweat beneath his arms. But he couldn't remove his jacket, run the slightest risk of imparting an air of informality to the interview. He would just have to stick it out. He wondered if Lineham were equally uncomfortable.

Harrow stood up. 'Then I can only inform you that you are making a grotesque mistake. And now, if you don't mind . . .'

'Oh but I do,' said Thanet softly. 'I mind very much. I'm afraid you're going to have to resign yourself to hearing me out. Sit down, please.'

But Harrow was not yet ready to capitulate. 'I just don't believe this. When I've heard tales of police brutality or callousness I've always thought that people were exaggerating. But to barge into the house of a man who's just lost his wife, and prevent him from going to arrange her funeral . . .'

'You shall arrange it, I assure you. Soon. As for your accusation of callousness, well, I don't like this situation any more than you do, but as far as I'm concerned it has to be dealt with and that's all there is to it. So, please, sit down and let's get on with it.'

Harrow hesitated a moment longer and then returned to his chair. He sat back, folding his hands primly on his lap. 'I don't seem to have any choice, do I?'

Thanet had had enough. He wanted the whole distasteful business over with. 'It's pointless to continue with this charade of innocence, you know, Mr Harrow. We not only know exactly when and how you killed your stepdaughter . . .' He paused, to give emphasis to his next words. 'We also know why.'

For the first time Harrow's composure slipped. Fear flashed in his eyes and he unfolded his hands, rubbed them again against his bulging thighs. 'I don't know what you're talking about.'

'Oh yes you do! But just to convince you that I'm not bluffing, I'll spell it out to you, chapter and verse.'

This time Harrow said nothing. He stared at Thanet like a rabbit mesmerised by a stoat.

'What happened on Monday night was, as we now know, the climax of a long process which began many years ago, the gradual destruction of your stepdaughter. A process which ended as it was begun, by you.'

Harrow's fear was even more evident now. A sheen of sweat had appeared on his forehead and his jowls quivered as his teeth clenched.

'Things might have gone on as they had for years if it hadn't been for an unfortunate combination of circumstances. Perdita fell in love with someone else and eventually plucked up sufficient courage to tell her husband she was leaving him and, on the same day, your wife was unexpectedly found a bed in hospital. And so it came about that when Perdita sought refuge here on Saturday night you and Stephanie were alone in the house and Perdita found that history was repeating itself in the worst possible way. She caught you in bed with your daughter.'

Thanet paused and his last words hung in the air, the disgust in his voice ringing in his ears. The atmosphere in the room was heavy with condemnation.

But Harrow was not ready to give in. He had, after all, too much to lose. 'I should be careful if I were you, Inspector. Those are very serious accusations.'

'I am well aware of that, Mr Harrow. And I certainly shouldn't have risked making them if they hadn't been corroborated.'

This time the fear in Harrow's eyes was stark, urgent, his voice so husky that he had to clear his throat, make two attempts to get the word out. 'Corroborated?'

'You must realise that I can only mean one thing. Yes, your daughter Stephanie has at last plucked up sufficient courage to lay evidence against you. Her mother can no longer be hurt by having to live with the knowledge of her husband's corruption of her daughter.'

'You realise that it's only her word against mine.'

'Oh, I don't think there'll be any problem there. In fact, I'm certain of it. But we won't waste time on that at the moment. Let's get back to the murder of your stepdaughter, or rather to Saturday night. Perdita, of course, was appalled. Having suffered so many years of abuse herself I'm sure she kept a watchful eye on Stephanie. But somehow Stephanie must have managed to reassure her that everything was all right. How did you manage to keep Stephanie quiet, Mr Harrow? Did you convince her that no one would believe her if she talked? Or that if they did believe her they would think she was the one to blame, for leading you on? Or paint a dire picture of what would happen to the family if it came out—you would lose your job, be put into prison, the house be lost because mortgage payments couldn't be kept up . . . And then, of course, there was the most powerful deterrent of all: what would it do to her mother—her mother who was so frail that such a shock would surely kill her?'

Harrow had lowered his head and was staring at the floor, unable perhaps now to meet Thanet's eyes.

'But I digress again. For Perdita this was the last straw. She saw now that she had been wrong to keep quiet about her own sufferings. By doing so she had simply ensured the same purgatory for Stephanie. I'm sure you begged and pleaded, but she realised that even if you promised never to lay a finger on Stephanie again, you were simply not to be trusted—the children at your school could well become your next victims. Quite simply, you had to be stopped, for once and for all, and she told you that as soon as your wife came out of hospital, she would tell her the truth.

'Nothing you could say would make her change her mind. She insisted that you arrange that while your wife was away Stephanie stay with a friend and she herself would stay only the one night. When, the next day, she arranged to go and look after Mrs Broxton's children for the week, she had of course to tell you where she was staying in case you had to get in touch with her quickly about her mother. So on Monday night you knew where to find her. You also knew that apart from the children—and you didn't think of them, did you, when you killed her?—she would be alone in the house. So you waited until late evening, then went. When you got there the place seemed deserted. You rang the bell but got no reply. You knew she must be in at that time of night because of the children, so you went around to the back of the house. The kitchen curtains were undrawn. You looked in and could scarcely believe what you saw. Perdita was lying on the floor. You tried the door. It was unlocked. You went in, saw that she was either unconscious or dead—I doubt that you even bothered to check—bleeding from a head wound. I don't know whether, up to that point, you had actually thought of murder, but now you realised that if Perdita were dead all your problems would be solved, and no one would ever suspect you of killing her. No one had seen you arrive, and you would make sure that you left no trace of your visit. But you had to act quickly. What could you use, to make absolutely certain that Perdita never woke again? Then you realised. In your pocket you had the perfect weapon. This.'

Harrow raised his head as Thanet felt in his inside pocket, took out his wallet, opened it and extracted a sample bag. Inside, clearly visible through the plastic, was another plastic bag, folded up and labelled. The temptation now, of course, was to lie, to tell Harrow that there were clear samples of his fingerprints on the bag. Many of Thanet's colleagues, he knew, would not hesitate to do so if they felt that it would be useful, give them an advantage, and would think Thanet a fool for not doing so. But he hated such tactics. Victory was so much sweeter if fairly won. Anyway, in this case deception was unnecessary. He had another card up his sleeve. And knowing that there were no traceable prints on the bag he had no compunction in taking it out, shaking it, holding it up.

Harrow said nothing, simply stared at the bag as though he had never seen one before. Or perhaps, Thanet thought, he was staring through it, beyond it, into the past, seeing instead Perdita's body lying on the floor, watching his own hands ease this very bag down over her head . . .

Thanet shrugged. 'There's not much more to tell. The deed was very quickly done. You couldn't have been there more than a minute or two.'

He stopped, waited. There was no tension in him, only relief that the unsavoury tale was told, and a weariness that was a result of the telling. He sensed rather than saw Lineham look at him expectantly.

Harrow too looked up. He was showing more resilience than Thanet would have given him credit for. 'If you've quite finished, Inspector . . . As far as the death of my stepdaughter is concerned, you have no proof of any of this. One plastic bag is, after all, just like any other plastic bag . . .'

So the fact that Thanet had not mentioned identifiable fingerprints had not escaped him.

'Ah, but that's where you're wrong, Mr Harrow. We do have proof.'

Once again Thanet took out his wallet, opened it. He laid another labelled sample bag on his knee. 'In here is a sample of woollen fibre, found in the plastic bag which was put over your stepdaughter's head.' He took out a third bag, laid it on his other knee. 'In this one is a sample of fibre taken from the woollen bedjacket which you took in to your wife on Monday evening before going on to see Perdita. Our forensic science laboratory has confirmed that they match.'

All three men stared at the two little plastic bags, the minute scraps of blue fluff inside them. It was against the rules to have borrowed them for this purpose, of course, but Thanet had been unable to resist the temptation.

Harrow looked up and Thanet could tell from the look in his eyes that he knew when he was beaten. 'What will happen to Stephanie?'

Thanet experienced a surge of anger and it was difficult to keep his voice level as he said, 'You should have thought of that before.'

20

'What's this Mrs Bonnard like?' said Lineham.

They were on their way to see Stephanie. Harrow had been charged, taken back to Headquarters and left to stew for the moment; as far as Thanet was concerned Stephanie's welfare now took priority. Mrs Bonnard was the mother of the friend with whom Stephanie had been staying and it was she who had rung Thanet that morning to tell him that Stephanie, released from silence by her mother's death and terrified that she would now be entirely at her father's mercy, had broken down and confided in her.

'She sounds very nice. Very concerned for Stephanie's welfare, even took the day off work to stay with her. She's known her for several years as a friend of her daughter and she's fond of her. She's very upset by all this, of course, could hardly believe it when Stephanie told her about the abuse . . . Turn into Wayside Crescent, then first right, second left.'

'Poor kid,' said Lineham, signalling then turning the wheel obediently. 'She's had a rotten time, hasn't she. Years of putting up with that and then, this last week, a positive avalanche of disaster—her stepsister murdered, her mother dead, and now her father arrested . . . I don't envy you the job of breaking that piece of news to her, I can tell you.'

They passed Harrow's house, its curtains still drawn as if to hide its secret from the world. Thanet experienced a spasm of revulsion against those overheated rooms, which like a hothouse had nurtured the monstrous bloom of perversion that had flourished there. Harrow had turned off the heating before they left and by now the temperature should have dropped, perhaps symbolically, to something like normal. 'I don't think it'll be that much of a surprise, actually. I forgot to tell you . . . Later on this morning, when I rang back to tell Mrs Bonnard

about the arrangements I'd made with the Social Services, she said tha
she was convinced Stephanie was holding something back, somethin
else to do with her father. She was sure that Stephanie wanted to tel
her but couldn't bring herself to do so. I would guess that somethin
Harrow has said or done since Perdita's death has made Stephani
suspect him. No doubt she witnessed the row between the two of them
on Saturday night and heard Perdita tell him that she was going to
report him to the police as soon as Mrs Harrow came out of hospital.
She must have realised how powerful a motive this gave him, and put
two and two together. This is the turning, I think. Yes, Meadow Drive.'

Lineham turned in. 'Number 14, wasn't it?'

'That's right.' Thanet was peering out of the window.

'Poor kid. If she did suspect her father, it must have been a great
temptation to try and get him off her back by getting him arrested for
murder, instead of sexual abuse. Much less of an ordeal for her. And
yet she chose to do it the other way around. She's got guts, hasn't she?'

Guts, loyalty or a desire for revenge? Thanet wasn't sure, and didn't
suppose that he would ever find out.

'She must be scared stiff about what will happen to her now.'
Lineham was scowling, leaning forward to peer out of the window as if
he were trying to read Stephanie's future.

'I know. She's very lucky that . . . Ah, there it is.'

Mrs Bonnard's house was much smaller than the Harrows', semi-
detached with a cramped garden and no garage. She had obviously
been looking out for them because the car had scarcely drawn up at the
kerb when she opened the front door. Her smile could not disguise her
anxiety. 'Inspector Thanet?' Her gaze went past him to Lineham, who
had stayed in the car. 'He's not coming in?'

Thanet shook his head. 'We thought it would be a bit overpowering,
if there were two of us. And as you're going to be present . . .' He
gave her a reassuring smile.

She was in her forties, heavily built and fair-haired, with laughter
lines at the corners of eyes and mouth. Thanet guessed that her usual
expression would be one of good-humoured placidity—just what Stephanie would need in these appalling circumstances. Her clothes were
clean but dowdy—a dark green sweater and brown Crimplene skirt.
Thanet knew that she was a single parent, having been divorced ten
years ago. She worked as a supermarket check-out attendant, and one
of his anxieties regarding the tentative arrangements he had made for
Stephanie's future had been that Mrs Bonnard's generous offer might

have been prompted chiefly by mercenary motives. Now, although he had been with her for no more than a few seconds, Thanet was reassured. This woman was not out for what she could get, he was sure of it.

She paused in the hall and lowered her voice to a concerned whisper. 'Is her father . . . ? Have you seen him?'

Thanet nodded, lowered his voice in response. 'Yes, but prepare yourself for a shock. He's been arrested and charged with Perdita's murder.'

She stared at him, her eyes opening so wide that the whites showed clear all around the irises. She was silent for a few moments absorbing the news and then she said, 'She suspected, didn't she, poor lamb. That was what she was holding back.'

Thanet nodded. 'Probably.'

'I wonder if this will . . . She really worries me. She's bottling it all up inside, hasn't shed a single tear, even over her mother's death.'

Mrs Bonnard opened a door to the right of the narrow hall and led the way into the room. 'Inspector Thanet is here, Stephanie.'

Like its owner, this room was clean but dowdy. It looked as though it had been furnished to last. The predominant colour was a safe fawn, the carpet a practical all-over pattern, the three-piece suite covered in a hard-wearing uncut moquette.

Stephanie was sitting bolt upright in one corner of the settee, arms folded tightly across her chest as if to prevent herself from flying apart. Her face was pale, the delicate skin beneath her eyes bruised by insomnia and anxiety. She was wearing her school uniform of navy skirt and blue and white striped blouse, and the mass of curly hair so like that of her dead stepsister was tied back with a dark blue ribbon. She looked heartbreakingly vulnerable and much younger than her thirteen years.

'Hullo, Stephanie. We met once before, at the hospital.' He gave her only the briefest of smiles, feeling that she would find it inappropriate to be less restrained in the circumstances, but the genuine warmth and goodwill he felt towards her must have communicated themselves because her expression lightened just a fraction and she gave a stiff little nod of acknowledgement.

Mrs Bonnard sat down beside Stephanie and Thanet took an armchair facing them. 'I was very sorry to hear about your mother,' he began. 'I'm not just saying that, I really mean it.'

Her lips tightened and she nodded again, her knuckles whitening as her fingers dug harder into the striped material of her blouse. Still she said nothing. Perhaps she couldn't trust herself to speak.

'But of course, that's not why I'm here.' He paused. Stephanie would be expecting him to talk to her about the matter of her father's prosecution for child abuse, but first he had to surmount the hurdle of breaking to her the news of his arrest for murder. There was nothing he could do to soften the blow. 'First, I'm afraid I have some very bad news for you.'

Apprehension flashed into her eyes and she glanced at Mrs Bonnard, who patted her knee.

'Your father . . .' He had to say it. 'Your father has been arrested, and charged with the murder of your stepsister.'

She stared at him blankly. Had she taken in what he said? Mrs Bonnard was watching her anxiously.

'I have a feeling,' he said gently, 'that you might have been half expecting this.' He waited a few moments and then said, 'Am I right?'

Her lips tightened and then she gave a barely perceptible nod.

Thanet hadn't known that he had been holding his breath. Slowly he exhaled with relief.

So far, he realised, she still hadn't said a word.

Now her lips parted. 'Where . . . ?' It was scarcely more than a whisper and she cleared her throat, tried again. 'Where . . . Where is he?'

'In custody.'

Stephanie's arms had remained tightly folded throughout the interview so far, her body stiff with tension. Now, at last, she stirred, the grip on her upper arms relaxed and slowly her hands drifted down to her lap. She looked at them as if they did not belong to her and then, gently, began to massage one hand with the other. If her fingers had maintained that tight grip for so long they were probably aching, Thanet thought. Did the fact that she seemed to have relaxed a little betray the extent of her fear that her father would be released and she would be expected to go back to live with him? Briefly Thanet was so filled with pity and anger that his throat closed and he had to swallow hard to speak in anything like his normal tone.

'I expect you're worried about what will happen to you.'

She stopped rubbing her hand and again glanced at Mrs Bonnard. 'Mrs Bonnard said I could stay here.'

Mrs Bonnard took her hand, squeezed it and nodded. 'Of course you can.'

'Yes. You will be able to. For the moment, anyway—and probably indefinitely,' he added hastily as he saw the fear flash back into the girl's eyes.

'Only probably?'

'Almost certainly.' Now it was his turn to glance at Mrs Bonnard. 'I don't know how much Mrs Bonnard has told you about the procedure in circumstances like yours?' He watched Stephanie absorb the implication: she was not a freak, there were other children like her, sufficient indeed for a procedure to have been established for dealing with them.

Mrs Bonnard shook her head. 'Not a lot, I'm afraid. I thought it would be best to wait until you came—beyond telling her that she was welcome to stay here with us, that is.' She glanced at Stephanie and squeezed her hand again. 'I don't think she's really been able to think beyond that.'

'I see.' Thanet became brisk, matter-of-fact. 'The situation has changed, of course, since your father's arrest. But even so, it's all quite simple, really, and I don't anticipate any problems.' *Especially now that I've met you, Mrs Bonnard.* 'When someone is left in your circumstances, Stephanie, and there is no relation to look after you—you haven't any relations, I understand?' He waited for her headshake before continuing. 'Well, in those circumstances, normally the child becomes the responsibility of the Social Services, and is put into care. No!' He held up his hand as panic flashed in Stephanie's eyes. 'I told you, in your case that won't happen, you'll almost certainly stay here.'

'But . . .' she interrupted.

'What?' he said, gently.

'You said, *almost* certainly . . .'

'Only because there are certain formalities to go through. You see, as I said, because the Social Services are responsible for someone in your circumstances, they really have to be sure that someone like Mrs Bonnard, who offers to look after that child, is a fit person to do so.'

'Fit?'

'Suitable, responsible, someone who will have the child's—your—welfare at heart.' He smiled at Mrs Bonnard. 'And as I'm sure there'll be no problem in Mrs Bonnard's case, I don't think you have anything to worry about.'

'So what will actually happen?' said Mrs Bonnard.

'A social worker will come here to talk to you both, look at the house . . . Just to make sure it's a suitable place for a child to live,' he added, as Mrs Bonnard gave an anxious frown. 'And I assure you, from what I've seen you needn't worry on that score. And then you will be made Stephanie's guardian, probably for a trial period. And finally, if everything works out, as I'm sure it will—it's not as if Stephanie is a stranger to you, after all—then eventually you will be made her permanent guardian.' He smiled at Stephanie. 'Does that help?'

She nodded. 'But what . . . ?' She glanced at Mrs Bonnard, bit her lip. 'It's a bit awkward . . .'

Thanet understood at once what she meant. 'You mean, about the financial side of it?'

She nodded.

'You're afraid of being a burden on Mrs Bonnard, is that it?'

She and Mrs Bonnard spoke together.

'Yes, I don't want to . . .'

'Stephanie, you really mustn't worry about that. We'll manage, somehow.'

'It shouldn't be as difficult as all that, Mrs Bonnard,' said Thanet, smiling. 'You will receive Stephanie's Child Benefit and also a Guardianship Allowance.'

'Really?' Her surprise was genuine, Thanet was sure of it. 'I thought we'd probably get the Child Benefit but I'd no idea there'd be any more.'

'It's not that much,' said Thanet, 'but enough to get by.'

'That's all we need,' said Mrs Bonnard, smiling at Stephanie. 'And I can't say it's not a relief. I do work, but I don't earn that much and it's a bit of a struggle sometimes. I'm not qualified for anything better, that's the trouble. That's why I always say to the girls, get yourselves educated. Then you'll always know you'll be able to support yourselves, whatever happens.'

'I agree, absolutely.'

'What will happen to our house?' said Stephanie.

'Nothing, for the moment,' said Thanet. 'There'll be plenty of time to think about that later on.' The Social Services had in fact told him that if Harrow were convicted and imprisoned the house would either have to be sold or rented out, in order to support Stephanie until she was of age. But there was no point in worrying Stephanie with this information at the moment. Let her have time to begin to adjust, first. Which reminded him. . . .

'There is one other thing that the social worker will want to discuss with you.' This was delicate ground and again Thanet cast around for the best way to put it. One thing was certain: he must be as matter-of-fact as possible. Above all things Stephanie must not be made to feel bad, or a freak. 'Children in your position, children who have been abused by their parents, usually need help to come to terms with what they have been through.'

Already Stephanie had hung her head, her pale cheeks stained with red flags of shame, and again Thanet had to exert considerable self-control to hide his anger at what this girl had had to suffer. He thought of Harrow's bulging flesh, his sweaty hands, and his flesh crawled. 'They often have to be helped, you see, to understand that what happened was not their fault, that they were not responsible for it, and above all that they are not bad, immoral or different in any way from other children who have not had to suffer as they have.'

He thought of Perdita and the seeds of self-disgust which Harrow had sown in her. Thanet was certain now that it was he who had made her feel a pariah, been the cause of her self-chosen isolation at school. No doubt it was he, too, who was responsible for her dark vision of the world revealed through her art, the sense of impending doom which had so distressed her mother. Had Stephanie been rescued in time? He hoped so, he fervently hoped so. But what about all those others, the secret victims of adult lust and perversion, those too frightened for one reason or another to betray their tormentors? It didn't bear thinking about. He would have to be satisfied that he had perhaps rescued one child from that particular purgatory.

Stephanie had still not raised her head but he could tell by her sudden stillness that she was listening intently. Had he said enough? Should he wait for her to respond, or just quietly leave? He desperately wanted to do the right thing.

She raised her head to look at him and he found he was holding his breath.

'You mean . . . ?' She stopped.

Go on, he silently urged her. *Go on.*

She must have sensed his silent encouragement because she tried again. 'You mean . . . they're not going to blame me?'

Thanet shook his head, filled with rage. What had Harrow said to her? 'No, I'm sure of it. Not in the least.'

'They won't say . . .' She glanced at Mrs Bonnard, who put her arm around the girl's shoulders and gave her a protective hug. Then she looked back at Thanet. '. . . I led him on?'

The desperation in her eyes was almost more than he could bear. Again he shook his head. 'No, Stephanie, they won't. Believe me, they won't.'

She stared at him for a moment longer and then, the first sign that her rigid self-control was beginning to crack, her lower lip began to tremble. A moment later a solitary tear tracked its way down her cheek and then suddenly her face crumpled and, turning her head into Mrs Bonnard's shoulder, she flung her arm around the older woman with the frantic grasp of a drowning man clutching at a rock, and began to weep.

Thanet knew that, heart-rending as the child's grief might be, it was far better that she should let it out. It was what Mrs Bonnard had been hoping for. She put both arms around Stephanie and began to rock her, to stroke her hair and comfort her as she would a much younger child. Over the girl's head her eyes met Thanet's and she nodded her satisfaction and dismissal.

His mission was accomplished.

He left.

21

Thanet awoke, remembered that it was Saturday and he didn't have to go to work, and stretched luxuriously. Yesterday had been hectic, completing all the paperwork inevitable at the end of a murder case, and Joan had been in bed when he got home. Knowing that she would be up early to tend to her mother he had left a note on her bedside table: WEEKEND OFF! As yet they had had no opportunity to talk properly since the case finished and he knew she would be eager to hear all about it. But there was no hurry. The delicious empty space of Saturday and Sunday stretched ahead of them. There would be plenty of time to relax, catch up.

He opened one eye and squinted at the bedside clock. Nine-thirty. Time to move.

He stretched again, sat up and swung his legs over the side of the bed. His nose twitched as he became aware of the beckoning smell of coffee and—yes, surely, bacon! He couldn't remember when they had last had bacon for breakfast, Joan's healthy eating campaign had banned it from their diet, except as the special occasional treat. Suddenly he was very hungry.

He went to the bathroom, showered and shaved. On the way back to the bedroom he paused at the half-open door of Bridget's room, peeped in. His mother-in-law was sitting up in bed, having breakfast. He went in.

'Morning, Margaret. How are you feeling?'

'Much better, thank you, Luke.'

She looked it, too. The unhealthy greyish pallor had disappeared and her skin had regained a little of its natural colour.

'You look it. Good.'

'I'm sorry to be such a nuisance, though. It's such a lot of work for Joan.'

He sat down on the side of the bed, took her hand. 'Look, the main thing is that you're getting better. If you start worrying about Joan you'll hinder your recovery and defeat the whole object of the exercise. You gave us a nasty fright, you know.'

'I can imagine. Even so . . .'

'I'm afraid,' said Thanet smiling, 'that just for once in your life you're going to have to resign yourself to other people doing things for you, instead of the other way around. Think how virtuous you'll make them feel!'

'You always did have the knack of turning things around,' she said, smiling. 'All right, I'll try.'

'Good. Anything you want?'

She shook her head. 'I'm allowed up for a few hours later. Not downstairs, yet, though, I understand.'

'No. Doctor MacPherson said you should wait a week before attempting to climb the stairs, and then only very slowly.'

She grimaced. 'I hate being treated like an invalid.'

'Look at it this way. The more you behave like one to start with, the sooner you'll stop being one.'

She shook her head, smiling. 'You'd better get dressed. By the smell of it your breakfast's just about ready.'

'See you later.'

He called into her room to collect the breakfast tray on the way downstairs. The kitchen was filled with sunshine and appetising smells. Joan turned to greet him, smiling. 'I thought you'd like a lie-in today.'

He put down the tray, went to put his arms around her, kiss her. 'Is the smell of bacon a product of my over-heated imagination?'

She grinned. 'A treat. To celebrate the end of the case. And the fact that it's Saturday. And that for once we've got the whole weekend free.'

Thanet nodded at the table, which was laid for two. 'Ben not here?'

'He left half an hour ago. He's gone into town.'

They ate in a companionable silence and it was not until they were on their second cup of coffee and Thanet had lit his pipe that Joan said, 'Now tell me all about it.'

'About what?' he said, raising his eyebrows in feigned ignorance.

'Luke! Stop teasing. You know perfectly well what I mean.'

'Oh, sorry, you mean the case. Yes, well . . .' he added hurriedly, seeing her eyes flash with pretended anger. 'Where d'you want to begin?'

He'd already told her the bare facts, of course, that Harrow had confessed, and why the murder had been committed, but very little more.

'Where we always begin. With how you worked it out. That's what always fascinates me. I can never understand how you do it. I'd never have guessed in a million years.'

'Don't exaggerate! You're simply trying to boost my ego.'

'No! I mean it, honestly. You'd told me everything you knew, everything you'd learnt, and I can honestly say the idea would never have entered my head.'

'That's because you hadn't met the people concerned. You hadn't seen how they behaved, how they looked, how they reacted. If you had—'

'I still wouldn't have worked it out, I'm sure of it. So come on, tell me how you did it.'

He removed his pipe, took her hand with exaggerated courtesy, dropped a kiss on the back of it and bowed his head. 'Your wish is my command.' Then he sat back, frowning. 'Though it's easier said than done. I'll have to think, if I want to get it in sequence.'

'All right then, think. I'll clear these things away—no, you stay there and concentrate on working it out.'

By the time she sat down again he had it all clear in his mind. 'It was after that conversation we had on Wednesday night. You remember? We'd been talking about the case, after supper, and I'd been telling you about Vanessa Broxton's visit to my office, how I'd suddenly realised that there must have been two people involved, not one.' He shook his head. 'I still can't understand why I didn't see that sooner. Anyway, if you recall, we had quite a long discussion about who the second person could have been.'

Joan was nodding. 'I remember.'

'And naturally, that was the question that was paramount in my mind that night, all the time, whatever else I was doing or thinking. Anyway, my back was playing up and you suggested I have a hot bath, so I did. I lay there for ages just thinking about the case, and about Perdita in particular. She was the key to it all, of course. Random violence apart, no one gets himself murdered without good reason. I knew that somewhere in her character, in her life, was something, I'd no idea what, which had brought about her death. So I turned over in my mind everything I'd heard about her from different people . . . I think that what I was trying to do at that point was put aside preconceived ideas, try to find a new way of looking at the case. It's so easy, as you go along, to formulate theories which, if you're not very careful, seem to become fact, which they're not. Then they get in the way.'

Joan was listening intently, nodding from time to time, chin propped on hand, grey eyes fixed unwaveringly on his. A shaft of sunlight falling on her hair turned the soft fair curls to gold. Perhaps it was this talk of Perdita that made Thanet, for the first time in his life, wish that he could paint. How, he speculated, would Perdita have painted Joan? But Perdita had never painted people, only drawn them. Why? he wondered.

He became aware that Joan was waiting for him to continue.

'According to her mother, Perdita never got over her father's death when she was ten. She'd always been a Daddy's girl, apparently, and found it very difficult to adjust to having a stepfather—Harrow had already told me as much himself. Mrs Harrow said she changed a lot, became withdrawn and gloomy and everyone—yourself included—told me how much of a loner she'd been at school. Mrs Harrow told me too that at one time Perdita became obsessed with death and then, a few years ago, when Perdita was having an especially difficult time with her husband, she said something which really shook her mother. She said, "I don't suppose it matters much, does it, Mum? I don't expect I'll have to put up with it much longer." When Mrs Harrow asked what she meant she told her that she'd always thought she'd die young. Mrs Harrow said it was almost as if she knew that she was doomed to die before her time.'

Joan shook her head in sorrow. 'Poor girl.'

'Yes . . . Well, everyone knows that the death of a father will have a profound effect on a child of that age but usually, if the child is reasonably well-adjusted, in time he'll get over it. But Perdita didn't. It seemed to have blighted her life. Not as far as her work was concerned, of course. On the contrary, she seemed to have poured all her emotion into it, which is presumably why it has such a powerful impact. You've seen her paintings, you must know what I mean.'

Joan nodded. 'After our talk on Wednesday night I hunted out an old catalogue I knew I had somewhere, of one of Perdita's local exhibitions.' She got up, disappeared into the sitting room for a few moments. 'Here it is.'

The catalogue was dated 24 October 1985, and there were several illustrations in it. Thanet glanced through them, aware that he was hoping to find a reproduction of the lilies in the garden. But he was disappointed. None of the paintings was familiar to him. All, however, had the same haunting quality. 'What a waste,' he said, shaking his head with regret. 'Think what she might have achieved, if she'd lived.'

'I know. It makes me so angry as well as so sad, when I think about it . . . But what I wanted to say was that looking at those illustrations I found myself for the first time trying to work out *why* they have such a powerful impact. And I agree with you, it must be because of the strength of emotion that went into them.'

'Did you come to any conclusions, as to what that emotion was?'

Joan looked diffident. 'I've thought about it a lot . . . I think, a combination of anger and despair.'

Thanet stared at her. Into his mind had flashed once more an image of the first of Perdita's paintings that he had seen, the one in her sitting room. He remembered feeling the power of that brilliant explosion of colour, noting the violent contrast with the cool neutrality of the colour scheme of the room and thinking that the effect was deliberately contrived to enhance the impact of the painting. He remembered thinking, in the bath, that it was anger which animated it, remembered wondering against what or whom that anger was directed. At the time he had not followed up this line of thought, but now he understood. It was anger at the way life had treated her in her impressionable adolescence, anger at being trapped in a loveless, claustrophobic marriage, anger perhaps also mistakenly turned inward against herself for somehow having been responsible for her stepfather's behaviour. It was no doubt this belief, reinforced later by the discovery of her attraction for men, which had brought about the despair, the darkness which lay beneath.

'Harrow made her feel guilty, didn't he?' he said grimly. 'He made her feel it was all her fault . . . And he was doing the same thing to Stephanie.'

He told Joan of Stephanie's fears that the social workers would blame her, think she had led her father on.

'Poor kid. Poor both of them . . . And I expect he also made them terrified of telling their mother because of what it would do to her. Her health has been poor for years, you said?'

'Yes. I can just imagine it. "It would kill your mother, if she knew . . ." Makes you sick, doesn't it, what these people put their children through.'

'It really does. I assume Harrow will also be prosecuted for child abuse?'

'Yes. It'll all come out at the trial anyway, of course, but in any case Stephanie is determined to go through with it. She wants to be sure that it goes down on his record so that when he gets out of prison he won't ever be able to be employed in a position of authority over children again. It's going to be a tremendous ordeal for her, but she has a lot of courage.'

'She must have. Do you think she'll ever get over all this?'

'I don't know. I hope so. She's lucky, in having Mrs Bonnard to fend for her, but she's been through so much . . .'

'Luke . . . I wonder . . .'

'What?'

'D'you think, if Perdita felt as Stephanie did, that it was somehow her fault, that people would blame her and believe perhaps that she'd encouraged it, that she could almost in some way—subconsciously, I mean —have precipitated her own death?'

'The thought had crossed my mind.'

'She marries a jealous husband, then fans the flame by telling him she wants a divorce . . .'

'And fate took a hand by arranging that she break the news to him and go home on the one night when unknown to her her mother is away and her stepfather is taking advantage of the fact to molest his daughter. D'you realise that if she had chosen any other time, she would still be alive?'

'Not necessarily. And you always say there's no point in saying "if".'

'I think Stephanie overheard Perdita tell him that as soon as she felt her mother was well enough, she would tell her the truth and report him to the authorities . . . He says, of course, that when he went to see her on Monday night, he just wanted to talk to her, to convince her he would never do it again.'

'Do you believe him?'

'I don't know. At this point I don't want to think too deeply about him any more. That's something the jury will have to decide . . . We seem to have got side-tracked.'

'Not really. You were saying you couldn't understand why her father's death seemed to have had such a profound and lasting effect on Perdita.'

'Ah yes, that's right. I couldn't make up my mind. Had it simply been that she couldn't reconcile herself to someone taking her father's place, or had there been some other, deeper reason?

'I then moved on to thinking about something that had really puzzled me all along, which was why Perdita had trained as a nanny instead of going to Art College. If you remember, you suggested it might have been because she wanted her independence but didn't want to hurt her mother by saying so . . .'

'Because her mother assumed that if Perdita studied art she'd go to one of the two local Art Colleges, both of which have a very good reputation.'

'Exactly. So if Perdita went away it would have to be to study something other than art . . . But I still wasn't satisfied. I knew Mrs Harrow was frail and would no doubt have been disappointed if Perdita had gone away, but she struck me as being a very sensible, well-balanced woman. I couldn't see that she would have been so desperately upset by Perdita saying she wanted to go to, say, an Art College in London. I think she would genuinely have wanted what was best for her daughter. No, I was very confused by the whole business. Even if Perdita had another reason for wanting to get away from home, surely she could still have studied art instead of going off on a completely different tack?'

'Perhaps she wanted to be sure that when she'd finished her training, whatever it was, she would have a cast-iron excuse for not living at home again, if her mother wanted her to?'

'Yes, that's possible. I hadn't thought of that. And nannying would be perfect, a live-in job. Yes, that could have been part of it.' Thanet shrugged. 'Anyway, I was still trying to make sense of it and I thought, Let's approach it from another angle. Let's assume that the decision had nothing to do with her mother, that Perdita was desperate to get away for a completely different reason. What if it was simply that she wanted to get away from her stepfather? I knew they didn't get on, her mother had told me so. But even then I still didn't see it. At that point I drifted off to sleep. I can't remember what I dreamt but you woke me up, if you remember, said I was having a nightmare.'

'And you said you weren't. In fact, as I recall, although you looked a bit dazed, you were really rather full of yourself . . .'

They exchanged reminiscent smiles.

'Well, I was in what we could call a celebratory mood. I suppose my subconscious must have gone on worrying away at the problem while I was asleep and when you woke me it hit me, like a revelation. Do you remember when we met Harrow and Stephanie at the hospital, after we'd been visiting your mother, the way Stephanie flung her father's arm off her shoulders when he was trying to comfort her? As I watched them go I was thinking how sad it was that they didn't seem able to turn to each other for help. I suppose that because of your mother's heart attack I was very aware of how much it meant to have the support of someone close at a time like that. I remember thinking how if—God forbid—it had been Bridget and I in that situation, we would have been depending on each other to see us through. Harrow, I thought, didn't seem to get on any better with his daughter than his stepdaughter . . . Now, as I say, it hit me. What if Perdita had wanted to get away from her stepfather for the strongest reason of all . . . ? What if she had been sexually abused, and what if, when she sought refuge in her mother's house on Saturday night, she found that Stephanie was having to suffer the same torment? Suddenly, it all fell into place. If this was what had happened, it would explain why Stephanie was staying at a friend's house while her mother was in hospital—no doubt Perdita would have insisted on it. And if she had told her stepfather that this time she wasn't going to keep quiet, that as soon as her mother was well enough she would tell her the truth and also inform the authorities, this would certainly give Harrow a powerful motive for the murder. He would not only lose his wife and daughter but his job, too, no one would want to employ an assistant headmaster convicted of sexual abuse. And he must have known his wife's condition was critical, that if he didn't act quickly and she died, Perdita wouldn't hesitate to go straight to the police. And, of course, he knew where Perdita was—she'd had to tell him so that he could get in touch with her if her mother's condition suddenly deteriorated.

'Then I remembered something else. Do you remember that the reason why I suspected that Vanessa Broxton might be guilty was because the one piece of concrete evidence we had was a scrap of blue woollen fibre found inside the polythene bag with which Perdita had been killed, and I'd remembered seeing Vanessa wear a blue woollen jacket on the night of the murder? Well, I then remembered that Harrow had told me he'd taken a woollen bedjacket in to his wife on the night of the murder, and I recalled seeing Mrs Harrow wearing the bedjacket when I interviewed her in hospital . . . It was blue.'

'And you thought that if he'd gone to see Perdita after visiting his wife that night, he might well have still had in his pocket the polythene bag in which the bedjacket had been wrapped.'

'Exactly! Which was, in fact, what happened. Of course, all this was theoretical until we could check that the fibres matched, but I was sure that this was the answer.'

'I suspected you had something up your sleeve on Thursday morning, when you left for work.'

'I didn't want to say anything until I'd got confirmation of the match, in case I was wrong.'

'But you weren't,' said Joan, smiling. 'Brilliant!'

'You're biased.'

'No, I mean it. I hope Draco was impressed.'

'I think he's too worried about Angharad to be impressed by any-thing at the moment. I do hope she's going to be all right. I don't know what he'll do if she doesn't get better.'

'No.'

They were both silent for a moment, thinking of the Dracos. Then Joan glanced at the clock. 'My goodness, just look at the time! I must go and help Mother get dressed.'

'Yes, she told me she was getting up later. She's looking a lot better, isn't she?'

'Yes, thank God. I'm not sure how good a patient she's going to be, though.'

'Don't worry, I've been laying down the law on that!'

'Ah, but will she listen?'

'I think so. I certainly hope so. Anyway, you go and see to her and I'll clean up down here.'

Thanet was halfway through the washing-up when the telephone rang. He hurriedly dried his hands and went into the hall, calling 'I'll take it,' up the stairs.

A telephone operator asked him if he would accept a reverse charge call from London. It must be Bridget. 'Certainly,' he said.

A moment later he heard her voice. 'Dad?'

'Bridget!' He was filled with joy.

'You've been very elusive this week. You've been out every time I've spoken to Mum. Been busy on a case, I gather.'

'Yes. I was sorry to have missed you.'

'How's it going? The case?'

'All finished.' He heard the ring of satisfaction in his voice and so did Bridget.

'Brilliant!' she said, unconsciously echoing her mother. 'That didn't take long. Was it an interesting one?'

'I'm not sure how I'd describe it. Anyway, enough about me. How about you? How are you settling in?'

'Fine.'

But he at once detected the reservation in her voice. 'Are you sure?'

'Yes, really.'

Now he was sure of it. Joan had been right. Something was wrong. 'Sprig,' he said, using her old nickname, 'what's the matter? Your mother told me she wasn't too happy about you. What's wrong?'

There was a brief silence, then a sigh. 'I might have known I couldn't fool you two.'

'Is it serious?'

'No.' This time she sounded more positive. 'I'll sort it out in time, I'm sure.'

'What's the problem, exactly? Are you homesick? It would be perfectly natural, you know, it's nothing to be ashamed of. In fact, we half expected it. It's the first time you've actually lived away from home, after all.'

'No, it's not that. Not really. At least, it wouldn't be, if . . . It's the other girls, really.'

Thanet was astonished. Bridget had always been sociable, had never had any serious problems in relationships with either fellow-pupils at school or colleagues at the restaurant where she had worked for the past year. 'In what way?'

'It's just that, oh, I don't know, they're so different from me. Most of them are much better off, for a start, they seem to spend money like water—not that that worries me in the usual sense. I mean, please don't think I'm complaining about being hard up or anything like that, I have all I need. It's just that, well, I suppose most of them come from such different backgrounds from me and they have such a different attitude to life. For instance, when they go out in the evening they seem to take it for granted that they'll go to a pub and spend the evening there, drinking and smoking . . . Oh, that sounds terrible, it makes them sound positively depraved, and they're not, it's just that that's not the way I want to spend either my money or my time, and it makes things a bit difficult, that's all.'

What it boiled down to was a clash of values, Thanet thought. And if Bridget was in the minority it wasn't going to be easy for her. 'Yes, I can see that. But surely all the girls aren't like that?'

'No. There is one girl, she comes from Yorkshire . . . And I'm sure there'll be others. It just takes time to find out, that's all. There's so much to take in all at once.'

'I'm sure you're right. And you've only been there a few days.'

'Yes. You mustn't worry about me. I wasn't going to say anything . . . How's Gran?'

'Much better. Hold on a minute.'

Joan had appeared at the top of the stairs, arm in arm with her mother, who was wearing a dressing gown. 'Is it Bridget?'

'Yes.'

'Tell her her grandmother'll have a word with her.'

Thanet nodded and the two women turned and made slow progress towards the door of Thanet and Joan's bedroom, where there was an extension.

'You can talk to her yourself,' he said into the receiver.

'She's up?'

'For limited periods, yes.'

He heard his mother-in-law's voice, firm, loving, reassuring as always. 'Bridget?'

'Gran! How lovely to hear you! How are you?'

Gently, he replaced the receiver, leaving the two women, one old, one young, to work their alchemy of love upon each other. He was happier about Bridget now. She would cope.

He returned to the kitchen. The washing-up water had gone cold and he pulled out the plug, watched the dirty suds swirl away. Then he squirted more liquid detergent into the sink and ran some fresh water. A few bubbles had escaped and he watched them float towards the window, iridescent in the sunlight. Like them he felt buoyant, light as air.

Life was good.